Troughton Company

Evelyn Rainey

ISBN-13: 978-1-946469-42-7

Sheltering Tree . Earth
PO Box 973, Eagle Lake, FL 33839

http://ShelteringTree.Earth

DEDICATION

Patrick Troughton was the first man I ever wanted to escape with through time and space. We did so, every afternoon from the time I was 8 until his regeneration the next season of **Doctor Who** in 1969. Thank you, all the wonderful Doctors I have known and admired. You helped shape my zeal for science fiction, my belief in true friends, and my hope for we humans whom you loved so much.

CONTENTS

ACKNOWLEDGMENTS

I have to take time here to thank the writers and producers of the *History Channel*, the *Discovery Channel*, the *Unsolved Mysteries* series, and yes, *Ancient Aliens*. I have learned so much from watching your shows. You made each episode intriguing and fun! Also, my appreciation goes to *Rand-McNally* Road Atlases, through which I travel vicariously with great joy.

Thank you!

1
MECHMONS

The boy slept fitfully beside Chrissy and Jerry. None of them slept well. She wasn't sure how he had come to be with them. They were all walking north out of Florida and he just sort of took up with them and they with him. He had quite an arsenal in his backpack – mace, strings he used for snares, a small hatchet, two knives, a fold-up and expandable fishing rod, reel, line and hooks, a compass and a first aid kit. Strapped to the bag was an array of water bottles, sunscreen and mosquito spray.

To balance the boy's supplies, the Troughtons had food – dehydrated vegetables and fruit, jerky, teabags, sugar and bouillon cubes. Jerry carried the kettle and the pot.

The road they traveled beside, Highway 301, hadn't been scoured by city-eaters. That's what the invaders were called – city-eaters. They were alien machines made up of one-hundred and forty-four mechanical monsters in a twelve by twelve linked grid. It did exactly what its name implied – it ate entire cities, one forty-eight-foot swatch at a time. The Troughtons had to watch out for individual mechmon (mechanical monsters became mechmonsters became mechmons over the six months since they arrived) but mechmons were easily evaded because the metal aliens made so much noise and traveled in packs of three. As long as humans didn't congregate too much metal together, they were pretty much ignored.

The highways were empty. When the mechmons first landed (actually, they were dropped off along the arctic tree line by the mother ship in thousands of bunches of one gross – like a factory spewing out one-hundred-forty-four four foot by four foot sized cubes at a time), humans stood and gaped in amazement. They went viral on the net, and people looked on them as harbingers of hope and a new alliance with whatever was *out there*. The mechmons, however, totally ignored their adoring fans and opened their mandibles, unfurled their appendages, and began to eat. Humans watched in disbelief as their world changed. The mechmons joined together into twelve by twelve masses – the city-eaters, and the ones left over joined into groups of three by three – the roadsters, or just stayed single. The mechmons were the scouts and moved in triplets, dashing around the countryside with their three appendages: the concave-shaped one hunting for metal, the spatula-shaped one communicating with each other, and the net-shaped one – the horrible net-shaped grabby-thing absorbing and infiltrating anything it came in contact with -- eating. Roadsters also moved in triplets; as scavengers attacking anything larger than a mechmon could handle in less than an hour – which actually and mind-numbingly was a great deal of metal. The roadsters traveled from the mechmons to the city-eaters and back again, like secret agents couriering the where-abouts of precious metals. Once the mechmons discovered roads, to be specific – cars on roads, the roadsters dashed back and communicated the information to the city-eaters, and humanity watched as the bulks moved at a slow pace to the roads, which led to small towns, which led to highways, which led to major cities. Humans were resistant to the idea that they were not, in fact, masters of the roads, and continued to use them as pathways of escape, clogging them with trucks, cars, motorcycles, busses and vans. Each city-eater would plod along the highway, scooping up every vehicle in its path. Cars disappeared inside it whether there were people in them or not. People disappeared inside the machines and were spewed out along with rubber and plastic and cloth and glass as great globs of gelatinous machine-generated excrement. The stench of a fresh pile was horrific for up to four months. Ants and roaches flourished, scouring sustenance from the minutia.

If the people got out of the vehicles and ran off the road, they were generally left alone. Occasionally, a mechmon would hoover down on a flock of survivors, confiscating metal coins, jewelry and glasses and any body parts that might still be attached to them.

Chrissy shuddered and rolled over, refusing to think about the poor soul yesterday. The old woman had had a metal replacement hip and thigh bone: surgical steel – too rich for a mechmon to ignore.

The boy sat up, looking around first in terror and then in resignation.

"It's almost dawn, Doug," Chrissy commented.

"I'll go check my snares."

"Would you teach me how to do that?"

Doug shrugged and then smiled, "Sure, Chrissy."

In Doug's four snares were a rabbit and a rat; the other two had been yanked away from their anchors. "I guess in time, we might need to think of rats as food, but not yet. Right?"

She nodded.

"You can make a snare out of any type of string or wire. But, I don't use any type of metal. I started out using shoe strings, but then you had that yarn. And you could use any type of string or rope, too. I read about snares made from grass woven together into a rope."

"That makes sense, since grass fibers were the first kind of yarn."

"You make a loop, like a slipknot on one end. Then feed the other end through the loop. Tie the noose a little above the ground and anchor it to a branch or shrub. Sometimes you need to hold the noose open with two little twigs. The noose has to be small enough for the head but not too big for the shoulders. See, the animal goes through the noose head first and gets caught. It struggles and strangles."

Chrissy tried not to show how squeamish she felt. Hunger took priority to the thoughts of cute little bunnies. So she nodded again.

Doug sighed. "The first time I set a snare, I caught a huge rabbit. My brother was so proud of me. But the second time, I caught a cat. It was a beautiful calico."

He glanced up at her. She had tears in her eyes, so he continued. "I cried. And my brother helped me bury her. I don't know what she was doing in the Green Swamp. My brother, he was great about it, though. Told me cats were wild once, and I'd actually just caught a wild cat, not someone's pet."

"I think your brother was a really terrific person."

"He was."

"Let's take the rabbit back to Jerry. And I'll unravel that shawl I tore and we'll be able to use the yarn for twice as many snares."

He nodded and gathered his strings.

Later that day, Jerry munched on broiled rabbit. "You know, Doug, you're a great hunter."

"I never thought of myself as a hunter, I just like to read."

"Well, you've done good, hunter. You're going to help us survive."

The teen beamed.

Doug had traveled Highway 98 north from Lakeland to Ocala where he met with Jerry and Chrissy a month ago. Together, they traveled north beside Highway 301 past Citra, Island Grove and Hawthorn. Skirting east of Gainesville, they cut away from the road and traveled due north to Earleton on the shores of Sante Fe Lake. They met up with 301 again at Waldo and followed it north-northeast past Starke. Near Lawtey, the three came upon a shallow grave and a hand-gathered bouquet of wildflowers. The flowers were still fresh.

Chrissy squatted down by the dirt, looking for a marker of some kind. "Well, at least this one didn't get creamed by the city-eaters."

"That's a little harsh," her husband readjusted his straps.

Chrissy stood, brushing the dirt from her pants.

Doug held up a hand and put his finger to his lips. They stilled and heard a deep rumbling voice.

"You're *gonna* have to walk, *chiquita*. I'm sorry your momma died, but we gave her a decent enough funeral. Best we could under the circumstances."

Chrissy pointed at the grave. Doug and Jerry nodded.

"Why won't you talk to me? You hungry? I ain't got nothing to eat, but sure as hell ain't nothing coming to feed us. Get on your feet and let's go. *Vamanos*!" The voice was from about one hundred yards off the road. The voice belonged to a tall, thin man who was speaking to someone seated in front of him, below the scrub brush line.

Jerry put his pack by his feet and raised his hands above his head. "Maybe food is coming to you. I have food and I'll be happy to share or barter."

"*Madre de Dios* - where the hell did you come from?" The young Hispanic stepped protectively in front of a teenaged girl.

"Orlando," Chrissy smiled.

"Lakeland," Doug added.

"You?" Jerry stood still, taking in the bright yellow stripes down the man's navy-blue slacks, along with the two tattooed tears on his left cheek – filled in without the circles. This man's tattoos boasted two murders.

A thin white girl sat on a stump behind him, swaying in a non-existent breeze.

"I'm Chrissy, and my husband Jerry. And our friend Doug."

"I go by Hunter," Doug stated.

"I am Emanuel. And *yo no se* - I don't know her name."

"Nice to meet you, Emanuel, and Miss." Jerry remained still. "We saw a fresh grave here."

"Her momma. She had the diabetes. She ran out of insulin about a week ago. They thought the clinic in Leesburg might have some."

"Leesburg has been wiped off the map," Jerry said.

"They found that out. Kept walking. Found me walking. We walked a while and then she died. I swore to her I would keep good care of the girl. But she never told me her name, and now I can't get the girl to speak, or eat, or move."

Jerry looked at his wife and as they had so often done, they carried out a complete conversation in just a look.

"Hunter and Emanuel," Jerry spoke softly. "I don't like camping this close to the highway. If my map's not mistaken, there's a thin stream runs just north of here. What would you think about the five of us pitching camp for the evening, having a nice meal?"

"I ain't leaving the girl." Emanuel puffed up.

"Of course he won't leave you, honey." Chrissy moved next to the teen.

It startled the young man with prison tats, this shift from *I won't leave her* to *he won't leave you*. But it seemed to assure the teen. She looked up at him for the first time since they'd laid her momma to rest.

"I won't leave you, Angel."

She stood and Chrissy wrapped her in her arms. They walked with the men to the stream.

Chrissy and Hunter worked together setting snares and fishing, so that by dusk, they had what amounted to a small feast.

A chunk of fish slid off Emanuel's stick and onto his slacks. He swore and retrieved the fish which had stuck to the fabric.

"You know," Jerry began gently. "Sometimes the smell of fish gets worse and worse. It becomes a terrible stench, especially if it's stained gabardine. Sometimes," he pointed at Emanuel's gabardine prison slacks. "The best thing to do is just burn the clothing and start fresh. If a man's willing to start fresh, that is."

"I'm willing." Emanuel looked deeply into Jerry's eyes, seeing the new beginning they offered. "But I've always gone commando. If I lose the pants, I'll –" he nodded at Chrissy and Angel.

"I think we're about the same size. And since we've been on the road for most of a month, I think we're all going commando."

The prison slacks and shirt added fuel to that night's flames.

Emanuel bathed in the stream and put on Jerry's extra pair of jeans and T-shirt.

Angel brought her blanket to him and they settled together beside the fire.

"Looking at this map, if we follow the stream, we'll get to Georgia faster and stay clear of most of the towns."

They looked at Jerry, waiting for more, but he waited for them.

"We'll have fishing and better catches in the snares close to fresh water. And if we boil the water, we can drink it," Hunter supported.

"And bathe in it," Chrissy swiped at her grimy neck.

Angel nodded at her.

"I've never heard of mechmons going very far off the roads," Hunter offered. "Sounds good to me."

"Whither thou goest, Love," Chrissy smiled at Jerry.

He looked at Emanuel. "You in?"

Emanuel looked at the girl. She nodded. He smiled. "*Vamanos.*"

After three days, they found an abandoned fishing camp along the Sante Fe River and slept in relative comfort inside the biggest cabin. They stayed for a week while Emanuel dried by stretching and rolling up the hides of all the animals snared. Chrissy dried as much fish as possible. After a day of watching, Angel (for lack of knowing her real name) joined in. By the week's end, they had a month's worth of dried squirrel, rabbit, possum, armadillo and fish for five people.

They rested well, which they all needed to do. And then, after listening to Jerry's suggestion, voted unanimously to follow the river north in three canoes they'd found. They packed up all the bedding from the camp, lanterns, fishing tackle – anything not tied down, and slipped into the stream. Jerry and Emanuel manned one canoe each and Hunter, Angel and Chrissy took turns on the other.

They gathered fruit from trees and bushes along the shore – avocado, papaya, mangoes, cherry laurels. Citrus wouldn't be ripe until winter, but cattail roots were a great starch dish, and wild escaped bamboo shoots added a nice crunch. They saved as much as they could, wary of how long their current bounty might last.

Sante Fe River goes west to 75 and then curls northeast to 231, five miles from Olustee Battlefield and the Historic State Park there. Just where the river bends before curling northeast, they camped in a sugar sand cove as evening approached.

"You know, that pile of skins is starting to stink," Hunter pointed.

Emanuel grinned. "Did you wonder about why I collected all those acorns? Let me show you."

Emanuel spread a towel on the ground and put a huge pot to boil on the fire, filled with about a gallon of water. He gathered two large rocks and the bag of acorns. The man and boy knelt beside the towel and as Emanuel crushed the nuts, Hunter scooped handfuls and put them in the boiling water. When they'd crushed about two gallons worth of acorns, Emanuel removed the pot from the direct heat and let it simmer beside the fire for another hour. While it was simmering, Emanuel and Hunter scraped the underside of the furs clean of meat, veins and fat and then soaked them clean in a plastic tub filled with a cup of laundry soap. Chrissy had taken the laundry soap from the fishing camp.

They rinsed the skins in the river until all the soap was removed and poured the soapy water into the soil rather than the river, knowing the ground would filter it before the water reached the aquifer.

"*Bien*. Now we roll the hides, one into the other – but not tight, until the bundle fits vertically inside this bucket."

They did so.

"And we pour the tannic acid into the bucket, covering the hides. This is why we had to roll them loosely, so the acorn juice gets in between all of it. We need to boil some more water in the acorns to completely fill the bucket and cover the hides."

Once that was accomplished, Hunter asked, "Now what?"

"Now we wait five days to let them soak."

"We're not going to stay here for five days," Jerry countered.

"Could you put the lid on that bucket and store it on a canoe? Would it be too heavy?" Chrissy asked.

"I've only read about doing this with turmeric and salt. Is it better to tan with acorns?"

"Well, Hunter. Me, myself? I don't know. I only read about it, I've never done this before. I had a lot of time to read recently. But since we don't have salt or spices and we do have an abundance of acorns, this works best for us."

"How are you going to oil the skins?"

"Brains, since we don't have neets."

While the men were working on tanning the collected hides, Angel tugged at Chrissy's arm and pointed. A doe stood above them on the ridge, watching.

"She's beautiful," Chrissy murmured.

The doe jumped straight up, clawing at the sky, then landed poorly. It trembled and fell off the ledge into their camp. They shouted in surprise.

As the body writhed, they noticed a wooden shaft protruding from its side.

"Somebody shot it!" Hunter squeaked.

"I did! Back away from my deer."

Instinctively, Chrissy grabbed her knife and pushed Angel behind her. She noticed the men and Hunter had also armed themselves.

Jerry commanded, "Show yourself."

"What, do I look stupid?"

Troughton's people looked at each other. Hunter laughed.

"I don't know. Maybe if you showed yourself, we could tell you – you know – if you look stupid or not," Jerry joked.

"Your deer isn't dead," Chrissy's voice quivered. "It's in a lot of pain."

"You should dispatch it with mercy. Quickly," came the voice.

Chrissy walked to the deer, knelt beside it, and mercifully slit its throat. Blood splattered her chest and face and pooled around her knees. Chrissy began to cry.

Jerry was at her side immediately. He put a steadying hand on her head and called, "Come get your deer. We won't harm you. And we have no need of your meat."

"I have children to feed," came the voice. "You understand."

Jerry conceded, "We understand the need to protect and feed children."

There was a slight pause. "I'm coming down. I'm trusting that you're not like some of the others I've met along the way."

Jerry looked at his people and then helped Chrissy up. "We'll go to the water's edge and leave you to it." To his group, he whispered, "Protect the canoes."

They waited by their laden canoes while a solitary figure made its way down the sandy dune. It seemed to be an older man with graying hair in very large, loose clothing with a bow slung over his shoulder.

They watched in silence as he slung the carcass over his shoulders and proceeded to climb back up the bank. The sugar sand shifted and slipped away from his every foothold up the bank. He finally reached the top.

"I thank you. God bless you for your honesty." The word *honesty* was drawn out into a yell as the man and carcass tumbled backward down the slope, winding up on his back on the beach.

Jerry was the first to reach him. He and Emanuel helped him to his feet.

Hunter gripped his knife and stood defensively between the stranger and the women.

"Easy there," Jerry reassured him. "If you have a rope, it might be easier to try to pull the deer up the embankment."

"My kingdom for a rope," the stranger snorted.

"I'm Jerry Troughton. This is my wife Chrissy and our friends, Emanuel, Hunter, and Angel." He pronounced it as Emanuel did: Ann-Hail.

"Pleased to meet you. I'm the Reverend Ned Chesterfield. May God richly bless you for the kindness you have shown this poor preacher today."

"We might could put the deer in one of our canoes and move it to your children. Are they up or down stream?"

The Reverend ignored Jerry's question. "You might want to wash off that blood before it congeals."

"Nice bow," Chrissy said in reply.

"Well, you know, all those years running summer camps, something worthwhile came out of it."

"Would you consider some sort of trade?"

Emanuel jumped in, "Not that we have much – *por que* – we don't. Five of us, living off the land."

"Living off the land, as God intended." The Reverend eyed them speculatively.

"Intentions are nice. Bows and arrows are better," Chrissy began the bartering.

"Well, there's only five of you, and I got more kids than food. You got food?"

"Some," Emanuel allowed.

"By the look of those pelts there, unless you're eating mighty

11

high on the hog, or you're wiser than you look and you've got plenty stored."

"Nothing wrong with putting things aside for a rainy day," Chrissy didn't smile.

"Well," the Reverend drew out the word. "There's rainy days, and then there's monsoons."

"How many children did you say you have?" Chrissy asked.

He ignored her. "That many pelts, you must know how to prepare the meat, you know, carve up a body. And cook it."

Hunter answered, "I do."

The preacher looked from Hunter to Emanuel to the dead deer at his feet.

Jerry added, "We know how to build a roasting spit for a deer, too. And how long to cook it until it's just tender juicy on the proper side of rare."

The Reverend licked his lips.

"Your children could sleep with full tummies tonight," Chrissy pushed.

"You gonna wash off that blood?" he retorted.

"*Tain't* no children, *verdad*?"

"Nope, Jailbird. I lied."

"Jailbird? *A quien llama* Jailbird, Preacher?"

"No offense!" He held up his hands. "I used to run a prison ministry, years ago, from the inside – you know. A little misunderstanding about extra cards up my sleeve during a poker game. I couldn't help notice the tats and tears."

Jerry held up a hand. "You lied? You have no children?"

"No children," Preacher confessed. "No fire, no knives, no clue how to butcher a deer. But I do have an overwhelming hunger, and a bow and arrows."

"Would the brain keep for five days until the hides tan?" Hunter asked.

"Who's brain?" the preacher asked nervously.

Angel laughed.

They spent two days on the beach, preparing the meat and dividing the loads to include Preacher and his small bag. Hunter was given the task of butchering the deer, but it took team work.

First, they hung the doe by its hind feet from an oak tree overhanging the beach. Hunter dug a small pit under the decapitated corpse so the blood had time to collect and percolate into the soil rather than run off into the river. While it was dripping out, Angel and Emanuel skinned it and added the scraped and cleaned hide to the five-gallon bucket of tanning hides. Then Hunter gutted it, carefully removing the inner organs. He set aside the bladder and the heart and everything else went into a hole he dug on the other side of the fire while Emanuel dosed the inside of the carcass with buckets of water several times to clean it.

"I'll need to wash in the river with soap, and thoroughly clean our knives with soap. Maybe sanitize them in the fire, too. I'm not real sure."

"Safer is better," Jerry concluded.

While they were doing that, Jerry, Chrissy and Ned collected scrub fronds and washed them in the river. These would be used to wrap the pieces of meat to keep them clean and bug free.

"If we had ice, we could age it a couple of days, but it'll be rotten by then in this heat." Hunter sharpened his knives.

"Animals would be attracted to it, too." Jerry squatted down and began sharpening his own knives. "So, how do we do this?"

"See these white lines here? They are the connective tissue running between each muscle group. We'll slide our knives along them and take the large pieces off the bone. We'll hand the pieces to you, Chrissy. Take them over to Emanuel's crushing rocks and you slice off anything that's white or shiny."

"I thought marbling was good in red meat," Ned questioned.

"In beef, yeah. But the fat and sinew in venison makes the meat taste funny if it's cooked with it."

"Where do we put the stuff we trim off?" Chrissy asked. "It'll stink and attract bugs if we leave it around."

"Fishing bait," the preacher suggested. "I'll set up some cane poles while you are butchering the meat and we'll use the trim for catfish. They love stinky bait."

"Good to know," Jerry smiled.

"We'll start with the backstraps and tenderloins, these long muscles along the spine. They are some good eating. They won't need much in the way of trimming. We'll grill them as steaks tonight."

Hunter continued talking – and teaching – while the others sliced and cleaned and began cooking the meat.

"The tenderloins are back here under the spine. Hard to get to, but well worth it. We'll cut them into smaller steaks. The shanks – the meat below the knees – you'll cut up into small chunks for stew or dry as jerky. This outside of the back legs is called rounds. They're good enough for steaks, but we won't be able to preserve them unless you cut them into half-inch strips and pieces and dry them. This here part of the front of the thighs is called top round or sirloin. If we had a meat grinder, we could use it for burgers or sausage."

Jerry handed Chrissy the so mentioned slab of muscle. "We'll put a meat-grinder on our shopping list."

Preacher snorted a laugh.

"Seriously," Chrissy said. "We find all sorts of things in abandoned houses and stores. I'll put it on our list."

"Rib meat is good for jerky or stew, but it's got a lot of white stuff, so you won't be able to trim it like you could the steaks. Shoulders and neck are the same. Just trim the large pieces of white away, and slice the meat into half-inch strips."

"We could cut drying stakes from these oaks and get the jerky going around the fire right now." Emanuel suggested.

Hunter looked at Jerry, who nodded.

"Good work, son," Jerry patted him on the shoulder.

2
TROUGHTON COMPANY

Two days later, they lazily rowed up the stream, taking their time and learning to become more self-sufficient. The morning of July Fourth just south of Lulu, their canoes slowed and they saw where Highway 100 crosses the river. Two people sat on the bridge with fishing poles. They jumped up and one grabbed up a rifle.

Jerry – as lead canoe – rested his oars and put his hands over his head, fingers spread. Jailbird and Preacher did the same.

"Hello the shore!" Jerry called.

"We come in peace," Preacher added.

Chrissy turned, "I can't believe you said that!"

"What? Time-honored greeting," he argued.

"Yeah," called one of the women on the dock. "Usually by invaders intent on pillaging."

"You're the ones with the gun; we've got our hands up." Jerry's voice was calm and sure. "Permission to come ashore?"

The women looked at each other. The older of the two, a black woman with dreadlocks held up in a kerchief, jeans and a long-sleeved pink shirt spoke, "Come ashore. You can tie up along the dock there to your right."

The women pulled out their fishing lines and watched as the

three canoes bumped against the wooden pier. The small dock was flanked by a wooden boathouse and a path led from it up to a ramp off the highway.

Preacher held the canoe still as Hunter climbed out. The women walked down from the road onto the bank and they all stared at each other.

Jerry spoke first, holding his hand out. "I'm Jerry Troughton. This is my crew."

"I'm Miss Olson." She laughed. "Fourteen years of teaching, I forget I have a first name: Jessica."

"I'm Ned, but most here call me Preacher." He took her hand. "This is Peggy."

"Hi," she spoke shyly and rested her rifle over her shoulder.

From the distance came the unmistakable roar of mechmon engines.

"Over there!" Jerry shouted. "Hide behind the boat house."

Everyone obeyed.

They peered around the wooden wall and watched as three mechmons approached them on Highway 100 from the other side of the river. They slowed at the bridge and backed up, turning toward the embankment leading down to the river.

"The canoes!" Chrissy hissed. "They're attracted by the aluminum canoes."

Jerry drew a deep breath. "Hunter, Angel, Preacher, Peggy and Jessica, Form a bucket brigade from the canoes to here. Chrissy, Jailbird and I will pitch up all our supplies. Get them emptied and our stuff to the shore ASAP."

Within five minutes, they had this accomplished. From behind the boathouse, they regrouped and watched as the three mechmons – which had made their way down the embankment - hesitated at the shore.

"Jerry, we've got to sacrifice the canoes," Chrissy proposed. "I think they'll follow the canoes."

He finished her thought, "If we untie them. Float them down

the river."

"Do it!" Jessica encouraged.

Chrissy, Jerry and Jailbird dashed back onto the deck as the mechmons headed into the water. Midstream, submerged, the bubbles escaping from them marked their path. They followed the canoes which floated down stream, leading the mechmons away from the Troughton's crew, beyond the bend.

The Troughtons stayed hidden, listening for the mechmons' return for ten minutes. They heard the sounds of crunching metal and then the sounds of massive metal beings moving back on shore and away.

Peggy and Jessica had a nice camp, centering on a large four-person tent and two bicycles. They had a dozen cane poles with all the fixings.

The Troughtons camped with them for two days and when it was time to move on, Peggy and Jessica joined them.

They traveled northwest through Osceola National Park to 441 and followed it north into Georgia. They skirted west of the Okefenokee Swamp. Halfway between Fargo and Edith, Georgia where 441 and 177 cross, the Troughtons moved swiftly off the road as the sound of motors approached. Rather than a triplet of mechmons, a dozen motorcycles roared past.

"Wow," Jessica exclaimed. "That's what we need."

"How come the mechmons don't chase them?" Preacher asked.

"They ignore our bikes," Peggy mentioned. "Maybe there's not enough metal in the frames."

"No, I've seen mechmons snatch rings off people's fingers," Hunter protested.

"Along with their fingers," Jessica added.

Angel stepped closer to Jailbird. He put his arm around her waist. Chrissy took Jerry's hand and Jerry put his other hand on Hunter's shoulder.

"Maybe it has to do with proximity combined with mass. Man, I wish I had my smartboard and laptop. There's got to be a formula. If we could figure it out, we could stay out of their way." Jessica shook her head.

"What's a smartboard?" Preacher asked.

"It's a whiteboard connected to a laptop," Hunter answered.

"I hate to ask, but what's a whiteboard?"

"You didn't have a white board in your church? In your Sunday School rooms?"

"I never quite got around to having an actual church."

"A white board is like a chalk board – no chalk. Magic markers, sort of," Jessica supplied.

"Smartboard, huh?" And within a day, Jessica's new name was Smartboard.

"Listen," Hunter held up a hand.

"Look, I know north. I'm pointing due north. I know Virginia is not due north but east-north-east. You want to go to Virginia; we're going to have to change our path and take 177."

The Troughtons stopped and listened as a man's voice carried toward them. Another man answered, "Man I spoke to said mechmons are scouring 177, so me and the kids don't go east-north-east. We'll take 441."

"Fine!"

"Fine!"

"So it's good-bye!"

"*Sayonara!*"

Their shouting grew louder, but cut to silence as more motors roared down the road.

"Clear the road," Jerry ordered.

"Billy, get off the road!" a woman shouted.

"Get the kids down!" the first voice demanded.

Returning from up the road, the same dozen motorcycles blew past them.

"Damn bikers," Preacher stood. Smartboard grabbed his arm,

yanking him back down beside her.

Behind the bikers, three mechmons pursued with deafening clanks.

The Troughtons backed away and met three adults and three children creeping away from the road, too.

The two groups eyed each other warily, taking refuge in humanity in the face of the alien threat.

"Dad, do you think those mechmons will be able to catch the bikers?"

"Quiet! They'll hear us!" the boy's mother cried.

"No, they don't seem to respond to sounds," Peggy countered.

"And they've already gone past us, so they don't come back unless it's at a ninety degree angle," the tubby man who had been speaking of directions reassured them.

"So, our two bikes didn't catch their attention; they won't come back?" Chrissy asked.

"I'm sure of it. Seen it dozens of times. I'm from Macon. Joe Lloyd, by the way." The plump young man held out a hand and Chrissy shook it.

The big, older man pointed to each person he named. "I'm Billy Hicks, my wife Daisy-Mae, Billy Junior, Shayla, and Tim."

Jerry introduced his people.

Joe blushed and gaped at Peggy. "She is a beauty, ain't she!"

Peggy blinked and began to smile.

"I love the skin."

Peggy and the rest of the Troughtons frowned.

"Open Country Concealment pattern, right?"

"Her rifle?" Jerry asked.

"You are such a moron," Billy grumbled.

Joe nodded, "Kimber Mountain Ascent Bolt Action rifle. What does she have? Point 280 Ackley improved caliber, twenty-two inch barrel. You got the lighter one, the four point nine pounds?"

Peggy nodded.

"Man! Bolt action, stainless steel barreled action with flute, removable muzzle brake with thread protector cap, three-position safety. She is such a beauty!"

"Yep, he's a moron," Billy shook his head as Peggy smiled.

Jerry looked at Chrissy but addressed the newcomers, "Looks like we're all heading north."

"I'm heading to Norfolk, Virginia." Joe affirmed. "I heard the army's holding the city-eaters off there. Thought I could lend a hand."

"Are you sure?" Jerry asked.

"Sure I'm sure. I heard it from a trucker who heard it from a waitress past Augusta, who heard it from a family out of Jessup and they say they saw it themselves – Army's holding back the city-eaters so the civilians can escape. Cause – as you know – City-eaters move about twelve miles an hour, but they don't leave nothing behind, and they're making their way through Norfolk."

"No," Billy shook his frowzy head. "You got it wrong. Mechmons move at fifteen miles an hour. Roadsters clock about eight. But City Eaters can only move two to five miles per hour, on account they're so heavy and all."

The Troughtons looked at each other, weighing thoughts without speaking them.

"What is it you think you can do against city-eaters, son?"

"Who are you again?"

"They call me Preacher."

"Well, Preacher, you ever heard of instant cement?"

"Yeah."

"Pour it down a mechmon's gullet, wet them down. Sludge turns solid. Mechmon stops in its tracks."

"Yeah, maybe." Billy mumbled. "But the other mechmons will turn on it, eat it, and move on."

"*Verdad*? They eat each other?" Jailbird asked.

"Damn straight. Where you been?"

Jailbird's eyes narrowed suspiciously. Angel took his elbow in defense.

"Shut up, Pizzaboy," Billy growled.

"Seems like a good time to take a meal," Chrissy soothed the stressful situation. "We'd be happy to share with you."

"What you got?" Tim asked, eyes wide.

"Dried fish and mangoes."

"We have corn fritters," Daisy-Mae smiled.

They decided on a clearing well off the road under the shade of pecan trees. The two groups blended well and while the children played and ran, the adults napped in the mid-July heat.

Late afternoon stretched into early evening and another meal.

"So," Jerry broached the subject of Virginia again after the evening meal was cleared up. "Where do you get the quick cement?"

"There's a whole bunch of building supply stores left standing around the country." Joe, aka Pizzaboy, named a half-dozen chains. He continued. "OK. We get a couple bags – easier to carry the five pound bags, but they normally come in eighty-pound sacks – so we could get those and divide them up - and enough water to set the cement."

"How do we get close enough to the mechmons without getting eaten?" Jerry asked.

"You can go right up and touch them, as long as you don't have any metal on you."

"Or in you," cautioned Peggy.

Jerry looked around the fire. "No metal in or out - Who does that include?"

Chrissy raised her hand. So did all of the adults and Hunter.

"Kids have braces, so we keep them as safe as possible." Daisy-Mae spoke softly.

"Have you tried this out?" Jerry asked Pizzaboy.

"Well, in theory, sure. Just not in reality."

"A lot like your love life," Billy laughed.

Pizzaboy reddened, glancing at Peggy.

"We should try it," Chrissy sounded excited.

"We need cement and a mechmon," Smartboard held up two fingers.

"The cement is easy. We just passed through Hoboken and their hardware store had been looted, but I'd imagine no one touched the cement."

"Yeah," Hunter laughed. "Who – in the middle of an alien invasion – wants to pour a patio!"

"Water in a bottle – we've got those." Jailbird held one up.

"So, how do we get a mechmon?"

"The canoes," Preacher stirred the fire. "They were attracted to the canoes and followed them downstream."

"So, what – Trojan horse something with wet cement and hope the mechmons eat it?" Jerry suggested.

"Well, that might work," Billy hummed. "But might not – not before the cement sets."

"And the city eaters eat everything – I don't think feeding wet cement to mechmons would work," his wife added.

"We pour it into the gills," Pizzaboy said it like it was the most natural suggestion in the world.

Everyone listening asked together, "Gills?"

"Well, sure." Pizzaboy blinked. "What, you never seen one up close?"

"No," Jerry looked around. "Anyone I know that got too close didn't survive."

"You're shittin' me!"

"Hey, language!" Preacher growled.

"OK," Pizzaboy took up a stick and began drawing in the dirt. "Mechmons are basic cubes – not to be confused with the Borg kind of cube – because those are just made-up TV science fiction – you know?"

"We know," Jerry said this seriously.

"Mechmons are real. Four feet wide and four feet deep. Right here, on the top of left front corner, are these vents that open and close."

Hunter frowned, "That's what they spew their stuff out of."

"Yeah," Shayla grimaced.

Pizzaboy continued, "Jab something pokey-like into one, bust out the vents, pour in the cement dust and water. Bam!"

"Pokey-thing has to be – what – wood?" Billy asked. "Like a pick handle." Peggy suggested.

"Wooden spear – sharpened at one end," Jailbird added.

"And available at the local hardware store," Smartboard concluded.

"OK, OK!" Jerry stood. "Then we'll need mechmon bait."

"Bicycles. I'll donate mine to the cause," Peggy stood, too.

"One bicycle's not enough." Chrissy spoke. "Is it? It hasn't been so far."

"If we're going shopping, seems we just need to put metal on our list."

Jerry nodded.

Jailbird put his arm around Angel. "Serious? We're going to kill a mechmon?"

Jerry took a deep breath and looked at their faces. "We'll take a vote. All in favor of kicking the aliens in the rear say *aye*."

The people cheered.

"All opposed?" Jerry's question was answered with silence.

There were people living in the small town. They looked out from behind blinds and drapes as Troughton's group of nine adults and two teens walked into town. They'd left their baggage in a safe hiding place outside of town, guarded by the three Hicks children. They each carried a whittled brand as a walking stick or as Pizzaboy called them – atlatls. They were similar to the Australian *womera* and the Alaskan *Nuquaq* in that they were long shafts of wood which cupped a fletched spur or dart at one end and was balanced by a thicker knob at the other. They had begun making darts and arrowheads from deer bones and bird feathers.

"You throw it overhand from shoulder-height, just like a spear. But the energy from your thrust is compressed by the shaft and the dart can be flung about two hundred yards with accuracy," Pizzaboy explained.

"Looks like a walking stick. Kills like a harpoon." Jerry nodded. "I like it!"

Preacher had his bow and arrows, Peggy had her rifle. Their knives were sheathed but in easy reach. They formed a loose circle so they could watch all directions and moved directly to the hardware store.

At the opening where the glass doors lay shattered about the ground, Jerry assigned Preacher and Peggy as guards. "Heads up inside. Don't take any chances. Shout out if you see anything wrong."

"Oh! Magazines!" Smartboard pointed.

"Teachers never change," Hunter laughed.

"We do change, because we can read new things – like this – how to bake a turkey in a can."

"Look, there's one on edible mushrooms," Daisy-Mae joined in.

"Focus, people." Jerry redirected them.

"Divide and conquer," Chrissy countered. "I see a sign for Archery supplies."

"Alright, stay in twos." He conceded. "Regroup here in fifteen minutes."

"Anyone still have a watch?" Jailbird asked.

Angel laughed.

Two minutes in, Daisy-Mae squealed, "OHMYGOD!"

They all reached her at a dead run. She had three jugs of laundry detergent clamped to her ample breasts and two more in the cart.

Jerry growled; Billy turned pink. Smartboard laughed, "You can't blame her – it's lavender scented."

"Keep a tally of what we take." Jerry turned to go back to the handles. "Shopping cart's a good idea."

Daisy-Mae smirked.

Within fifteen minutes, they met at the front and used a yellow pad to write everything down: twelve five-pound bags of quick-crete, two dozen shovel handles, seven extra-large plastic funnels, nine gallons of lavender-scented laundry detergent, two five-man tents, four magazines, six sleeping bags, an economy size bag of toilet paper, and – presented with a flourish – three sets of bow and arrows.

"I'm still not sure two bicycles will be sufficient bait," Jerry said. "Wait here." He grabbed an empty cart and headed to the nail department. They heard the unmistakable rattling of chains. Then Jerry retuned. "Four yards of heavy steel chain. The sign said it was thick enough to anchor a yacht. Write it down, please."

Smartboard did so.

"*Porque excribamos todos?*"

"Because we are not thieves and we are not looters." He took Smartboard's pen and paper and wrote:

Approximate sum of goods:
3 deer, 1 bushel of dried fish, and 2 gators.
Due within one month.
Sincerely,
Jeremiah Troughton & Company

He then dated it and used a patch of silver duct tape to attach it to the post of what used to be the front door.

As they each pushed a cart up the road, Peggy leaned in to Chrissy, "Is it my imagination, or is your husband swaggering, just a bit?"

"I do believe he is!"

"I do believe you'll get a little something in the bedroll tonight."

"God, I wish! We haven't had any privacy since we left Orlando, months ago."

"You know, my parents used to go sasquatch-hunting."

"Excuse me?"

"Yeah, about once a week, we'd all have an early dinner and mom would send us to bed with the warning that she and dad were going sasquatch-hunting that night, so no matter what fierce growling or other noises we might hear, we weren't to come into their room, because we might get mauled by a sasquatch."

"Sasquatch-hunting!"

"Yep. We could drop a spare sleeping bag a ways out of camp – safe and close – but distant enough for privacy."

"Jerry looks great swaggering up the road."

"Chrissy, if you don't take your husband sasquatch-hunting tonight, I will!"

Beet red, Chrissy grinned.

"It sounds like that sasquatch is eating Chrissy up," Hunter sat up in alarm.

"I'm sure he probably is, little one," Peggy rolled over.

"They're not really hunting sasquatch, are they," Hunter's voice cracked.

A few adults giggled.

"Well, son, they might not bring back a sasquatch, but maybe they'll give you a baby brother next year."

"I ain't your son, Preacher; nor theirs."

"Well," the man's voice bore no umbrage at the rebuke. "Jerry loves you like a son. You could do worse than the likes of him for a dad, adopted or real."

"I did do worse," Hunter growled. "Jerry's great. He'd make the best dad. Better than mine ever was."

Pizzaboy sat up. "I'd like him to be my dad, too."

"Shut up, moron. You're the same age as Jerry," Billy rolled up against his wife.

"Shut up, Beer Belly," Pizzaboy countered. Billy was irrevocably called Belly from then on.

"Oh. Jerry God Jer-" came a passionate refrain from the sasquatch-hunt.

"*Madre de Dios!*" Jailbird threw back his blanket. "You cannot sleep that close to me tonight, Angel. God almighty, you are – what - fifteen?" He walked away and settled on the opposite side of the camp.

"OK," Smartboard tried to sound logical. "Next time, we'll suggest they go a little further afield for their sasquatch-hunt."

"Is that a hoot owl?" Preacher asked.

"Shut up, everyone. Go to sleep!" Belly grumbled.

Hunter began giggling. So did Shayla and her brothers and Angel. As hysteria and joy swamped the campers, they settled back in their spots.

"Troughton and Company."

"What's that, Hunter?" Preacher asked while everyone else listened.

"Jerry signed that paper *Troughton and Company*. I like it – we're all Troughton and Company."

"Hoyah!" Pizzaboy's guttural affirmation was joined by everyone.

"Oh yes!" Jerry's shout seemed to agree with them.

It was a lot simpler than Troughton and Company had imagined.

They piled the chains in the middle of the road and took positions on either side. Each pair had specific tasks. One person would run in from the side, jump on top of the cube, shove their wooden pike into the gills, and gouge as big an opening as possible. The partner would shove the business end of a funnel into the opening and pour in the powdered mix. The first person would dump two pints of bottled water into the gill opening once the funnel was removed. Then they would both jump down and run away.

Chrissy and Jerry, Jailbird and Angel, Peggy and Belly were the pairs. Daisy-Mae would keep the children safe at camp. Preacher and Smartboard guarded the roads, ready to step in as substitutes if necessary. Pizzaboy – as the strategist, observed from the boughs of a pine tree. Hunter was scout and kept a few yards ahead of the mechmons.

They disavowed themselves of any metal – including zippers and bra underwires. They piled the bait in the middle of the road. Hunter got on one bike and headed north. Within an hour, he came flying back, three mechmons in pursuit.

Chrissy and Jerry chose the central beast – the hardest to get to, leaving Jailbird and Angel to take the east one and Peggy and Belly the one on the west. They had practiced each step, chanting each step until they were memorized, and now it was for real:

1) mount, stab, twiddle the vent open, step aside
2) jab funnel into hole, unroll already opened bag and dump it into the funnel, jiggle the funnel until the powder was inside, jump off
3) first person pours both bottles of water into the opening and jumps off.

They all dismounted about the same time, no more than three minutes start to finish.

The mechmons ignored the attacks on their exteriors, intent on devouring the rich metal chain.

The Troughtons retreated to a very safe distance and observed the mechmons finish the chain, sniff the area with the hose-like protuberances that morphed into grabby-things and back again, and then continued their journey south.

The Troughtons followed. Nothing happened for ten minutes. Then the aliens slowed. They chugged. Rainbow tinted translucent fumes seemed to curl up from their choked vents and their protuberances flailed about.

Then they stopped.

In the ensuing silence, Pizzaboy spoke, "I don't suppose I've earned a sasquatch-hunt?"

"Abso-fruiting-lutely!"

"Not you, Belly," Pizzaboy frowned.

Peggy flung her arms around his neck and tried to suck his wisdom teeth out. "Abso-fruiting-lutely," she whispered.

Hunter took a canister out of his hoody pocket and shook it vigorously. He stared at the three bulks with his head tilted, still shaking the can. He glanced over his shoulder to Jerry – to make sure he was watching. Jerry was. Hunter uncapped the canister of red spray paint and in large letters, wrote: TROUGHTON & Co. WAS HERE.

Jerry whooped and threw his arm around the boy's shoulder. "Come on, son. I do believe we're having fried fish for dinner."

They had the opportunity to practice on two other sets of mechmons before they needed to resupply. They used the already stopped monsters as bait. Hunter tagged the second set as the first: TROUGHTON & CO WAS HERE. On the third set, he wrote MECHMONS BEST BE A'FEARED.

Smartboard approved and sounded it out like a cadence. The company joined in as they marched back to camp.

They headed into town the next day, planning to restock. On the yellow legal paper they'd taped to the hardware store, they found large red letters scrawled across their receipt: PAID IN FULL. GOD BLESS YOU, TROUGHTON COMPANY.

It was a slow journey: from Hoboken up 203 to Blackshear, north on 15, taking 121 through Surrency, Mendes, and Manasas, around the totally eaten Ft. Steward and Savannah, continuing on 121 to Millen, staying in Magnolia Springs State Park for a few days, then 25 north to Augusta. They had planned to join the Army in Virginia, but by September, the army had fallen back to Augusta. Troughton Company camped alongside Highway 25 and watched as hordes of people fled on foot, bike, horse and an occasional motorcycle from the gorgeous town of Augusta, Georgia. The city-eaters' paths gouged three columns north to south, forty-eight feet wide each, barely inches apart but twelve miles ahead of each other. They had been munching their way through buildings and streets for two weeks now, having left a smeared path behind that used to be Norfolk and points in between.

"We'll get a good night's sleep and then head towards the southernmost city-eater first thing tomorrow." Jerry stretched out and pulled Chrissy into his arms. She smiled in contentment and offered him a piece of her guinea fowl.

"If we go past the two and hit the northernmost," Hunter suggested, "and then the middle one, and then the southernmost, we could kill all three in a week."

Jerry nodded. "You're a good strategist, Hunter. But by my way of thinking, if we take out the south CE, the next two will stop to investigate and recycle it. My intention is to slow their progress to allow the citizens more time to escape. We'll have all three of them in the same spot, so we won't have the danger of travel."

Preacher leaned his shoulder against Smartboard's knees. "But, it'll still take time."

"Time to re-stock on cement and rods." Jailbird nodded.

"Time to teach the army how to do this, too," Chrissy added. "Ya'll heard those refugees yesterday. The 74th Cavalry is being wiped out because they're still trying to fight with modern weapons."

"Maybe," Peggy held up her hands. "I know this sounds harsh – but maybe it's a good thing – for our purposes – to have the army keeping the mechmons distracted. At least until we hit the first CE."

Belly smacked his wife's rump as she walked past him. "We've never killed a CE before. At most, we've done well with the roadsters. That's nine of them linked, but they were still mechmons. Are you sure CE's are just linked mechmons?"

"Yes. Twelve wide by twelve long. Linked just like the

roadsters." Sally – a voluptuous blonde - had joined the group at the beginning of August. She had been from Chicago, when there was still a Chicago.

"So, how do we do this? Which positions do we sting?" Jerry asked his company.

Smartboard drew a twelve by twelve grid in the dirt. "If we're still doing this in five pairs, I suggest we form diagonal lines from the left foremost corner in toward the center. First pair stings the first mechmon and then runs like hell to the left furthest back corner. Second pair hits the mechmon linked cattycorner to the first and then runs to the other end. Third through fifth pairs, the same way. They'll have the furthest to run at first, and less to run next, so we should be stinging the back-left diagonal at the same time. She filled in each box of the grid as she explained. "Left side front then back. Then run like hell to the back right, sting them and run up to the front right." Her grid started with a /, became a >, then a Y and finally an X. "Jump off. Run back to cover."

"Just in time for the quick-crete to set in the left side." Preacher whistled.

"Excellent." Jerry's one word said everything.

3
HISTORY CHANNEL

"In 197 BCE, a Macedonian Phalanx was being opposed by a Roman Legion. They had twenty-foot spikes which served to kill when held parallel to the ground, and could deflect air-born projectiles when held at forty-five degrees. However, the soldiers wielding them could not change directions unless the spikes were held straight up. So, Flaminius changed the rules of battle, and attacked the Macedonians from the rear."

The Troughtons looked down over the overpass of the intersection of 25 (Gordon Highway) and 56 (Doug Barnyard Parkway) onto the colonel and the 74th Cavalry below. The colonel stood head and shoulders above the rest of his soldiers but wasn't on any type of platform. His broad shoulders and tight ass were made prominent by his khaki uniform. Muscular thighs and arms – the kind that came from hard work, not just nights at the gym – put him at about two-hundred twenty pounds.

"Where are their horses?" Pizzaboy asked.

Jailbird pointed, "Bikes. Two Harleys, an Indian, a Kawasaki, and a couple of custom jobs by the look of them."

"Mechmon fodder," Smartboard growled.

The colonel tilted his head and listened to a messenger, who spoke excitedly and pointed onto the overpass where the Troughtons had gathered. The colonel shook his head. "We regroup, get behind this CE, find its weakest patch."

Jerry kissed his wife and hugged Hunter. "Let's go sting them where it hurts."

Chrissy cupped her hands over her mouth and bellowed, "Hey, History Channel, watch this!"

They began running and chanting, "Troughton Company is here. Mechmons best be a'feared!"

The colonel held up his hand and his troops watched in trepidation as ten civilians ran toward the city-eater. They climbed onto the front left corner unmolested.

The pairs worked with speed and agility, calling out to each other encouragements and accomplishments.

"One-Left, done!" Jailbird shouted. He and Angel ran to the back corner.

"Two-Left, done!" Jerry grabbed Chrissy and dashed to the backside.

It continued with precise timing. A line became a chevron, then a Y and finally a massive X began to appear on top of the CE.

"Twelve-Right, done!" was shouted at the same time as "Six-Right, done."

The four pairs were scrambling down the east side of the CE just as Jailbird shouted, "One-Right, done!"

They ran, out-pacing the slow creature and jumped back on top of the overpass just as the CE chugged. It shivered and the Troughtons cheered. It began flailing its nozzles about and the individual mechmons gleaning its path returned to its side. The 74th rose in a frenzy of cheers.

The CE stopped. It didn't die, but it couldn't move.

"Private," the colonel called the messenger over. "Go to Troughton Company and give them my compliments. Ask them to parley."

Colonel Peter Glynn watched as the Troughtons kissed and

hugged each other. Two of them – a fat, pot-bellied man in his fifties and a chubby man in his thirties mooned the disabled CE. Some members of the 74th did the same. He observed as the private deliver his message to the bearded man holding onto the red-haired woman and blond teen. Jerry Troughton – Glynn presumed – a legend in these parts – noted for guerilla attacks on mechmons – successful ones – shook his head and raised his hand. His company stilled and listened to him. He pointed northwest, toward the middle CE.

A plump woman in her forties and three children pulled the tarp off a shopping cart they had brought with them. Glynn watched as the Troughtons grabbed five stakes and a satchel and a funnel.

The private arrived out of breath. "Troughton Company sends their regards, Colonel. They respectfully decline your invitation but counter with an offer of their own."

"What offer?"

"They request ten of us to join them in the next assault."

Another messenger – a corporal -- interrupted. "The middle CE stopped dead and has begun moving southeast, straight at the disabled CE."

"Straight at us."

"Yes, sir. Should be here in three hours or less."

"Major Crumbley!"

The tall woman saluted.

"Gather eight of your best soldiers. Make damn sure Mickey's one of them. Mount up! We've been invited to repeat what we've just seen done."

"Yes, sir!" She quickly assembled her team. They rode up onto the overpass within fifteen minutes; two hours and forty-five minutes to spare.

Jerry met the colonel with a handshake. "Welcome, Colonel. We thought you might like to go with us on the next volley. Depending on how well you do on the second, we might just let you take the third one out by yourselves."

"The third one is twenty-four miles away." Major countered. "Six hours at best but going due south."

"Mechmons are attracted to the biggest mass of metal. Right now," Hunter pointed at the CE. "That's it."

Chrissy handed Hunter a bottle of water. "When we take out the second one, the third one will head this way, too. They'll have to stop and go directly east and then stop again and trace their first one's path."

"They can't shift diagonally," Hunter added.

"We are quite aware of how CEs move," the major growled.

Daisy-Mae stepped up. "There's enough metal in those bikes to attract the feeder mechs. Get them out of here."

Glynn glared.

Jerry supported Mrs. Hicks. "We have children here. We know what we're doing. Trust me. Take the bikes away. If you're to do this, you can't have any metal on you. No zippers, no steel-toed boots, no braces even. We can crawl all over these mechmons, roadsters, and City-eaters without raising their alarm – but only as long as we have no metal."

"Empty your pockets, too." Chrissy added. "You've heard loose lips sink ships? Well, loose change, lose your hips."

"That's a little harsh," Jerry whispered to his wife.

Glynn nodded at the major, "Make it so." He bent down and unlaced his boots.

"I'm sorry, colonel," Chrissy spoke gently. "You'll have to take off your wedding ring, too."

He looked down at her five-foot-three frame from his six-foot-four height and deep sorrow forced its way into his rugged features. He shoved the emotion back and away and yanked off his ring.

Jailbird ordered, "Put all your stuff in the saddlebags of your bikes. But get someone to take the bikes back to your camp."

"Mickey," Glynn shouted. "Time?"

"ETA, an hour."

"Talk fast, Troughton. The next monster is on its way," Glynn growled.

Smartboard grabbed a stake. "They've got gills at the front left corner of each unit. It doesn't matter how deep or how shallow you hit, just slam your rod in and gouge the gills open." She demonstrated jabbing down and pulling the stake back and forth.

Preacher took up the instructions. "Second member of the team jabs this funnel into the hole and first person holds it steady while second pours the bag of cement into it." He and Smartboard knelt side by side; she held the funnel and he pretended to pour from a sealed bag.

She finished the process. "Second grabs the stake and runs to the next gill flap while number one pours a gallon of water into the funnel. And then runs after her partner just in time to stab the funnel into the hole that's been gouged into the beasty."

"Beasty?" Mickey laughed.

The Troughtons tensed at yet another seeming barb from the 74th.

"We've dissected one. There's no flesh inside. It's a toaster."

"Play nice, Mickey," Glynn cautioned.

"Point is, Colonel. It is simple, but you've got to work as a team. And once the cement starts thickening, you've got to be clear of the beasty, because those nozzle apparatus-things come out to make repairs and to defend. They can slice a man wide open or suck him straight inside in two seconds flat, whether he's got metal on him or not."

Glynn never made snap decisions. He faced Jerry Troughton and weighed his thoughts based on what he'd seen and heard. He nodded.

"OK." Jerry pointed, "Mickey? You'll work with my wife. Major, you're with Hunter. Colonel, you'll go with Angel. She doesn't speak, so I hope you were paying attention." Jerry paired them all up. They grabbed supplies and watched as the second CE munched its way toward them.

A band of soldiers ran up from camp and drove away on the bikes, much to Daisy-Mae's relief.

"We can't let them touch. If we do, they'll just trade out working units for disabled ones and ingest what's left behind." Jerry tugged affectionately on Chrissy's braid. "One down, two to go. Let's go sting them where it hurts!"

They took off running and shouting their motto.

It took longer to disable the second CE. The Troughtons had worked together for months; they made assumptions that the 74th didn't understand. But it worked. Within thirty minutes, two CEs rested side by side, flailing black nozzles, but unable to move.

Twenty volunteers awaited them on the overpass, armed with stakes, funnels (some make-shift), bags of cement and gallons of water. Daisy-Mae and Sally had already given them instructions, and they were naked of anything metallic.

"OK," Jerry shouted. "Experienced, take a new partner. We'll go in as a straight line and hit the gills in an upside-down V. So, hit the corners closest first, next pair step up a unit sequentially and then race to the opposite side and hit them in a V from center point. Then jump off in any direction other than the direction it is moving and rendezvous here."

"Any questions?" Glynn asked.

Chrissy spoke, "Troughtons, rest and recoup. Drink plenty of water."

Sally winked at Mickey, "You can always pee in the gill hole."

"Sally, don't be vulgar."

"Sorry, Preacher."

"And Pizzaboy, get your hands off Peggy. You can go sasquatch-hunting tonight. Save your strength."

"Yes, Preacher," they answered together.

"Sasquatch-hunting?" Glynn asked.

Chrissy blushed. "You can figure it out."

"Oh! Sasquatch-hunting!" Jerry nuzzled into Chrissy's neck. She gave him a passionate kiss and then pulled away. "Save your strength."

"Yeah, ETA is less than an hour for the third CE," Glynn agreed.

"I meant, save your strength for tonight," Chrissy grinned at Jerry and sat down.

Glynn looked down and away, thinking about the wedding ring he had just relinquished until this battle was over.

As the third CE approached the two writhing ones, mechmons swarmed toward it, like bees to a hive. The CE slowed and then stopped a mile from the Troughton's perch on the overpass.

Jerry and Glynn stood next to each other, watching.

"What the hell are they doing?" Glynn mused.

"They're communicating." Jerry turned back towards his people. "Watch out for accommodations and modifications. They're not stupid; they're logical linear machines. They adapt. Like Flaminius of the Roman Legions, they're changing the rules. You see a nozzle, you abandon your mission and jump off. Hear me – no heroics. We're just here to slow their momentum. You can't kick tin butts if you're dead!"

The two disabled CEs began to tremble. Feeder mechmon dashed from one to the other, grinding noises filled the air as the two beasties broke apart, shifted and reformed, moving the twenty dead cells out and away from each CE. The first CE broke even farther apart and twenty cells left it to attach to the second CE, completing it. Eighty-four cells of the first CE divided into nine roadsters (nine cells each) with three mechmons left over to join the other feeders. The roadsters began moving in threes east, south and west. The newly complete CE continued its path south. The third one, waiting, turned south also.

"Snap."

"Preacher, you don't usually cuss," Smartboard took his arm.

"You're right, darling. Holy Snap. Is that better?"

She clung to him, but smiled.

"Colonel," Jerry looked exhausted. "Two complete CE, plus nine roadsters. That's three-hundred-sixty-nine cells. If we could hit them all at the same time, we'd be heroes. You got any cement?"

"I think that's the only way. If not, they'll just keep reforming."

"Dad, we've got thirty five-pound bags of cement left. That's it."

Jerry took Hunter's shoulder. "Roadsters move faster than the CEs and are more viscous around people. If we hit every cell in a roadster, we can kill three of them."

"If you leave the center cells, they can't break free by themselves. That will give us three more bags of cement, enough to stop a fourth roadster."

"Good thinking, son. Troughtons! We'll hunt the roadsters that went south and east."

"Now wait a minute. You can't make that kind of a decision."

"Says who, History Channel?" Chrissy grabbed her braid and glared at him. The rest of the Troughtons took similar stances.

"You've got all of the cement and stakes. You're going after smaller roadsters while we're staring down the gullets of two full-sized city-eaters."

Jerry stepped towards him and spoke firmly. "Glynn, not my place to tell you how to run your army. Not your place to tell me how to run mine. But I'd strongly suggest you pillage each and every hardware store within the area for bags of cement, funnels and wooden stakes, not to mention gallons of water. You've got about one-thousand men, I've got thirteen. Do something brilliant: adapt."

Chrissy shouted out, "Let's sting them where it hurts!"

The Troughtons split up and ran.

Jerry went with Hunter, Preacher and Smartboard after the

eastward roadsters. The rest of them followed the ones going south. Since the intent was to destroy all three of them, theirs was the safest path. The four Troughtons tackling one out of three roadsters left them vulnerable to attack.

They accomplished their objectives and met up with the shopping cart and Belly's family at their campsite in the early hours the next morning. They ate, slept, and went sasquatch-hunting and finally met as a company late that afternoon.

The 74th had not fared so victoriously. They split their resources between the two CEs and while these were being stopped, foraged the countryside for more supplies. By later afternoon, while the Troughtons were sharing a meal, the 74th had moved camp and were trying to recoup. They'd lost thirty men to the black nozzles, but what was left of two complete CEs by midmorning amounted to seven roadsters. Those, along with the other five that escaped, were being hunted down.

"Find them. Kill them. And find me the Troughtons." Glynn stuck his wedding band back on before collapsing onto his cot in his tent.

4
HEY, MICKEY!

"Damnation," Belly hissed while handing his binoculars to Pizzaboy. "The 74th is louder than moose in heat!"

"Meese? Mooses?" Pizzaboy speculated.

"What do you call just one moron?"

"I don't know," Pizzaboy held the glasses to his face.

"Pizzaboy," Belly snorted.

"What?"

Preacher shook his head.

"What do you suppose they're looking for?" Pizzaboy sat up.

"Us," Preacher and Belly both said.

"Question is," Preacher continued. "Do we let them find us or not?"

"Let's go tell Jerry." They all-but-silently made their way back to camp.

Daisy-Mae had two buckets and a shopping cart in front of her. A laundry soap jug, a long stick, and a collapsible clothes line were all within reach.

"I'm washing darks today. Get a pile going next to the big tub."

Belly dropped his overalls on the spot, blinding everyone with his shiny white ass.

"Hey! Some decorum, Mr. Hicks!" Smartboard covered her eyes.

"Yeah baby, this decorum's why my wife's smiling all the time." He kissed Daisy-Mae profoundly, dropped his overalls onto the pile, and sauntered into their tent.

"We have got to find a store that still has underwear," Jerry whispered to Chrissy. She laughed and finished filleting a fish.

"Preacher squatted down beside them. "74th's got soldiers out beating the bushes. They're led by that sergeant with the pretty eyes – Mickey."

"Well, they've got about a thousand civilians they're moving west, plus the soldiers make up about five hundred; they must be running low on food."

"No, Chrissy, they're not hunting animals, they're hunting us."

"Makes sense," Jerry nodded. "We're independent; Army-folk don't like independent factions."

Pizzaboy handed Jerry the binoculars, "Rogue Warriors. I like it!"

"So they're looking to – what? Subjugate us?"

"I wish you'd stop using those fifty-cent words, Smartboard. Makes me hot!" Preacher patted his chest.

Smartboard rolled her eyes and walked away.

"Preacher?" Pizzaboy grinned. "You and Smartboard been sasquatch-hunting?"

"Thinking about it," he smiled.

"Well done!" Jerry clapped him on the back. "Congrats."

"I'm not moving. I've got washing, rinsing, waiting and a clothes line full. We're tired and we need to rest up and restock."

"Daisy-Mae, don't worry. We all need to keep camp here. But the question remains – what are our options when the 74th does find us?" Chrissy kept working on the fish while she spoke.

"They'll need our expertise on stinging the mechmons. So they'll come at us nicely." Jerry stuck each fillet with a thin dowel,

42

preparing them to be dried. "We've been under martial law for a year now, so that gives the army the right to conscript civilians as needed."

"We're not just civilians, we've got children here," Chrissy argued.

Preacher lowered his voice so Daisy-Mae couldn't hear. "We've only got six children under the age of reason – Biblically speaking – thirteen. If they conscript us, Hunter, Angel, Little Bill and maybe Shayla will be tapped, too."

Jerry matched Preacher's volume. "Then they'll most likely split us up into twos and threes – just enough to pass on what fighting strategies we've learned and divide what authority and loyalty we have."

Chrissy glanced at Hunter teaching Shayla how to improve her aim with the bow. Her heart caught in her throat. "They're not splitting us up. We're family. We're the Troughtons. They're not splitting us up."

"Steady on, Love." Jerry took her elbow and kissed her cheeks. "We're the Troughtons, but they're the law."

The people around Jerry exchanged glances but didn't vocally disagree with their leader.

"I'm going to suggest we rest up here for a while. If they get close enough to find us, we send out an ambassador. I'm thinking Sally would do nicely."

Chrissy grinned and snorted a laugh.

"If they want to play nice, we play nice. If not, Pizzaboy, Sally and Peggy can lead them on a wild goose chase while we disappear into the woods. I'm thinking we meet up at that little camp we found just out of Brunswick."

"We can pack and run within three hours."

"Yeah," he nodded at his wife. "Tell the kids to keep close to camp. And ask Daisy-Mae if she'd make sure that stretchy pink sweater Sally wears is clean."

"You know, Mickey," the feminine voice hovered in the trees above the scouting party's head. "You sure have the prettiest eyes."

Mickey slowly raised his hands; his two soldiers did likewise.

Sally and Pizzaboy dropped from the pine trees and smiled nicely.

One of the soldiers cocked her head, "It's the end of summer. Isn't that sweater hot?"

"It sure is," Mickey agreed.

Sally grinned and stuck out her hand to shake his.

"What you doing so far from your people?" Pizzaboy asked innocently.

"We're looking for you. We have a proposition the colonel wants to make to Jerry Troughton."

Pizzaboy looked at Sally. She spoke, "You come. They stay here."

"My team stays together."

One of the team – the tag on his badly ripped and repaired uniform stated Yolanski – offered, "We brought food."

"You got whiskey?" Pizzaboy asked.

Yolanski paled, "That's illegal now. Colonel's orders."

"Snap, no wonder you boys and girls look a little peaked."

Sally drew a deep and admirable breath and let it out, "What else is illegal under the colonel's reign?"

"Gambling," the woman growled.

"Preacher will hate to hear that."

"Pizzaboy, right?" Mickey shook his hand. "I'd really like to meet with Troughton. This is Todd Yolanski and Megan Edwards. My people and I brought food as a peace offering."

"What you got?" Sally tilted her head.

Mickey nodded. Yolanski knelt down and opened his pack. A jar of peanut butter, two boxes of saltines, and a box of breakfast cereal peeked out.

Sally shook her head sadly. Pizzaboy grinned and took the

peanut butter. "The children will like this. Thank you."

"You'll take us to Troughton?" Mickey asked.

Sally answered, "We'll bring Troughton to you."

"And we'll bring you food." Pizzaboy added. "Go a half a mile that way. There's a nice clearing and an old water well. Wait there."

"And don't follow us."

They waited until Mickey's team walked out of sight.

They returned in two hours with ten pounds of dried venison, a small burlap bag full of pecans, and another one full of peanuts. Plus, Sally had changed into skinny jeans and a thin cotton sleeveless blouse. She'd wanted to wear Daisy Dukes cut-offs, but Jerry shook his head.

Jerry, flanked by Chrissy and Hunter, came into the clearing behind Pizzaboy and in front of Sally. Mickey stood first, smiled friendly-like and stuck out his hand.

"Mr. Troughton, Colonel Glynn sends his regards and the entire 74th Cavalry wishes to thank you and yours again for your assistance last week."

Jerry shook his hand and stared him in the eyes while his team each picked a member of Mickey's team to watch. They didn't smile friendly-like.

"You came a far bit just to say thanks."

"That's not the only reason we came. Colonel would like to discuss a few things with you."

"Does this discussion have to be face-to-face, or can you do some of the speaking for your colonel?"

"I've been authorized to begin negotiations."

"I see you found the well; it draws clear and clean." Jerry nodded.

"May I offer you a cup of water, Mrs. Troughton?" Yolanski asked.

"That's very kind of you, Mr. Yolanski." She smiled. "We brought two dozen empty bottles. I'd appreciate your help filling them."

Yolanski glanced at Mickey, who nodded, before holding out his hand. "I'd be delighted to, Mrs. Troughton."

They walked together to the well.

Pizzaboy put his sacks at his feet. "The children liked the peanut butter. They thought you might like some venison jerky and nuts."

Megan Edwards licked her lips and stared hopefully at the bag.

"If you've got a pot or pan, I'll show you how to soften it into stew."

Edwards nodded eagerly and Pizzaboy followed her to the other side of the campfire.

"Mr. Troughton," Mickey began again. "I'm authorized to offer you a commission in the US Army as a major in the 74th Cavalry. Your leaders can have officer standings as well, commiserate with training and skills."

Jerry kept a deadpan expression, "You play poker, son?"

"Poker?" Mickey tried not to read an insult into the term *son*, but both men were about the same age. "That's a card game, right?"

"If that's your opening bid, I can't help but wonder if you're bluffing, or desperate."

"We're desperate, sir."

"Well," Jerry put his hand on Hunter's shoulder. The boy sheathed his knife. "I've never been interested in being an officer, but since Sally here says you've got the prettiest eyes she's ever seen, I'll give a listen. What's Glynn want in exchange?"

Mickey pointed at the campfire and they sat out of the heat but close enough to the smoke to keep the mosquitoes away.

Hunter nodded at Jerry, "I'll take first watch."

Jerry smiled, "Thanks, son."

The boy beamed and swaggered to the edge of the clearing.

"Would you like to pull up a patch of grass and join us,

Sally?"

She looked at Mickey as if he'd just asked her what her sign was. Then she rolled her shoulders, managing to expand the opening of her blouse to show rock-hard cleavage.

"Sally is my knight-at-arms right now."

She glanced at Jerry.

Jerry continued, "We don't know you, and you shouldn't be so damn trusting of us."

Mickey tensed.

"I'll be the first to put an arrow through your throat, should you or yours become deceitful." She quickly snatched an arrow from her quiver, set it, pulled back and relaxed it again.

Mickey took a calming breath and crossed his hands over his lap – because she hadn't pointed her arrow anywhere near his throat. "You're not quite the homespun militia the colonel thought you were."

"We're the Troughtons," she stated, end of subject.

Jerry scratched his ear. "So, what does Glynn want in exchange for honoring us with official ranks?"

"Guidance, expertise in the field of battle." Mickey sniffed the rich smell of venison jerky simmering in boiling water over the fire. "And lessons on how to live off the land. He's got about a thousand civilians and over five hundred grunts. Orders are to move everyone west to the farming countries of the mid-west. Cities are all going the way of Charlotte and New York – nothing but rubble and mechmon poop. Scientists have sent word that the land is reclaimable. There's no nukes or disease involved."

"What about Atlanta?" Sally argued. "Pizzaboy said that Atlanta --"

Jerry held up a silencing hand.

Mickey answered her anyway. "Disease in Atlanta was man-made. Cholera, mostly. We were there. Colonel's wife was a doctor. She died. Three hundred of the 74th died. God awful way for a man to die."

"I'm sorry for your loss," Jerry was sincere.

Mickey nodded and swallowed his sorrow. Sally told their children years later that this was the moment she knew she loved him.

"We'll be picking up stragglers and joining other battalions along the way. The more we can train how to – what did you call it? Sting? The mechmons, the greater chance we have to save what bits of civilization we've got left."

"You know how; we've taught you Pizzaboy's Dance. You don't need us to teach it. You teach it."

"Pizzaboy's Dance?" Mickey glanced across at the man who was dazzling Edwards with his venison stew recipe.

"It was his idea." Jerry nodded.

"And it worked?" Mickey squeaked.

Sally snorted an unfeminine laugh. At that moment, he later told their grandchildren, he knew she was his one true love.

Jerry grinned, "Are you familiar with the phrase that ends *where angels fear to trod*?"

Mickey looked up, trying to remember. "Oh! Yeah." He laughed.

"So, you don't need us to destroy the aliens."

Mickey nodded, giving Troughton credit for his logic. "The Troughtons are a good, solid unit. We've got one thousand civies – dumb as sheep – and we'll need units to help shepherd them along."

Jerry scrubbed at his face, "I see no incentive in that scenario."

"As Army officers, you'll pull full combat pay plus benefits."

"We're actually very wealthy, as far as nomadic post-apocalyptic people can be."

"Underwear," Sally whispered.

"What?" Mickey's top lip suddenly broke into a sweat.

"We're wealthy nomads, but we wouldn't mind finding fresh skivvies."

"You're not," Mickey glanced up at Sally, but not higher than her hips. "You're not wearing nothing?"

She thumbed the top button of her jeans. "Are you?

"So, sergeant," Jerry spoke loudly, trying to regroup. "What else you got to offer?"

"A thousand dumb-ass civies, and not a golden-arches in sight. We need a way to keep them fed and moving."

"That we can help with. We can provide some food, teach others to hunt and gather, but there are millions of people between here and the Mississippi River. The land can't support you. Take half your people back up north. They need to be planting crops in the mechmon poop that used to be the east coast."

Mickey's lips twisted and he looked down and away.

"You have a very honest face, Mickey," Jerry stated.

The sergeant looked up.

"*The east coast is toast.* We've been hearing that phrase for two months. Is that the way of things?"

Mickey's eyes filled with tears. He gritted his teeth and nodded.

Sally threw her arms out, "What stupid fruiting bastard thought that up?"

"Do you know who our president is?"

"I know who my president is," she growled. "Jerry Troughton."

"Oh." Mickey blinked and stood up. "Snap."

"Sit down, son," Jerry ordered. "Why would the US government order a nuclear strike on its own soil? Soil that's already been eaten up and spit out by the aliens?"

Mickey glanced around him and noticed for the first time that the Troughtons had divided his team into the far corners of the clearing. He looked down at Jerry Troughton with his five-foot-nine inch, one hundred sixty-five pound frame, his threadbare blue oxford button down and faded Levis. He looked into his intelligent eyes and kind expression. And Mickey stopped hearing '*son*' the way a mulatto child had been raised to hear it. He heard it as a term of respect and family. And he sat down.

"When city-eaters get full, they stop. They close up every vent and crack and become one solid berg of metal. They are impenetrable. Immovable. And scary as hell."

"We've seen it," Jerry agreed.

"Our president believes that nuking them is the only way to totally destroy them. Hit them while they're hibernating. Before they wake up and do even worse damage."

"Or," Jerry stirred the fire with a long twig. "Nuke that much solid metal and you have enough resulting energy to rule the world."

Mickey stood. "No."

Jerry shrugged.

"No!" Mickey sat back down. "The United States government wouldn't do that! Not just for financial gain; they have scientists that must have studied this. We're the good guys."

"We've seen what happens when you shoot a mechmon with automatic weapons." Jerry's voice was gentle.

"Bounces off with greater force, directly back at the sender," Sally supplied. "I used to live in Chicago, when there was a Chicago. I saw first-hand what happens when you try to electrocute a mechmon. It fried half the city. What the fruit's it going to do with a nuke?"

Jerry stood. Pizzaboy and Chrissy immediately grabbed up their bags and walked toward them. "So, Mickey, tell your colonel thank you for the honor of becoming part of the glorious 74th, but the Troughtons will pass."

"Yolanski, Edwards. Take this news to the colonel."

"Yes, Sergeant," Yolanski saluted. Edwards glared.

"I would ask permission to stay with you for one month, to learn all you can teach me about living off the land in that time." Mickey stared directly at Jerry.

Jerry waited for twenty seconds before answering. "You may be our guest for one month. You will abide by our rules, work as one of us, and leave the second we tell you to, whether the month is up or not. We're nomadic; don't expect your colonel to track us. We let you find us. We can just as easily leave you behind."

"I won't swear loyalty to you; I'm an American."

"I'm an American, too, soldier. I don't need your loyalty. I just need you to understand. We're the Troughtons. No government is going to tell us how to live or where to live. When we find our spot of heaven on earth, no government is going to make us move from it. Mechmons can be stopped by a bag of cement and a thirty cent funnel. So how come your government wants to nuke the entire east coast? Join us, observe us, learn from us. But never expect us to bleed out our lives for saber rattling a year too late and cause too shady."

Mickey saluted Edwards and Yolanski. "Eat that stew quickly. No reason to waste it. Then join back up with the 74th. In a month, Glynn should be just at Gatlinburg, if he holds to his plans. I'll meet him there."

Edwards glared specifically at Sally again and took the pan off the fire.

Sally took a scarf from Chrissy and grinned. As she wrapped it over Mickey's eyes, she whispered, "In a different time and place, this could be the beginning of a very interesting scenario."

"How am I supposed to walk through the forest blindfolded?"

"Just hold on to me."

He reached out and grabbed her left boob. She yelped and they both laughed.

"Hold onto my shoulder, Sergeant."

"That wasn't your shoulder?"

About eight inches higher, if you please."

"Are you sure? It felt very firm and muscular. Maybe I should try again."

Pizzaboy took his hovering hand and placed it firmly onto Sally's shoulder.

"Spoil sport," Mickey laughed.

They wandered around for an hour, retracing their steps and bamboozling their guest as much as possible. Then they went southwest for three miles and Hunter – on point – began whistling like a cardinal. He was answered by a mockingbird.

Sally reached up and took off Mickey's scarf. "Welcome to Troughtonville."

The camp was larger than he imagined, with more people than they had speculated. Nine large family-sized tents were circled around a huge campfire. Beyond the tents was a wide slow river. Fishing rods and nets freckled the water's surface. On the eastern edge of the large circle, bedrolls and rolled pup-tents vied for space among backpacks and cloth shopping bags. Children peeked out from tent flaps and behind adults. The smell of fried fish and roasting meat made Mickey salivate. He sniffed again, savoring the smell of soap-washed bodies and leather.

Peggy and Angel rushed to Chrissy and whispered furtively. Chrissy glanced in alarm at her husband and followed the women into Belly's tent.

"You'll bed down with the bachelors and orphans – Steve, Andrew, Preacher, Beverly, Mary. The others are out on patrol or hunting."

Mickey looked at the people Sally introduced but spoke to her, "You're not a bachelorette?"

"I sleep with the women elders. You have to earn a tent here."

"Elder, like a church elder?" He tried not to show his disappointment. "Like a nun?"

She tried not to grin at the disappointment on his face. "Like an officer."

"So I'm sleeping with the grunts?"

"Set your things over there; wash up, then report to Preacher. He'll start you on the patrol schedule and fill you in on light duties."

"I'll see you later?"

She grinned and started to reply.

"Sally!" Chrissy stuck her head out of Belly's tent.

Sally ran to her and disappeared inside.

"I'm telling you, Preacher," Pizzaboy sat next to him, eating. "There's something going on with the women."

"It's probably that time of the month," Preacher supplied.

"You ever notice how they all start around the same day?" Hunter grimaced.

"Yes, Smartboard tried to explain it to me, how all their menstrual cycles line up with the full moon because we've gone back to being clans."

"I know, Preacher, but it's more than that," Pizzaboy insisted.

"What's more than what?" Mickey grinned a friendly grin and sat down.

"Just," Pizzaboy mumbled. "Something's wrong with the women-folk."

Mickey spoke around a mouthful of cornbread, "There ain't nothing wrong with your women. You got fine women here. Specially that one."

"Keep your eyes off our women-folk," Jailbird commanded.

"She yours?"

"She don't belong to no one. She's a Troughton."

"And you ain't," Hunter snarled.

"So keep your eyes to yourself."

Mickey glanced between Hunter and Jailbird.

"Pizzaboy," Sally came over. "Your wife needs a word."

"Thanks." He got up and handed his plate to Belly's oldest, Bill Junior. "You likely to grow another three inches before morning, here you go."

"She's in the Hick's tent." Sally crossed her arms. Mickey didn't meet her gaze. She growled. He took another bite of his meal, looking steadfastly at his food.

Her nostrils flared and she turned to storm off when Mickey

spoke, "If I'm not allowed to look at your women-folk, can I at least tell them how pretty their feet are?"

"You what?"

"Now, Sally," Preacher held up a hand.

"Who you calling *your women-folk*?"

Mickey pointed at the men around him. They scrambled to their feet. "They told me not to look at you 'cause you belong to them."

"That's not what we said." Preacher found he had three men cowering behind him.

"Is not what we meant," Jailbird whined. *"Lo siento, por favor*, Sally."

"You men – time like this - and you go all caveman on us! Here you stand, cowering behind the one man who puts sanctity in front of his need for sasquatch-hunting."

"What do you mean – a time like this?"

Hunter's question was overwhelmed by Sally's next exclamation. "And you, Pretty Eyes, don't you dare turn them my way. You're not taking me sasquatch-hunting and then leave me behind with a baby – even if he or she will have your pretty gold eyes! You hear me?"

"Yes. Yes, ma'am. My eyes are down here, looking at the dirt. No eyes looking nowhere but down here."

"And you jack-asses," she snarled. "Lincoln done freed the slaves." She stormed away.

Mickey cussed with conviction.

Preacher snorted, "Welcome to the full moon with the Troughton women."

"Hunter?"

The band of men jumped.

Chrissy laughed, "You guys ok?"

"Yes ma'am," Preacher answered.

"Hunter, when you're finished eating, ask your dad to come to our tent, please. I need to speak with him."

"Yes, ma'am."

The men settled back down as Chrissy walked away.

"Can I look at your mom?"

"No!" they all growled.

5
WOMEN-FOLK

"I don't understand why the women-folk don't want Belly and the rest of us to know." Jerry stretched out in his tent, speaking to his wife. She was seated on the ground beside him.

"What is this *women-folk* crap? Ever since WWII, we have been people first, equals! Now suddenly, once we have come back to building fires and sleeping under the stars – living off the land – we're women-folk. Like we're separate species."

"What you just told me is exactly why we men are going to treat you women differently than just *one of the guys*. You are vulnerable in a way men will never be."

Chrissy tried to respond with a logical argument. Jerry let her think her way to a calmer plateau.

"Is anyone else pregnant?"

"There are only the three of us that are actively sexual – that I know of. It's not like we babysit the bachelorettes. Peggy, Daisy-Mae and I are married. Peggy's got a stash of condemns, though."

"Yeah, I'm amazed that's lasted this long." Jerry mused. "Preacher mentioned he and Smartboard are considering going sasquatch-hunting."

"And then there's Angel and Jailbird."

"He's a man of honor; they're still celibate."

"She's got to be at least seventeen and this winter's going to be a cold one."

Jerry grimaced. "Well, that was less than romantic."

"There's nothing romantic about sasquatch-hunting in the piney woods, love." She smirked and then lay down beside him. "But those wild roses you picked for me last time were very sweet."

"Are you ever sorry that I can't get you pregnant?"

She nuzzled against him. "Right now, I'm grateful that we can't get pregnant. I can't imagine going through a pregnancy out here. The closest thing to an OB-GYN is Peggy who took an online midwifery course."

"Do you suppose the 74th has doctors?"

"That's not enough of a reason to join them."

"Hum," he slipped his hand under her shirt. "If we're real quiet, do you suppose we could go sasquatch-hunting right now?"

She grinned and kissed him.

"Jerry!" Preacher yelled from outside of the tent. "We found a bee hive. Pizzaboy thinks he's got an idea. Come on!"

"We'll start you with the jeans. That's why we announced at breakfast today's jeans day. Anyone with dirty jeans will start piling them there."

"Beside the pile of white or whitish clothes?" Mickey asked Sally.

"Yeah, well, we're a little behind in the laundry. I'll take care of the whites, you do the jeans."

"So, announce the flavor of the day, wait for the clothes to pile up. I think I'm getting a hang of this *living off the land* mojo."

"Put twelve jeans at a time in that tub there. Shake them first, to make sure there's no bugs. Check the pockets – carefully."

"Bugs?"

"Or worse. Especially Timmy Hicks. Smallest jeans. That child finds every squishy critter interesting and collects them – in his pockets."

Mickey made a face but assured her (and himself), "I can do this."

"Use one cup of laundry detergent and fill the tub with water from the stream."

"Don't I have to boil it or something?"

"Not yet."

"Oh, two words that offer such promise."

Sally pointed.

"What?"

"Get the stick."

He did so, and held it vertically between them.

She placed her hand caressingly at the top of the stick, placed her other hand on the shaft and then used it to demonstrate her words. "You know how, in an engine, when the pistons go up and down, up and down, and up and down, faster and faster until the engine just screams with heat?"

"Yeah? Oh yeah. Up and down."

"Once the tub is full, you work your mojo with the stick – with the clothes in the tub. Like a hot engine."

"Screaming hot."

"Can you guess what happens next?"

He leaned in toward her, "Not yet."

"You let them soak while you fill that second tub with boiling water."

"Steaming. Hot. In a tub."

"Use a cup of laundry soap."

"I like bubbles."

"Take the clothes out of the first tub and put them in the shopping cart to drain. Then dump the tub that way."

"Toward the little ditch in the dirt?"

"It leads away from the river towards the latrines."

"So you don't foul the river."

"We have a chance at a new start here. Jerry says we need to treat the earth like grown-ups, not like the generations before us."

"President Troughton has an environmental policy."

"Yes, Sergeant Mickelson, he does." She crossed her arms.

He licked his lips, recognizing how much ground he'd just lost. "So I dump the dirty water while the first load drains. Then put them in the hot water bucket, piston them for a while and what?"

"Fill up the first tub again for the next load. While it's soaking, use the shopping cart to drain the hot load. Dump that tub. Put the water on to boil again and while you're filling the second tub, dump three buckets of cold water over the load in the shopping cart, let them drip a bit and then hang them on the line. Use the cart to drain the cold tub, put them in the hot tub. Dump, fill, repeat."

"The line's going to get full, looking at that load of jeans."

"Jeans take two days to dry in this humidity. When the clothes are dry, fold them on that table. We each mark our clothes, so everyone will come and get them before dinner tomorrow."

"What you need is two shopping carts."

"What we need is new underwear."

"Oh, baby, I love the thought of you in a new, fresh out of the lingerie store, thong."

"Oh, now that was just a cheesy line."

"Hey, cut me some slack here, I've been out of practice this past year."

She handed him a bucket and took one herself. "So, how many wives and girlfriends did you leave behind?"

"None that belonged to me."

"How about children? I'd like to think there are a dozen children with such beautiful eyes."

"No, not yet. I never wanted a woman to have my child unless I was sure she was my one true love."

Sally blinked. He leaned in to kiss her. She smirked, "That was a great line."

"Ladies tend to like it. You?"

She filled her bucket and handed it to him. "It has potential."

As she walked away, she reminded him, "Be careful checking the pockets."

"You did a good job today, Mickey. Seven loads is almost as good as Daisy-Mae can do."

"I had a good teacher, Troughton."

Sally winked. "Once the jeans are dry, we'll finish the lights tomorrow and the colored the next day."

"We're staying put for a while? I thought the Troughtons were nomads, wandering the face of the earth."

Jerry's lips smiled, but he looked down at his plate. The women around them grew silent. "We'll rest up for five more days. Get your laundry done, we're a little behind."

"It's been raining."

Mickey glanced at Chrissy; the woman didn't lie well. He wondered why anyone would lie about laundry.

"If we washed the bedding tomorrow, let those dry a full day while I pre-treat the whites, we'll be clean and ready to roll whenever Troughton says."

"Clean bedding," Pizzaboy leered. "It's been quite a while since we went sasquatch-hunting in clean bedding."

"It's been a while and it's gonna be a while longer, too." Peggy snapped.

Pizzaboy handed his bowl to Preacher and turned to his wife. Softly, he began, "I'm sorry, Peggy. I swear, I'm so sorry. Whatever I did, I swear, I'll never do it again. You know I love you. You are my shining star."

"Oh, God," Andrews moaned. "Not the song lyrics again."

"You didn't do anything wrong, Pizzaboy," Chrissy spoke. "Peggy didn't mean to make you feel like you had."

Peggy shook her head, "No, honey. It's not your fault."

"We're having a women's meeting tonight around the fire. Men are going snipe hunting or some such."

"How long?" Preacher asked.

"As long as it takes," Chrissy growled.

"We'll ring the all clear on the triangle," Smartboard suggested.

"Men and children will go with me to the river. Nice night for crap fishing," Jerry supported.

"Women – and that's all of us including you, Shayla, since your mother tells me you've started your period," Chrissy began.

"OHMYGOD! Did you just tell the entire Troughton Nation that I'm on the rag?"

Chrissy blinked, "Yes, I did. And if we lived a thousand years ago, we would have had a celebration for you – a rite of passage."

"Um, darling," Jerry leaned toward her. "I think the men should stay."

"You what?"

"Shayla was mortified that you would tell us all that – well – that she's – you know."

"She is menstruating. It is a normal part of life."

"OHMYGOD JUST SHUT UP!" Shayla wailed.

"You mentioned it this morning; these are the things that divide us." Jerry turned to his people. "If we mess up tonight, we're going to let the things that differentiate our people divide us into unequal parts. As my wife said, and no offense or embarrassment intended, little one, but menstruation is a normal part of life. We joke – we men joke – about Troughtonville on the full moon. We know it is a part of our lives – not just the women. It affects us all. And it leads us all to matrimony and sasquatch-hunting and lo and behold – to new life."

Stunned silence faced him.

"And with new life in this post-apocalyptic world comes horrendous challenges and miraculous joy." Jerry looked each of them in the eye. "But we're Troughtons. We have faced and defeated devil spawn from the blackest reaches of the universe."

Cheering broke out.

"We can handle a baby."

"OHMYGOD!" Shayla wailed.

"We know what causes babies."

"Sasquatch-hunting!" Pizzaboy cheered. Peggy smacked the top of his head and then kissed him.

"Birth control pills are gone; condoms are sparse." Jerry nodded at Pizzaboy. "Sasquatch-hunting is a natural part of life, thank God! But we need to be careful. We have a midwife and a very cold winter ahead of us." Jerry looked to Chrissy.

She completed his thoughts, "Let's be very careful."

Into this came Mickey's voice, "The 74th has doctors and condoms."

Jerry nodded and pierced him with a frank expression. "Duly noted, Sergeant."

"So, who's pregnant?"

"I am!" Belly roared to his feet and did a victory dance.

The Troughtons cheered. Andrews brought out his fiddle. Jailbird brought out his bags of wine – well – almost wine. People danced and sang.

Sally handed the leather bag to Mickey. "You ever had peach brandy?"

"Yeah. A bit fancy for my taste, but it'll do."

"Well, Jailbird started this with peaches. Just, if you start going blind, don't drink anymore."

Bedding, colors and lights were done in three days. Daisy-Mae allowed the tubs to be used by anyone who wanted to wash their own socks and small clothes – if they had any. During those two days, the Troughtons taught Mickey how to tan hides with acorns. He already knew how to trap, track and hunt.

Sally waved him over to her side by a collection of hides. She was scooping a thick liquid out of a bowl and smearing it into the undersides of a piece of rabbit fur. He joined her and sniffed.

"Brains?"

"Yes. Brains. Are you going to go all squeamish on me?"

Mickey pressed his lips together and reached his hand into the bowl.

She nodded as he grabbed up a piece of fur and began rubbing the goo into the backside. "That's right. Rub it like it was hand lotion. Then we'll stretch them out in those frames."

"Those round hoops? They look like what my auntie used for quilting."

"Amazing how things are easily adapted to new purposes. Quilt hoops become stretching racks. Compost tumblers become tanning containers. Shopping carts become the new mode of transportation. I guess if you think about it, you can adapt anything."

"My grandfather used to tell me I didn't have enough brains to tan my hide." Mickey rubbed harder. "I never knew what he meant. Now I do."

"I think your grandfather was wrong about you. You're really good with reading tracks."

"My grandfather had a story he told every chance he got – about how we came from wild and fearless hunters of the African plains. He said hunting is in our blood."

"Africa, huh?" Sally fitted an oiled hide into the quilt frame and took another one from the pile. "So, how are you with a spear?"

"My spear's long enough to do what needs doing, and I've never had any complaints."

"Snap, Mickey. If you'd stop trying so damn hard, I might actually think you were serious. But you're not sincere. So just stop pushing so hard with your damn African warrior stick. I'm not impressed."

"What, is this a racial thing now? I tell you my heritage is

Black and you don't want babies with my pretty golden eyes anymore?"

"Racial?"

"As in the color of my skin, or yours."

"You're joking, right? We have aliens munching their way around Earth and you think I'm prejudice? You think anyone in their right mind divides the human race in that way anymore?"

"Twenty-eight years, I've put up with *Your daddy's black, your momma's white; what's that make you?*"

Sally took a step closer and lowered her voice, "My mother was white, too. We have that in common. Actually Mickey," she leaned closer. "We have a lot in common. But there's something huge that divides us. It's not the color of our skins; it's the color of our uniforms. You're 74th Cavalry; I'm a Troughton. We haven't joined you. We may never join you. And if and when Jerry Troughton gives the order to move on, away from the 74th, I'm going with him."

"Join the Troughtons, you join for life, that it?"

"It's not joining the Troughtons. I am a Troughton. And yeah, I'll be one to the day I die."

Mickey touched his forehead to hers and whispered, "I'm an American soldier, Sally. I know where my duty lies."

"So stop trying so damn hard to go sasquatch-hunting with me. Because if we did, it'll break my heart when the Troughtons have to leave you behind."

"Sasquatch-hunting, huh?" He pulled away with a sigh.

"That's what we call it." She picked up the next skin and her scraper.

"Sally," he smeared the ointment into the leather. "If I were to ever ask you to go sasquatch-hunting – if – I wouldn't leave you nor forsake you. That's the Bible truth. If I ask you to go sasquatch-hunting, it'll be because I want my true love to be the mother of my children."

"Daisy-Mae, you start feeling faint again, or weary, you let Shayla run tell me. We'll stop for a while. We don't have a schedule to keep, just the road ahead to travel."

The expectant forty-three year old smiled and adjusted her straw hat. "That was real sweet, Jerry. I'll be fine."

"Shayla," he called her. "Stay by your momma."

"Yes, Jerry!" Shayla shouldered her pack and grinned at Hunter who marched beside Jerry.

Sally helped Mickey adjust the shoulder straps that bound the two nestled wash tubs to his back. The laundry soaps, buckets, pots, pans along with his kit filled the shopping cart.

"So, where are we going?"

"Northwest. Always." Sally stepped back.

"Why?"

"Montana. Troughton thinks we can find a large enough homestead in Montana, with land for plowing and planting, pasture for horses and cattle, sheep or goats. And houses that were intentionally built off the grid."

"You know how cold it gets in Montana in winter?"

"There are ways of staying warm," she grinned when Mickey stumbled. "You got a better idea?"

He looked around the two dozen men, women and children, all laden with packs, bags and bundles. "Do you know how long it will take this bunch to walk to Montana?"

Preacher's voice carried across the Troughtons. "God, you gave us a promise in Jeremiah 29:11 that you have plans for us. We thank you for that promise, and we march towards it under Jerry Troughton, together as family. We ask you to guide and guard our steps, our hearts and our minds. And lead us home."

"Amen!" the Troughtons shouted.

"Nice prayers," Mickey said. "So, Jerry Troughton's like Moses – chosen by God to lead the Israelites in the desert."

"Moses led his people *through* the desert. Jerry's leading us through, too."

"Moses may have led his people through the desert, but as I recall from my vacation Bible school days, Moses didn't get to go into the Promised Land."

Jerry encouraged the Troughtons as they began to march, "Keep your eyes and ears open for stragglers and highwaymen. Scouts are out in all directions, but stay vigilant."

"Highwaymen? What's that mean?"

Sally helped steady the shopping cart until they could get to the road. "Not everyone is nice, or hadn't the 74th come across any bad guys?"

"No looting. No rape. No murders. Martial Law tends to keep the bad guys away." Mickey spoke with passion. "We could keep you safe."

She pulled the shopping cart onto the tarmac and then retorted, "I am safe. Jerry Troughton keeps us safe."

He frowned as he watched her walk away.

The Troughtons were close enough to Macon that they followed alongside 75 and skirted west around Atlanta. Diseases, especially cholera, were still rampant in the metropolis. They continued northwest to Chattanooga, which they again skirted, and headed toward Nashville.

6
BIG BOOM!

"Birmingham's gone, sir." Major Crumbley never sugar-coated anything. Glynn admired that in her, but she'd never make colonel if she didn't learn to soften her blows.

"Last intel we had said mechmons and city-eaters pretty much ignored Alabama."

"It wasn't mechmons. Birmingham burnt to the ground, three weeks back."

"Survivors?"

"Scattered across the countryside, foraging as best they can."

"Atlanta is still rife with cholera, right?" Glynn was counting on taking 20 from Augusta through Atlanta and on to Birmingham. The civies could travel the three hundred miles safely without having to deal with the mountains.

"Yes, sir."

"Crap almighty!" With Birmingham burnt to the ground, he'd lost shelter for the winter. Two thousand civilians plus six hundred soldiers, starving, freezing come winter. Glynn poured over his maps for alternatives. "If we take 78 north to Athens and follow 129 northwest into Gainesville and then 53 west to 75, we could take 75 north through Dalton and into Chattanooga. That's what?

Two hundred sixty miles? Divided by twenty miles a day marching, plus two days' rest for every three marched."

The major rolled her shoulders, "There's a Wal-Mart about ten miles out. I sent Yarborough and his team to take anything not tied down."

"Have him give the requisitions officer – Dilts - a copy of the script," Colonel popped his neck and pulled out his maps. "Original gets posted –"

"I know the fruiting routine. Original gets posted on the door."

"Excuse me?" Glynn sat back and stared at Crumbley. "Insolence will not be tolerated in the 74th, Major."

"My apologies, sir." She saluted and left.

"Colonel," his valet Private Matthews set a tray of stew in front of him. "The major had a brother and his family who lived in Birmingham."

Glynn glanced up in remorse. He nodded and pushed the stew away. "I hear Rodrigues' team just picked up five orphans. Take the stew to them."

"Begging your pardon, sir, but the orphans are fine. Eat the damn stew." Matthews picked up a load of laundry and headed out of the tent. Glynn had the maps open, the stew forgotten.

"Eat it before it gets cold, 'cause God knows what it will taste like then."

Glynn shook his head but picked up the bowl. No spoons, he sipped the greasy broth and used his fingers to pick up what few chunks of vegetables and meat there were. He tried not to think about the taste – something between dishwater and barbeque, with some chunks soft and squishy while others were so hard they like to break his teeth. But he ate it.

What he needed were self-sufficient groups, instead of these dependent, helpless whiny civies. What he needed were people like the Troughtons. "Snap, I forgot about Mickey." Glynn shouted to his corporal outside the tent. "Johnson! Find a way to get word to Sgt. Michelson. Tell him to forget the rendezvous at Birmingham.

Tell him," he perused the map. "Tell him we'll meet up at Nashville and head toward St. Louis for the winter. And tell him we need the Troughtons. No holds barred."

"I'll send Yolanski and Edwards in the morning."

"No. Tonight. Mickey's got one more week with the Troughtons and rumor has it they're traveling toward Montana. So," Glynn used a pencil and ruler on the map. "Tell Yolanski to head south along 75 with due haste."

"Yes, sir.

That night, as his stomach churned on the greasy sorry-excuse-for–stew, his mind raced along map lines and boundaries: mechmon territory, chewed up landscapes, diseased and burning cities, and open terrain. Highways invited mechmons, but there was no way to transport that many people through woods and mountain passes without losing too many to death and injury. Highways were easier to travel, strenuous paths demanded more calories to burn which meant more food and supplies like boots, socks and medicines.

Glynn rolled over on the thin cot and grunted. He couldn't sleep; hadn't slept, had to sleep. He had to move his people as far away from the east coast as possible before it was too late. He sat up and bowed his head. "God, don't let them nuke the world. OK? Just – help us find a way without that. Amen."

He lay back down and didn't sleep.

"Hell, Mickey, if I'd known you'd go domestic on us, I would have brought you an apron." Yolanski's words were tempered by a huge grin. The three members of the 74th hugged each other.

Edwards clung to him and whispered, "I have some laundry you could wash."

Mickey stepped back quickly, jostling the tub of hot water.

"We need to speak to Troughton, ASAP, Sergeant." Yolanski gently put his arm on Edward's elbow.

She looked at him and shrugged, "Nothing ventured."

"I've been telling you for months, Edwards, Yolanski would be happy to wash behind your ears."

"Who says he hasn't been?"

Yolanski blinked and his mouth popped open.

"See that man over there?" Mickey pointed. "He's Preacher. Don't play poker with him, 'cause you can't bluff worth a plug nickel."

"Welcome to Troughtonville, Mr. Yolanski, Miss Edwards." Jerry walked to the three, flanked as always by Chrissy and Hunter.

"Sir," Yolanski saluted. "We need to talk. Is there someplace private?

"No."

Yolanski blinked again.

"Smartboard, ring the bell for an all-call." To the Seventy-fourthers, he explained, "Anyone not on duty will come to the fire. We'll hear what you have to say together."

Andrews brought up two bowls of gumbo and handed them to the soldiers. Edwards took hers with a gruff grunt; Yolanski smiled gratefully at Andrews. Their fingers brushed under the bowl and both men blushed.

The Troughtons assembled quickly.

"The floor is yours, Mr. Yolanski," Chrissy held out her hand.

"Colonel Glynn sends his regards and asks that you rendezvous with the 74th at Nashville."

"I thought the 74th was going to winter at Birmingham. You can't get to Birmingham from Nashville, can you?" Sally asked.

"Birmingham burned to the ground about a month ago," Edwards stated.

"But," Yolanski glanced first at Mickey, then at Jerry and finally rested his gaze on Andrews. "We just skirted around three city-eaters and they're headed directly toward Chattanooga. They're headed north, which is damn peculiar. Most ones we've ever encountered travel north to south, unless they've turned towards a major source of metal. They'll get there about the same time the 74th will, and the 74th is dragging two thousand civilians in its wake."

Jerry observed his people while they murmured to each other. While they quieted, he asked, "Have you noticed any adaptations? Have their gill vents modified?"

"Yeah, about two weeks back, we destroyed three roadsters, but it was hard because they had face-plates over their gills. We had to pop those off to get to the gills."

Yolanski added to Edward's comment, "We lost a dozen people before we got them stopped."

"Again with the gills. Why gills? They don't breathe," Preacher groused.

"They must use them for exhaust of some kind," Smartboard offered.

"What – oh!" Pizzaboy stood up and bounced. "I love this – what if we plugged their gills – you know – sealed up the edges?"

"I got some duct tape!" Belly offered.

Jerry waited, thinking. Then he grinned, "Who wants to go duct-hunting?"

A dozen hands shot up.

"OK, Troughtons, let's solve this," Jerry encouraged.

"We'll need to lure some mechmons away from the CE's," Sally said.

"We'll need to cut the tape into sections before getting near them," added Hunter.

"Gills were – what? Six inches both ways? Seven inch slabs of tape, times four for each monster," Daisy-Mae said.

"Tape their gills, then jump off to a safe distance and observe," Pizzaboy concluded.

Jerry paced, "What are we expecting?"

"Big boom," Jailbird said.

"How so?"

"If the gills are putting out exhaust and we block it, the build-up either causes an explosion or poisons them."

"They're not living creatures," Mickey reminded them.

"How big an explosion?" Chrissy asked.

They shrugged.

Hunter scowled. "They'll most likely just stop and use their nozzles to tear the tape off."

"That's a possibility. But stopping them even for fifteen minutes is a good thing, too." Jerry stopped pacing.

"So, let's go practice on a mechmon." Peggy grinned.

"All in favor?" Jerry asked.

Everyone shouted, "Aye!"

"Tomorrow morning, we'll need you to lead us close to the CE. Main camp will stay here. Anyone with duct-tape, kindly deposit it in the shopping cart before breakfast."

"I'll show you where to bunk," Andrews offered.

"I'd like that," Yolanski whispered,

"Mickey, may I have a word?"

"Sure, Jerry." He winked at Sally and walked around the fire.

"You want some brew?" Brew being a combination of herbs and chicory simmered in water all day.

"No, thanks."

Jerry stared at the man. Mickey shifted his feet but remained silent.

"Good night, darling," Chrissy kissed her husband's cheeks. "Good night, Sergeant."

"Good night, Ma'am." Mickey watched her enter the tent. "So, I'm back to being sergeant."

"We've enjoyed your visit."

Mickey bit his bottom lip. "Yep. Nice visit."

"You're welcome to stay with us as long as you want."

"I appreciate that, I really do. But it's not up to me."

"Yes, it is, Mickey. It really is."

"I don't fancy being shot for desertion."

Jerry nodded, "Well, that tells me where your heart is – here with us."

"If my heart leads me to disloyalty to my country, it's leading me the wrong way."

"What if it's your country that's leading you in the wrong direction?"

"Don't." Mickey held up his hand. "Please don't, Jerry. I like it here just fine, but I am not a Troughton. I'm an American soldier. And that's an end to it."

"Good night, Sergeant Michelson."

"Good night, Mr. President."

"Look, three feeder mechmons leaving the CE to scavenge," Sally pointed across the prairie.

"Intel says they act like worker bees, locating stores of metal and then when they return to the CE, they communicate with those nozzles there and the CE adjusts its path accordingly."

"Like bees to the hive, only the entire hive moves," Andrews expanded on Yolanski's observations.

Chrissy grunted and tugged on her braid. "It's the nozzles we need to target. The spatula-shaped one is for communication. It just presses anywhere along the surface of the CE or any mechmon. That's what I think."

"We all know what that net on the end of the long hose does." Hunter growled. The Troughtons grimaced en masse. The net latched onto living flesh and infiltrated it – quickly – and then pulled it inside the mechmon's cavity through the mandible-like doors at the base of their nozzles.

"It's that third one – the one looks like a Dalek's toilet plunger – that we think is the metal detector." Mickey tried not to get too close to Sally. His heart ached with the thought of leaving her.

"We think so, too," Jerry agreed.

"If we could find a way to cut those off, but we can't," Chrissy mulled.

"I was with the National Guard outside of Portsmouth when

they first came," Edwards spoke softly. "We had some volunteers who tried to saw them off – stupid idiots used steel hacksaws."

"Bullets bounce off at equal velocity," Pizzaboy added.

"Blow torch might work," Belly grunted. "But you can't get an acetylene torch close enough."

"We tried flame throwers," Mickey bit his bottom lip. "They just sucked their nozzles in like a turtle into its shell."

"Those mandible doors seal solid. Had a cousin who tried to bust them open with a wooden stake and rubber mallet."

"What happened, Andrews?"

"Mandibles opened."

"I'm sorry for your loss, son." Jerry said while Yolanski patted his new friend's back.

"Well, let's forget the nozzles for right now and center on the gills." Chrissy released her braid.

"OK Pizzaboy. Tell us how to work this." Jerry commanded.

"We'll chase after the next triplet of feeder mechmons leaving the CE. Mount them as usual, but we'll have those sections of duct tape. It will take too long to try to peel them off the rolls, so we stick five sections of them on our arms. One for each side of the gill plate and one to spare. Jump up, tape over the sides, jump back and then we all follow them at a safe distance to observe."

"Three Troughtons: Hunter, Chrissy and Sally." Jerry pointed at each.

"I respectfully request the three of us Seventy-fourthers accompany the Troughtons."

"Watch and learn only. No heroics and no independent John Wayne bravado. Understood?"

"No cowboy diplomacy, Mr. President. You have my word." Mickey saluted.

"Divest yourselves of anything metal."

"Jerry," Andrews stepped forward. "I'd like to go and earn myself a nickname."

Jerry hid his grin with his hand. "The day's young, Andrews.

Give it time.

Yolanski bumped his shoulder against Andrews. "I'll save you a dance."

The CEs made slow progress but three mechmons headed toward the Troughtons within thirty minutes. Hunter, Chrissy and Sally each had five strips of silver tape flapping from their left arms.

"Oh!" Pizzaboy laughed. "Less hair on their arms!"

Jerry nodded. "The rest of you might consider long sleeves if you want to use the tape."

The hairy-armed men shuddered.

"Let's do this. Slow. Cautious. Abort at the first sign of nozzles."

Chrissy shouted, "Let's sting them where it hurts!"

The six took off running toward the mechmons, jumped on top and quickly applied the strips of tape. They jumped off and ran back to the waiting Troughtons.

Within five minutes, less than one-fourth of a mile, the mechmons began circling themselves.

"Twisting to the right only, each one," Sally pointed.

"No nozzles," Hunter squeaked.

"Does the air above them look shimmery to ya'll?" Pizzaboy pointed.

"Like heat?"

"Yeah, Jerry, just like heat off the top of an oven."

The mechmons continued to spiral their way in a northerly direction, but they didn't make much progress. Eventually, two of them collided. Their nozzles flashed out and they began disemboweling each other. The third mechmon stopped. Its nozzles came out, too, but wormed their way up to the gill plate and sliced through the tape. A blast of rainbow colored gas shot up and away.

"Snap!" Sally gagged. The Troughtons and the Seventy-fourthers all covered their noses even though they were a good distance away.

The smarter mechmon reached a tentacle out and untapped the other two, which were now so badly disabled they had stopped moving. The same rainbow-shimmered gasses escaped, and the human's eyes watered. Yolanski threw up.

They watched as the surviving mechmon consumed the other two and turned back toward the CE.

Andrews jumped up. "We can't let it touch the CE. It'll tell what happened and they'll adapt before we can use the duct-hunt again."

Jerry handed him the roll of tape. "Make it so."

Andrews grabbed Yolanski's arm and they began to run.

"That smelled like methane," Chrissy snorted.

Jerry nodded.

"Methane explodes."

Again, the pensive nod.

"Oh!" Pizzaboy held up a hand. "Oh! I love this. This is gonna be so cool. Well – hot. But – you're gonna love this!" He took three arrows out of his quiver and squatted down, pulling twine from his pocket.

"Walk that way until you don't smell the gas anymore," Jerry commanded.

"Hunter, you're the fastest runner. Grab an armload of that there kindling and toss it onto the mechmon, then make it clear to the Song and Dance boys to run like hell. As soon as ya'll clear past me, I'll shoot three lit arrows onto the kindling. It'll catch fire about the time the gasses build up."

"Big boom!" Belly bellowed.

"Oh yeah!" They knuckle bumped.

"What if it doesn't work?" Edwards scowled.

Peggy glared, "It'll work. This is Pizzaboy. His ideas always work."

"Except maybe for the moonshine I made from skittles and m&ms," Pizzaboy countered.

Jerry laughed, "Even a genius is allowed one mistake."

"Go on, Hunter, run like the wind!" Chrissy touched his arm.

"Alright now, ya'll back out of range that way," Jerry pointed and started jogging with Pizzaboy toward the escaping mechmon.

Song and Dance, as they would ever here-after be called, were jumping off as Hunter flung the armload of brush up onto the beast. They could see him give verbal warning and the three ran fast and hard past Pizzaboy and Jerry.

Jerry took out a rare bic and lit each twine-wrapped arrow as Pizzaboy shot it. Two landed on the brush, the third one sailed over the mechmon. The men started to run. They passed the place they had been observing from when they heard a scream. It sounded like a forest full of children being eaten alive. The explosion knocked them all to the ground, Jerry and Pizzaboy at one-quarter mile from the mechmon, the rest of the Troughtons and soldiers at one-half a mile away. Fire raged through the air, igniting autumn-dried trees and tinder. They all staggered to their feet and kept running. The blast stretched a mile radius in all directions with the fireball's penumbra at one-third a mile. Pizzaboy and Jerry were scorched, but ecstatic.

Then they noticed the CE had turned and was moving in their direction.

"How much tape do we have left?" Mickey shouted.

Jerry shook his head. "Too dangerous. One mechmon toasted a mile in diameter. One-hundred-forty-four of them, and we couldn't run fast enough or far enough before it blew a chunk out of the state."

"But think of it! Total destruction of three CE – with duct tape and a bic lighter! We could save the world!"

"Sergeant, I'll not endanger my people. And I won't allow you to do so, either."

"That CE is headed this way. Like it or not, we stop it here and now or it eats the Troughtons for breakfast."

"It'll take the CEs two to three days to move that far. In that amount of time, I'll have my people in Mississippi."

"If we hit them now, you won't have to move!"

"Shut up, Mickey!" Sally punched his shoulder. "They deflect energy exponentially."

"Huh?"

"They're not going to blow twelve miles by twelve miles; the blast radius will most likely be twelve times twelve miles. One-hundred-forty-four miles each way."

"Most likely," Mickey turned back to Jerry. "You're not sure."

"Listen here," Jerry grabbed the sergeant and shook him. "I am sure of one thing, and one thing only. I will find a place of refuge for my people. You want to play the martyr, here's a roll of duct tape and my very last bic."

Mickey bit his bottom lip while everyone else held their breath. In the distance, a roadster was scavenging through the blast site. The CE stopped and turned back on its course toward Chattanooga.

Mickey snatched the items from Jerry's hands. "Yolanski, Edwards, move out. We'll get this news to the 74th. Mr. President, thank you for your hospitality."

The three soldiers began to run. Only Yolanski looked back.

"If we could trap the CE in a valley, hit them from above, contain the explosion," Major Crumbley was just thinking aloud.

Glynn was using a compass to lightly draw circles of 144 mile diameters around the map.

"If we just tape the bastards, it sounds like they start eating themselves," Captain Rodriques offered.

"Six inches of tape times four sides per one-hundred-forty-four gills," Yolanski was fingering the digits in the air. "Times three CEs and what – sixty yards of tape per roll?"

Glynn raised an eyebrow, wondering why anyone knew the amount of tape on a roll. He decided Yolanski showed promise.

"Five rolls, and watch them dance!"

Glynn smiled at the young man. "Sergeant Michelson, get me five rolls of duct tape and twenty-four volunteers."

"Yes, sir."

"We ride motorcycles to the farthest CE. Attack from west and east sides since the only side with mandibles open is the one in the direction it heads. Each soldier is responsible for sealing the vents of six units. Then run back to the parked bikes and ride as far and as fast as possible to the next CE. The CEs stagger themselves twelve miles south but barely inches east from each other. We hit the back one first. Either the middle one will turn to help or it will keep going. If it turns back, tape it too. It'll be caught up in the chaos. If not, we can deal with it later. Finally, you will ride to the closest CE and repeat the procedure. Tape only, gentlemen. We don't have a clear one-hundred-forty-four mile corridor."

"You realize," Crumbley crossed her arms. "They'll adapt after this. This may be our only chance."

"We can blow the heck out of individual mechmons to your heart's content, Major. But roadsters will blow eighty-one miles wide, CE's one-hundred-forty-four miles and I will not risk the civilians."

"Volunteers who knew the risk," she countered.

Glynn growled, "You know what you can do with your suicidal volunteers? You can get them to kick civie asses faster and farther along the trail. They're slow as molasses in winter and we have yet to find shelter." Glynn took a deep breath. "Mickey, do it. The rest of you, dismissed."

Two days of hard riding took Mickey's squadron past the first two CE's and close enough to the last one that their bikes got the feeder mechmons excited. Mickey went past them five miles and then walked back to one-fourth mile of it. The squadron began sticking twenty-five seven-inch slabs of tape along their shaved arms and thighs. Mickey fingered the bic in his top right pocket then solemnly removed it and stuck it with the binoculars he was leaving behind.

"We'll live to tell our grandchildren about this," he told the waiting soldiers. "Well, let's sting them where it hurts!"

They ran. They followed Glynn's plan; half took the west edge, the other the east edge. Once they had taped the gills of six units each, they jumped off and ran back to their bikes. Once there, they waited for all to return. Then they mounted up and roared toward the middle CE and repeated the duct-hunt since it had turned and was sluggishly going diagonally toward the back CE. The 74th continued riding and discovered the first CE had also turned north. They duct-taped it, too. They arrived at camp amidst cheers.

"I left two men at each CE to observe and report." Mickey took the canteen Glynn's yeoman Matthews offered him.

Within three days, news arrived that all three CEs had consumed each other and what few mechmons and roadsters had survived continued spiraling to the right, even without duct-taped gills. Individual mechmons were torched – carefully.

People began to have hope.

By Thanksgiving, the Troughtons joined the 74th and their civies at Nashville.

7
WINTERING

"Sir, President Troughton requests the pleasure of your company at the Thanksgiving dinner, along with Sergeants Michelson and Yolanski." Matthews pulled out Glynn's dress jacket and began brushing it.

"RSVP an affirmation on my behalf. Order Michelson and Yolanski to do the same."

"I already did," Matthews grinned. "I heard they've got real turkeys. And women. Beautiful women."

"Yes," Glynn thought of Mrs. Troughton – fearless, sassy and beautiful. "Yes, they do."

Matthews paused.

"I'll save you a slice of turkey."

Matthews blushed, "Thank you, sir." He began brushing the wool fabric again. "I'll find you a pup tent. This one's too big to carry with you. But I can make sure your cot travels with you."

"No, leave it here; I'll take my bedroll. Do we have anything I can take as a hostess gift?"

Matthews gave diligent attention to a stubborn stain on the right cuff. "Rumor has it, and now, sir, it's just a rumor, but rumor has it that when Yarborough liberated the Wal-Mart outside of

Ashburn, he found chocolate."

"Chocolate?" Glynn tried not to salivate.

"To be more exact – chocolate-covered blueberries."

"Oh," Glynn swallowed.

"Actually, to be precise, Queen Anne's Chocolate-covered Blueberry Cordials. In the blue box. All the cherry ones were gone."

"Blueberries," Glynn nodded. "What would Yarborough consider a fair exchange for two or three boxes?"

"I don't rightly know, sir."

"Find out. Discretely, Matthews. And I'll give you three pieces if the price is right."

The yeoman nodded. "I'll have your answer by noon."

"Blueberries," Glynn got a vision of Mrs. Troughton popping one – slowly – very slowly – between her lips and of him standing close enough to her to watch the sugary cordial spurt out and across her bottom lip.

Glynn had never cheated on his wife. He'd never had an affair. He didn't want an affair. He pulled out his maps again and ignored the thought that he'd envisioned Chrissy, not his late wife, eating the candy.

Glynn and his men arrived on two Harleys. One was a FSXB Breakout with a sweet little Soft tail chassis and a long wheel base, steep-looking rake, chubby one and a quarter inch drag handlebars and a fat back tire. Glynn's six foot four body looked a little cramped, but he rode well. The other was a Forty-eight with subtle modifications, like the Licks Cycle ten-inch Z bars and a screaming Valkyrie custom paint job. They had their tents up and gear stashed within thirty minutes. Glynn accompanied Smartboard to visit their one-tent schoolhouse. Pizzaboy, Jerry, Chrissy and Mickey watched as Song and Dance embraced and walked away.

"Love is in the air! Dew dot dew, dew dot do. Love is in the air!" Pizzaboy sang the phrase and walked away, too.

"Speaking of love," Chrissy raised an eyebrow.

"Is Sally real mad?" Mickey hung his head.

"About what?" Jerry asked.

"About me leaving. Without saying good-by."

"I don't think she noticed." Jerry turned to his wife. "Did Sally notice Mickey had left, dear one?"

"Not a bit," Chrissy lied.

"So," Jerry grinned. "How are you going to play this? She knows you're here. She's been sobbing since you left. What are you going to say to her?"

"I'm going to say, 'Hey Sally, I got a powerful desire to go sasquatch-hunting. Want to join me?'"

"You cannot honestly plan to use that line to ask Sally out," Jerry cautioned.

"Sure, why not?" Mickey put his huge hands on his narrow hips.

"She's a woman. You're not supposed to just say exactly what you want." Jerry lowered his voice and looked at his wife for support.

"Oh, no, Mickey. You're supposed to make subtle allusions to nature."

"Birds and bees, yes."

"And talk about how beautiful her children are going to be."

"I what?" Mickey paled.

Jerry picked up his line, "He then speaks to her about her intelligence and how she makes him feel all manly."

Chrissy grabbed Mickey's elbow, turning him away from her husband. "Sit next to her at dinner. Press your knee against hers. Offer her some of your food."

"Yes!" Jerry took his other elbow. "Show her you can be a good provider."

"You two have been married – what – ten years?"

"Fifteen," they both smiled.

"Married young?"

"Right out of high school."

"Dated much before then?"

They exchanged glances. "Each other," Chrissy said.

"Since eighth grade," Jerry beamed.

Mickey shook his head and saw Sally walking past. "Hey Sally. I got a powerful desire to go sasquatch-hunting. Want to join me?"

"Sure."

Mickey smiled smugly at the Troughtons and took Sally to his tent.

"Mrs. Troughton?"

"Yes, Mr. Troughton."

"I got a powerful desire to go sasquatch-hunting. Want to go?"

"Sure."

The Troughtons moved with the sprawling 74th from Nashville to St. Louis and camped with them the week before Christmas with the intention of wintering there. Together, they weathered freezing temperatures and snow flurries. They taught the civies hunting, fishing, tracking, snares, gathering and sanitary techniques the army had not relaxed enough to allow.

In turn, the army taught the Troughtons weaponry and how to ride motorcycles. Together, they scoured the country side and provided for humanity. They kept vigilant watch against CEs, roadsters, and the occasional mechmon, but after the three city-eaters basically ate each other outside of Chattanooga, very few aliens came their way. Intel stated that most CEs seemed to have stopped, as if they were hibernating. But there was a great deal of hopeful speculation that the CEs had a communication system which recognized the threat the Troughtons represented and stayed away. "Mechmons best be a'feared" had become more than a rallying cry – it became a promise.

Glynn visited Troughtonville often – probably too often. He

admired Jerry Troughton immensely. He realized he had what amounted to a school-boy crush on Chrissy Troughton – one she either ignored or was blind to. Hunter saw it and resented Glynn for it.

Glynn was planning to start his people moving again in February. The rivers were frozen hard and thick enough to carry the weight of almost three thousand people. City eaters and roadsters had devoured every bridge north of St. Louis along the Mississippi. Glynn wasn't sure how they were going to cross the Old Man; it never froze over. But his orders were to clear the east half of the US by spring.

"If we travel north along the Mississippi banks to the Red River and cross there, like the pioneers did," Jerry offered. "We could be in the plains by July – at the earliest."

Glynn exhaled and took another sip of the peach-sort-of-wine. "What I don't understand, Troughton, is why we haven't met up with any other units. We have intel coming in from them, but they stayed in Virginia and North Dakota and Pennsylvania. Why are they risking atomic destruction?"

"Perhaps they believe their president will see reason."

"Reason? You have studied history, right?"

"My wife calls you History Channel, not me."

Glynn blinked, thinking about Troughton's wife. He pushed the tangled mess of puppy-love and desire behind him. "US Presidents are known for greed, war-mongering, and deceit."

"Steady on, Colonel."

Glynn snorted a laugh. "You're the only president I've known who shows reason, fortitude and honor."

Jerry's lips smiled. "The peach brandy takes some getting used to."

Glynn snorted again and took a deep swallow. "I miss my wife. I miss my children. I miss my Gosh-Darn barbeque grill in my back yard."

"Hunter?" Jerry called.

"Yes, Dad?" He rounded the corner.

"Help me get the colonel to his tent."

"Yes, sir." The fifteen-year old groused.

"If you go sasquatch-hunting with Shayla, her daddy is gonna skin you alive."

"We're just kissing."

"Yep. That's how Chrissy and I started. And look at us now."

"Shayla and I are going to get married one day, Dad. And we'll give you a dozen grandchildren."

They dumped Glynn unceremoniously on his bedroll and exited the tent. As they walked back to their tent, Jerry said, "You're the best gift God could ever have bestowed on me. Please realize that, Doug."

Hunter's eyes filled with tears but he only nodded.

"Now, go kiss Shayla for a while so Chrissy and I can go sasquatch-hunting tonight."

Hunter grinned and obeyed.

Between December and February, the president of the US who advised nuking the eastern coastline was assassinated. His replacement died of a massive coronary, and her replacement advocated evacuating the masses to metal-neutral locations all around the nation. City Eaters were becoming still – hibernating in glut and satiated states. People were trying to find their way back, cautious of the still aggressive roadsters and pillaging mechmons. A thousand CE's still munched their ways across the continent, but the end of winter brought a sense of relief, of hope, of second chances.

"Oh no." Glynn held up a hand. "I vaguely remember the peach brandy. From the smell of that, sweet potato wine's not going to be any better for my brain cells."

"You don't know what you're missing." Chrissy poured dark amber liquid from the skin bag into her mug.

"Neither will you if you drink much of that."

They laughed and she sipped the sweet potato wine while he poured some real coffee into his mug.

"The gift of coffee was very nice, Colonel. Thank you."

"The gift of the boar was very nice. Coffee is nothing in comparison."

"We're glad to help."

"I wish we weren't so dependent on you."

She frowned.

"That came out wrong. Let me start again. I wish those sad-ass civies would start providing for themselves."

"Jerry says it's because they don't feel like equals. There's the glorious 74th – hoojah! And then the 'sorry-assed civies'. Your words. They know it. The only ones you've incorporated into your inner circle are the men and women with military experience. Old folk are a nuisance. Children just get underfoot. You think you've got an attitude problem and you do – but it's coming from your end, not theirs."

"Civies are always going to bitch and moan. You're only hearing their side."

"I heard the words come right out of your mouth, History Channel. 'Sad-assed civies. Bitch and moan.' I would imagine Spartacus and his slaves heard similar descriptions. Remember what he did about it?"

"What were you before the war? A sales clerk?"

She grabbed her braid, "I was a secret shopper, thank you very much. You know what made a store successful? It wasn't the products, it was how the customers were treated. I took what I knew before the war and I've applied it to how we run the Troughtons. You were a soldier before the war and you're still a soldier, but you haven't changed. You were rank and file then and you're rank and file now. Well, civies aren't rank and file, and neither are the Troughtons. The aliens are! They move one direction only – forward. They can't back up and they can only turn at ninety degree angles. Lucky you! You're both alike!"

"You're out of line!" He was standing, too.

"Out of line! Exactly! You made a pun and didn't even get it because it doesn't fit in your rank and file world! Now we – we Troughtons are out of line! And we kick ass."

"Yeah, with your caveman technology – bows and arrows and 'sting them where it hurts' brouhaha!"

"No, you asshole. We kick ass because each and every one of us belong to each other. We are Troughtons. We are one unit. We live as one, we hunt as one."

"Don't forget the sasquatch-hunting. You probably do that as one, too."

"Is everything alright?" Neither Chrissy nor Glynn had noticed Jerry pulling back the tent flap.

Glynn sat back down. "Yeah, sure. Your wife has just convinced me to stay away from your sweet potato wine."

"Fruit you," she hissed and pushed past her husband to the outside.

"You have three children; two boys and a girl, right?"

Glynn blinked at Jerry's sudden question. "Grown now. Well, I hope. They were in South America on vacation when the aliens landed. They were exploring some ancient Mayan ruins that were supposed to show evidence of alien visitation. Can you imagine the irony?"

"Irony, yes. Peggy brought word last night of another still birth in your camp." Jerry pursed his lips. "We can't have children. Chrissy – she really wanted babies. You'll forgive her."

"Oh hell, hand me the wine."

"No, it curdles in coffee. Trust me."

The men smiled with their lips. They did like each other, but had they met before the invasion, they would never have become friends.

"I need to tell you, we're moving south at the first sign of thaw. I want the Troughtons to come with us."

"What the hell's south of here?"

"Texas. It's pretty big. You might have heard of it."

Jerry shook his head, "Walked into that one, didn't I."

Glynn smirked and then drew a deep breath. "I also need to take your wife's advice, although I didn't realize it until just now. I need to make the civies part of the 74th."

"What, not just refer to them as scum of the earth and an albatross around the 74th's neck?"

Glynn flinched and scrubbed his jawbone before responding. "I would appreciate any suggestions you might have, Mr. President."

Jerry held up one finger, then stuck his head out of the flap. "Smartboard," he hollered. "Ring an all-call!"

The triangle began to clang.

"Hunter, get the Hicks' kids and bring your stats."

"Yes, Dad!" Hunter's voice sounded from the Hick's tent.

"Sally, leave that man alone and both of you get out here."

"I just got here!" Mickey shouted.

Preacher came out of his tent pulling on a thick sweater. "For everything there is a season, and a time for every sasquatch-hunt under heaven."

"Why, when I ask for your advice, do you insist on getting everyone together?" Glynn growled following him out of the tent to the campfire.

"Because everyone is important. Everyone's a Troughton. Just like you're going to make everyone a member of the 74th. So they know you know everyone's important."

Chrissy came up beside the men. "You fight for what's important. You abandon what isn't. Those civies are clinging to you for dear life, because they're terrified of being abandoned – again."

"Everybody got a blanket?" Jerry looked around his Troughtons. They beamed at him. "Colonel Glynn has it in mind to utilize the civilians. But he's a busy man, so I thought we might could fill in some blanks for him. Demographics, talents, etc. Hunter, you and yours did a survey of skills and trades. What did you find out?"

Hunter stood up with a notebook. He looked beside him and Shayla and Billy Junior stood, too. "We only surveyed one-half of the civilians, so we'll have to guess that the rest is about the same. Half of the civilians graduated high school. We have plumbers, electricians, mechanics; most are just hard workers – lawn services, roads, construction. A third of them have college: teachers, preachers, store managers and computer geeks mostly. One hundred have doctorates, in fields of divinity, education, business, and medicine."

"I know we have seven doctors."

"You have fifteen people with medical degrees – doctors, dentists, nurses, and two psychologists – just in the half of the population I questioned."

"See?" Shayla showed her teeth. "We paid a dentist three rabbits to remove our braces."

"We convinced him to take the braces off of all children in the camps. Make them safer from the mechmons," Daisy-Mae explained.

"So we can go duct-hunting," Billy Junior boasted.

"What else did you find out?" Glynn asked.

Shayla opened her book. "Most everyone speaks American, but a whole section of people – about two hundred speak only Spanish, and there's thirty-five Amish who speak mostly German with a little bit of English. Twelve speak Cajun-Creole, and a family speaks something called – I can't spell it – it sounds like Hu-jer-a-tee."

"The father's a surgeon," Hunter added. He nodded for Shayla to continue.

"The religions are Protestant, Jewish, Catholic, Hindu, Muslim and Pagan and they all have different holy days and eating rules."

Billy Junior swallowed hard and opened his book. He cleared

his throat and Hunter nodded encouragement. "In the 74th, only ten percent are girls – well, women. Females."

Jerry nodded.

Billy Junior continued, "Yeah, females. In the civilians, forty percent are female, thirty percent are children, and fifteen percent have died since the 74th left Augusta. I heard half died the year before in Atlanta, with cholera and all that. But all told, cause of death is disease, heart failure, food poisoning, and accidents in equal measure. Death-by-aliens are mostly in the soldiers, not the civilians."

Glynn scrubbed his jaw again, mostly to keep it from dropping open in surprise.

"Good work." Jerry was sincere. The three passed their notebooks down to Glynn.

"Preacher, what did you find out?"

Preacher stood and wrapped his blanket around Smartboard. "Seventy-five percent of the people I spoke to know how to build and light a fire, catch and cook a fish, and have a stash of supplies they've been bartering between them. Twenty-five percent are hunters by hobby and know how to track, hunt, skin and cook any mammal, fish or fowl they can find."

"Why don't they provide for themselves, then?" Glynn frowned.

"Well to quote one old gentleman, they're not 'flaming pinko-commies.' You don't let them keep what they catch. You confiscate any and all meat and then dole it out in that God-awful stew you feed them."

"You've got quite a black market going on," Jailbird added. "We've been getting rich off of it, providing meat and roots, as well as those twenty-five percent of your civies."

"Your soldiers are suffering the most, those that are honest and follow your laws." Sally snuggled into Mickey's arms.

"Here's a list of the hunters and those who have basic survival skills." Preacher sent his notebook around the campfire.

"You also have a brothel being run by a woman goes by the name Arquette." Peggy sent an index card to him. "We're not being judgmental, but they're not using condoms. Aides and STDs didn't die out when the aliens landed."

Glynn looked at the notebooks and papers in his lap. "What do you suggest?"

"Autonomy. Democratic autonomy. Like statehoods, but under your command. A military governance, much like Rome in the Holy Lands at the time of Christ." Chrissy let go of her braid. "We make the rules, you keep the peace."

Jerry continued, "Three thousand civilians. Ten groups of three hundred each. Let them fuss and fume for two weeks and come up with democratically elected leaders and officers."

"Like the Troughtons?"

"Don't judge what you weren't here to see, Colonel." Pizzaboy pointed. "Jerry's our president because we elected him so."

"Ten groups of three hundred each," Glynn repeated. "Who chooses the groups?"

"You don't have to, but I'd start with the hunters. People know and trust and depend on them. Let the hunters include their families and closest friends. They should divide themselves pretty evenly. How they want to divide up into the three hundreds is up to them."

"History shows that perfect clan size is two dozen adults," Glynn relaxed.

"Works for us," Belly laughed.

"This is sort of exciting." Glynn almost smiled. "So, it'll take – what – a month to divide into groups and then we spread out a bit so we're not tripping over each other and head south."

"It'll only take two weeks at the most – they're already in family groups, if you'd taken time to notice."

Glynn glanced at Hunter.

Jerry interrupted gently, "Why south?"

"According to the map –"

"Colonel. Glynn – do you have a first name?"

He glared at Chrissy. She shrugged and continued, "History Channel. Why should the 74th's eleven states move south? They have got to be given a reason that makes sense to them that they can believe in and vote on. It doesn't have to be unanimous, but they'll go with you a sight better than being dragged and pushed just because."

"Ten states. Three thousand divided by three hundred. You said eleven."

"What? The Troughtons aren't good enough to join your merry band of sad-assed civies?"

"Chrissy, do you have to snap at everything I say?"

"Peter," Jerry drew the colonel's attention away from his wife. "There will be eleven states, plus the 74th. For now. The Troughtons will maintain our independence from you until or unless we vote otherwise. But for now, you need us."

Colonel Peter Glynn choked. "That, dear president, is the understatement of the century. We'd never have survived without the Troughtons. And if we're to continue to survive, we'll need you more than you might be willing to accept. When I counted the ten states, it was because I included the Troughtons in with us, the 74th."

"No. We're separate and independent of the army. That's got to be understood." Jerry pierced Glynn with his eyes.

He drew a deep breath before answering. "The Spartans were the elite warriors of the Greeks. They were Spartans first, Greeks second. They came to their country's aid when it suited them. And when it didn't suit them, Greece was nearly destroyed."

Chrissy's expression softened as well as her voice. "But when the Spartans fought, they were magnificent. We'll be your Spartans, Glynn. You'll be our Greece."

8
A POINT ON A MAP

A messenger arrived the third week of February. Glynn was calling a general assembly in one week to discuss relocation. He welcomed suggestions and asked that one leader with two flanking officers would attend for each unit, including the Troughtons. Not near the three hundred mark of each of the other ten units, still, the Troughton's numbers had doubled to fifty over the winter. In addition to civilians, a dozen soldiers were made honorary members of each legion, as someone tagged the units.

"We'll be there." Jerry nodded at the messenger. "Have a bite to eat before you head back."

"Thanks, Mr. President," the young woman smiled. "Also, Colonel asks if you and your delegation would dine with him the night before the meeting begins. In his quarters."

Jerry glanced at Chrissy, who was crocheting a fishing net out of boiled and spun Spanish moss. She nodded and continued crocheting. "Tell him we'll be honored, and we'll bring some honey-wine, if he's brave enough to try it."

The messenger blinked, not sure if she should be insulted on her colonel's behalf or not.

"Thomas, have you met this young lady?"

The Troughton bachelor looked up (not far, since he'd been casting sideways glances at her since she came into camp). "How do you do, Private?"

"Are you carving that wood with flint?"

"Yes, ma'am. Can't use metal. I'm from Kentucky. Mines are full of flint rock. Grew up making my own knives and arrowheads with flint."

"Thomas, would you mind getting the private a bowl of gumbo?"

He put his flint knife and whittling piece down and stood.

"Could I interest you in bartering for a flint blade or two?" She walked around the fire toward him, totally forgetting about Jerry.

Jerry grinned as he observed the two flirt.

"Never hurts to have another fighting member in the Troughtons," Chrissy whispered in his ear.

"Was I that obvious?" He wrapped an arm around her shoulders.

"You're such a romantic. Have I told you how much I love you?"

They kissed.

"If History Channel wants a private meeting with you, it's because he wants you to back his relocation idea."

"He hates it when you call him History Channel."

"That's why I do. It lets him know flat-out that he's not our colonel, but he's earned a Troughton nickname."

He sighed. He had overheard Hunter tell Shayla last week that Glynn was sweet on Chrissy. Jerry wanted to ask her about it. But he didn't want to ask her about it, either. "Well, wife, do I have any clothes clean enough for dinner with the Commander of the Seventy-Fourth Cavalry?"

"That shirt there," she pointed to what used to be a blue oxford but was now blah-grey hanging on the lines. "And your jeans could be aired tonight."

"What about you? I seem to recall a sexy black silk dress with glass beads."

"I wouldn't wear something like that for him," she snapped. "If I still had it. Which I don't."

Jerry's eyebrows furrowed at her unexpectedly passionate response.

"He'll just have to make do with my Levis and hand-crocheted sweater."

"I'll see that Hunter's got new pants. He's grown six inches this winter." Jerry pushed his suspicious thoughts away. "Mickey says he'll trade me a pair of his camos for two rabbits and a fishing net."

"Jerry, are we still going to Montana?" she said it softly so no one else could hear.

"Where ever we go, it'll be to a place we can all live and work the land. Safe. Where ever we end up, it will be home."

Matthews served the colonel's table with roast venison, mashed potatoes and French styled green beans from cans liberated from an abandoned housing development they had passed by sometime in August.

"Doug," Colonel addressed Hunter. "Would you say grace?"

Hunter bowed, the others did likewise. "Heavenly Father, we sit at this man's table, ready to eat his food and hear his plans. May both be used to sustain us, nourish us, and lead us to Montana."

Chrissy snorted.

"Amen." Glynn shook his head while Jerry grinned.

Matthews slapped an angry dollop of potatoes on the boy's plate.

"Preacher's been teaching Hunter how to play poker." Chrissy smirked.

"Well, might as well pour me some of your honey-wine, Mr. President. Seems we have skipped the diplomatic finagling and jumped right to the brass knuckles."

"We Troughtons tend to go for truth first, because we could be dead before the dance ends." Hunter held up a plastic cup.

Glynn looked at the serious sixteen year old and stopped smiling. When everyone had wine, Glynn stood and held up his cup. "To truth."

The three stood and joined his toast.

"OH MY GOD!" Glynn began coughing. His eyes blurred and his nose began to run. The Troughtons roared with laughter and Jerry poured everyone another round.

The meal was enjoyable and they all talked and joked about different pre-war and current things.

As Matthews cleared away the plates, Glynn turned to the business at hand. "I need you to support me tomorrow."

"I need to hear your plans before we vote on it."

"I'm not taking the 74th to Montana."

"You still heading south?"

Glynn shook his head. "South is just a point on a map. I'm heading us back to Georgia."

Chrissy and Jerry exchanged silent looks.

"We'll head south at first, following the Mississippi River. We'll start planting the legions in farms we find along the way. Eventually, we'll have a band of viable farming communities from Missouri to the Gulf and from the Gulf to the Atlantic coast."

"To start again," Chrissy whispered.

Glynn nodded at her and then turned his attention back to Jerry.

Hunter numbered each item on his fingers. "It's good farming land. Winter's not too intolerable. Dairy and cattle do well. Gentle summers."

"I thought you wanted to go to Montana?" Glynn asked.

"It's like you said, South is just a point on a map. Montana is what we Troughtons call home. We'll know it when we find it."

Glynn looked around the table, they were all in agreement.

"Your son's wise beyond his years, Troughton. You must be very proud of him."

"I am," he gripped Hunter's wrist.

"Matthews, bring out the atlas. Let's pick out a piece of Georgia as pretty as Mrs. Troughton is."

Hunter scowled; Jerry smiled with only his lips. Chrissy blushed and then refreshed everyone's wine.

The next morning, thirty-three delegates joined the colonel and two majors in the dining tent. They walked around the floor and loudly got reacquainted. Politics and bartering mixed with social alliances until Glynn stood and the room quieted.

He explained his plan, and as if the Troughtons had no idea beforehand, Chrissy stood when he opened the floor to questions.

"With us all being scattered across a thousand miles, who's going to hold the authority?"

Glynn looked pensive. "The legions were set up to be autonomous and self-sufficient. Active members of the 74th attached to each legion are answerable to the US government which at this time is embodied in myself. Each of you, as heads of states, govern your own group, but together, we form a union where – like today – we meet and flesh out ideas, policies, and affairs of state." Glynn paced for a few steps and then turned back and faced them. "I don't see that changing. I would like to propose a central location to set up as a governmental capitol, but the location of that is up to you."

Before lunch, the delegates were to choose, debate and vote on the location of the new seat of government as managed by the 74th Cavalry. It didn't take long. Hunter waited for four suggestions to be made and then walked up to the six by six-foot map. "I know I look like a kid, and if this was still the United States of America, I couldn't even get a learner's permit until last month. But ya'll know me. I'm Hunter Troughton. I used to go by other names two years ago, but so did most of you."

Jerry nodded to himself; his son was a natural leader.

"I was standing there, looking at this map and thinking we need a central location for the 74th. Some place they can come to our aid quickly and easily if the need arises, but – no offense, History Channel – but someplace they won't be underfoot and in our business, either."

The crowd murmured in agreement.

Hunter took a stance in front of the map, hands on hips, head tilted to the right. He traced the areas on the map as he spoke. "We're going to be spread out from here down to the Gulf along the Mississippi, and then from the Delta to the Atlantic, like a giant L. If the 74th stayed inside these two lines, they'd best set up shop at the delta. But then they'd be really far away from the people homesteading in Missouri and in Georgia. What if the 74th was centralized, not along the route, but here?" His right hand came up and he stuck it onto the map, as if spurred by sudden inspiration. "Rome, Georgia."

He circled his finger, showing that Rome would be equidistance to any location on the L.

"Wow," Glynn murmured loudly, as if in surprise.

Hunter faced the delegates. "Before the Troughtons took me in, my brother got a scholarship to a college in Rome, Georgia. He was going into the forestry sciences. He loved the piney woods."

"Is he there? Is the college still there?" a voice questioned.

"The college is still standing, last I heard. But my brother – he joined the army and went to defend our country's interest in the oil fields of Arabia. He made it home by way of Dover Air Force Base. The Army gave us a real nice plaque to put on his grave."

Hunter squared his shoulders and addressed the colonel. "Well, if my brother's college ain't good enough for the 74th, then I'll write it down for one of the Troughtons."

Glynn blinked and realized he was up. "Hunter Troughton, the 74th Cavalry would be damn proud to locate the central government of our legions at your brother's college. If there are no objections."

Chrissy and Jerry started the applause and it was a unanimous if tearful conclusion.

She leaned into her husband's ear. "What else is Preacher teaching our boy?"

"No," he looked down into her lips and then her eyes. "He was telling the truth. His brother died, his dad became a drunk, his mom married another man. Then the first day of his eighth grade year, aliens landed."

Glynn smiled gruffly at the delegates. He watched as Hunter was embraced by the Troughtons. "Well, it seems that, yet again, all roads will lead to Rome! Let's go eat. We'll all be back in two hours. Those of you who still have watches, kindly help those who don't."

Crumbley stood next to him. "I believe we've just heard from the next president of the United States of America."

Glynn snorted, "Abso-fruiting-lutely."

When they adjourned for lunch, it was with the proviso that they return with three choices of one-hundred by one-hundred mile pieces of land along the L-shaped corridors between St. Louis and the Piedmont Plateau in Georgia. Three choices, each choice written on an index card and placed in a ceramic bread bowl. They would use a wooden ladle to stir up the cards – thirty-three times. First card pulled got that plot of land, and so on. Once a legion had the land, their other two choices were discarded if pulled. But that would take place after the two-hour lunch break. Matthews and Chrissy played a game of chess behind the map, handed out the cards and pencils, and said they were guarding the empty bowl so no one could claim unfair advantages.

When the delegates returned and placed their cards in the bowl, Glynn asked Matthews to stir the cards and then draw them out one at a time. Matthews did so, and handed the first card to Glynn.

"The legion known as the Fighting Cajuns. The location, one thousand square miles, one hundred by one hundred miles surrounding Jackson, Mississippi."

The crowd cheered. Chrissy kept her face averted. She knew they were from that area originally, so when she overheard them – as she played chess with Matthews – she surreptitiously wrote it on a card. They were a popular legion with gifts for brewing hooch and playing soccer.

"President Olaf, would you come and put your mark on this land claim?"

The barrel of a woman jumped forward, arms above her head in victory. She babbled a joyful refrain from a Cajun folk song and grabbed up the pen Glynn handed her. "Lincoln freed the slaves, but Colonel Glynn done brought us home!"

Everyone cheered. So the next card was accepted as joyfully. "The legion of the Troughtons. The thousand-square mile area around Tifton, Georgia."

Glynn had worried that someone might have seen Matthews slip the two cards out of his sleeve but no one protested. "Mr. President Jeremiah Troughton, would you come forward?"

Jerry nodded. He accepted the pen, signed the deed and worried at the ease by which his wife and son had contrived with Glynn to rig this land grab. Theirs was the richest farming land in the column.

"Well," Glynn shook his hand. "Now we'll have two great presidents who are peanut farmers."

Everyone chuckled.

Nine other pieces of the southeast were deeded out that afternoon, but those were honestly chosen by the card lottery. And at the end of the day, everyone was happy.

The next day was spent pitching proposals and voting on them. Each petitioner had the floor for seven minutes and three minutes for questions and rebuttals. Then the assembly voted by show of hands and the number counted and displayed. Majorities won; others were put aside for further debate until the next session – three months from today.

The brothel was allowed to continue, bartering for trade, as long as the women and men were examined every two weeks for disease and abuse. The drinking limit was dropped to fifteen as was the age of vote and marriage. Marriages were what each legion considered them to be. Pairs, multiple partners, homosexual and/or heterosexual were determined by the legions where the people planned to live. Joining a different legion was tantamount to divorce and desertion and could only take place with special dispensation by the CO of the 74th. Records of birth and death were to be kept by one clerk per legion with a copy sent to the 74th every three months, taken by the delegates to their meeting and filed in the National Archive, yet to be established by the 74th Cavalry.

Murder, rape, child molestation, theft, and abuse were to be handled on a legion-basis. Inter-legion disputes and crimes were to be handled by the 74th every three months.

As they had been stationary since December, it was determined and ratified that "moving day" would commence the third week of March. That gave them three weeks to gather and store foods and supplies they might not be able to get as they journeyed across the continent. They planned to walk twenty to twenty-five miles each day for three days and rest for two days.

Glynn asked the Troughtons to dine with him at the close of the convention. This time, they had ham, black-eyed peas and something crunchy in a brown gravy. They also had a lot of honey-wine.

It was close to dawn when they left. Glynn and Jerry thumped each other on the back, then Glynn hugged Hunter, who actually hugged him back. He turned to hug Chrissy and stopped. She blushed and kissed his cheek before being enveloped by her husband and son's arms. She didn't look back at him. He was relieved she didn't. She was adamant that she would not.

9
FRUITING CRAZY

"Well, if it isn't the Prince of Troughtonville," a scrawny teen jumped onto the path in front of Hunter and the Hicks children. Three teens assembled behind the acne-pocked bully.

"I'm Hunter Troughton. You're one of the Rutherfords."

"I am the next President of Rutherford. My daddy is the current President. But here you are, Prince Troughton. Makes me want to bow, don't it?" He spoke to his plebes. They snickered.

"If you feel the need to bow to your betters, go ahead," Shayla snarled.

"Oh, is she your girlfriend?" Rutherford stepped closer. "She has to be your girlfriend, because the law says all dogs have to be leashed."

It went downhill from there. When the Troughtons got home, Hunter had a wound down his right arm that had to be stitched, Shayla had a black eye and bloody nose, Billy Junior had lost a tooth, and Timmy had dislocated his shoulder.

They lumped all four kids into Jerry's tent so Peggy could tend their wounds. While they slept with Jerry keeping watch, the rest of the Troughton elders sat around the fire, plotting revenge.

It wasn't hard to lure the Rutherford brat and his minions

away. A new Troughton bachelorette liberated by Peggy from the brothel took the task to heart and led them into the trap. The bullies were quickly stripped of all clothing except their footwear and tied to trees about a mile north of camp. The bachelorette went sasquatch-hunting with two bachelors and the rest of the avengers went to their own tents and spouses, feeling glorious.

A messenger showed up about noon. "Colonel Glynn requires your presence to answer to an immediate dispute between the Legions of Troughton and the Rutherford on the charge of kidnapping."

Chrissy yanked her braid. "Jerry, this is just nonsense. Why don't you stay with Hunter and the Hicks. I'll handle this."

"I don't like it; not if some of our people took it upon themselves without my knowledge."

Chrissy patted his arm. "We would never do anything to dishonor the Troughton name."

"Honor," Jerry caught her hand. "It has a very wibbly-wobbly definition."

"You used to trust me with the grocery shopping; trust me with this. No one's been hurt except our children."

"You had a hand in this?"

"No. If I'd had a hand in this, the Rutherford brat would be facing charges at the 74th."

He looked at her and it broke her heart to see the hesitation in his eyes. But it wasn't just this incidence, either. Somewhere along the lines of their marriage, doubt had insinuated its way inside.

She left the tent without another word. She went directly to Pizzaboy and Peggy's tent. "Get out here!"

They both emerged as did the Song and Dance men and three other bachelors from around the fire.

They stood and faced her. She glanced over her shoulder at her tent and lowered her voice. "You better hope to God those brats aren't hurt. Go, get them, escort them to the colonel and have a brilliant idea ready to explain to Jerry when we get home. I'll tell them to expect you in less than two hours from now, since you had to have taken them to the outskirts of the camps."

Peggy was the only one courageous enough to say, "Yes ma'am."

"Where are they?"

"Remember that tree that looks like an ogre straight out of the Hobbit?"

"Fifteen minutes east of here."

"We tied them to the trees nearby."

"Wolves. Sasquatches. Raccoons. Freezing temperature. Water and food deprivation. If they're dead, I'll charge you all with murder."

"We kept watch. We took turns. They're safe."

"Who's watching them now?"

"Belly."

"Have you seen Belly's kids? You want to stand there and tell me your prisoners are safe from him?" Her scalp hurt; she realized she'd been yanking on her braid. She had been shouting and just now heard the motorcycle as Glynn pulled up beside her.

"Mechmons, a triplet of them. You're the farthest camp and it looks like they're headed straight here."

"Where?" Pizzaboy grabbed his wood spears from beside his tent as his wife grabbed up her kit.

"Scouts say there's a tree looks like a giant ogre, about a mile from here. They seem to be heading straight for it."

Savagely, Chrissy turned to her people. "What did you do? What did you leave on those children?"

"Nothing!"

"I swear it! We stripped them naked."

"Except for their boots."

Glynn leapt into the conversation, "Steel-toed boots. Rutherford was really proud of them. Is his son wearing those boots?"

Pizzaboy began to shake. "I think so. Work boots. He said we couldn't take his boots or his daddy would kill him."

In slow motion, as if she were three different people watching from above, below and beside, Chrissy went into her tent and came out with her bow and quiver. Her husband trailed behind her. She jabbed her finger at the vigilantes. "You go cut those boys loose and get them safely home or don't come back."

She threw herself onto the back of Glynn's Breakout. "Ride."

The mechmons were one and a half mile from the Troughton camp, one-half mile from the four naked boys tied to the trees.

"Get me as close to the mechmons as you can, then drop me off and help those morons to get the boys home."

"You can't defeat a mechmon with just a bow and arrow."

"I don't mean to defeat them, History Channel. I mean to distract them as long as possible."

"Mechmons aren't going to be distracted by arrows."

"I have on an underwire bra."

The bike swerved.

"We were going sasquatch-hunting tonight. It's the only time I wear it."

Glynn braked the bike and spun three times before he could stop. "You're crazy. Do you know that?"

She dismounted and began to run as she notched an arrow in her bow. He caught up with her and they ran together towards the metallic four by four foot cubes.

"Hey, your mother was a toaster and your father was – Help me out here, History Channel. Electronic insults. I can't think of any."

"Your father was a vacuum cleaner."

"Good one, History Channel."

"What's the plan, Battle Braid?" He plunked her braid.

"Battle Braid?"

"What? Troughtons are the only ones who can bestow colorful nicknames?" He grinned. She laughed.

"I thought I'd run up and shoot the bastards."

"With arrows?"

"With arrows."

"What about the bra?"

"Eventually, if I get the chance, I'll take it off and throw it between them."

Glynn stumbled.

At one hundred yards, Chrissy stood her ground and took aim. Glynn circled back to her side. She centered herself and exhaled. Her arrow flew true and imbedded itself in the center of the three appendages. Two hundred yards away from where her arrow was lodged, the Troughtons were untying the Rutherfords.

"What is that noise – and smell?" Glynn covered his ears and then his nose. The sound of children screaming pierced their ears as the methane-like gas escaped from the puncture in the base of the appendages.

"I know that sound. And that smell. We call it mech-thane." She squatted and plunged her hand into her quiver, withdrawing three arrows; their shafts were entwined with moss-yarn. "History Channel, do you have a lighter?"

"We're one hundred yards away. You fire that fruiter this close, you'll be caught up in the blast."

"Not if we run really-really fast." She'd never felt so calm. "Troughtons!" she hollered. "Get past the mech-thane. Run like the wind, Troughtons! Then climb above the mech-thane layer." To Glynn, she whispered, "Light this. I shoot. We run. Get behind the ogre and hold our breath."

"Easy peasy," Glynn responded from somewhere beyond sanity. He reached into his breast pocket and pulled out a lighter.

"Three. On my mark. Then we run. Yes."

"You're fruiting crazy."

"One." Lit, fired, next one. "Two." Lit, fired, last one. "Three." Lit, fired. He grabbed her hand and they flew into the woods.

The screaming gas became a roar which chased them. She got

behind the ogre tree and pulled him with her. He clung to her, pressing her against the dark side of the bark as the flames raged past them to scorch one-third mile each way.

Pressed against the tree, she felt every sinew of the man in her embrace. He was hard and aroused. She forgot who she was, that was it; she forgot who and what she was and turned her mouth up to his. He engulfed her, pinned to the tree, more enflamed than the scrub around them. She thought fleetingly that this was the way a tsunami felt, crashing ashore and engulfing a pitiful little island.

Just as suddenly, Glynn stepped back; his hands up in the air. "You are fruiting crazy."

She gasped, realizing he was right. "Yes." She grinned. "Let's go sting the other two."

He followed her. What else was he supposed to do – he had the lighter. Each time they shot fiery arrows into the mechmon, they raced back to the ogre tree, but these times, they didn't kiss. She turned her face into the tree trunk and he pressed himself against her exposed back.

Three toasted mechmons and one square mile of burning forest later, Chrissy and Glynn made it back to Troughtonville, singed but glorious. The elders of the Rutherfords had also arrived, but Jerry soothed their fears and offered honey-wine in exchange for a keg of their blinding brew.

Talk about vigilantes and school-boy bullying was blatantly laid aside in exchange for battle strategies about fiery arrows and damned mechmon nozzles.

Glynn sipped mind-numbing brew while recounting for the third time the afternoon's heroics. He looked at Chrissy, fully ensconced in her husband's arms, her back to his chest, his legs wrapped around her.

Somebody started singing about an American soldier. She turned and caught him watching her. She bit her lip and he watched as color rose in her cheeks. Then a tear swelled and fell on her cheek and she turned away.

"Let's go," he read her lips. Her husband kissed her and they stood up and walked toward the outside of the camp.

"Sasquatch-hunting," Glynn murmured.

"Yeah, those two go sasquatch-hunting a lot," Pizzaboy responded. "I tell you, Chrissy and Jerry's love for each other is what keeps us Troughton's strong."

"I can only imagine," he answered truthfully.

10
PHILISTINE PRECISION

March came in like a lion. Daisy-Mae began nesting and it was all the Troughtons could do to keep their clothes, tents and beddings from being dumped into the laundry tubs every evening when they prepared for their journey. They insisted that she not lift the clothes onto the lines over her head. Her three children and other orphans took on that responsibility. The shopping cart was refitted into a mobile crib and playpen.

Each of the Troughtons, singly or in pairs, bestowed gifts to the Hicks the second week of March. Jailbird and Angel gave the expectant parents three bunting outfits made from rabbit pelts. Hunter and the three Hick's children wrote out babysitting coupons, "for when sasquatch-hunting season comes back around."

"I ain't never going sasquatch-hunting again, Hunter Troughton!" Daisy-Mae hollered.

Belly, however, collected the coupons and tucked them inside his overalls, grinning.

Chrissy and Jerry presented a crocheted cap, jumper, booties and blanket Chrissy had made.

Daisy-Mae went into labor on the full moon and a new Troughton joined the ranks within twelve hours. Peggy served as midwife with Belly as Daisy-Mae's coach and Shalya as assistant for both of them.

A victory celebration broke out around the camp with the first peels of Georgia's voice. Glynn put off "moving day" for three more days, finding one excuse after another to afford the Troughtons time to ensure the mother and child's health. For the next week, everyone went out of their way to be quiet, but eventually, normalcy returned and the Troughtons just adapted and adjusted and welcomed the new child.

Of course, Shayla assured Hunter that if he ever touched her or kissed her, she'd hit him. And that only lasted about a week, too.

Moving day went better than Glynn had feared. Eleven Legions were gangly and spread for miles, but had been nomadic units for eighteen months now – since the aliens landed. He scattered his troops in small units between the bands, constantly sending runners between them and him. He sent pairs of scouts out three miles north and south along the column with instructions to disable any mechmons they came across, but to warn the column about roadsters and God-forbid city-eaters. The plan was to stop the column and part it to allow roadsters access across the path, like Moses parting the Red Sea, but the Legions were the waters. Since the aliens tended to move north to south or east to west in precise lines, it only took Jerry – with Pizzaboy's ingeniousness – to convince Glynn to stop the Legions and allow a two-mile gap between them when mechmons and roadsters were sighted. Once there was sufficient room, the Troughtons and/or Seventy-fourthers would rush the beasties, taping gills on the roadsters and simply 'blowing the crap' out of the individual mechmons.

The third time the Troughtons attacked a mechmon threesome in this manner, the last one exploded earlier than predicted. Belly's overalls caught fire and his left arm suffered second to third degree burns.

The next evening, as everyone was setting up camp, Glynn rode into Troughtonville on his Harley. He rolled directly to Chrissy.

"The Philistines went against the Egyptian forces of Ramses II on chariots. Each had two people, the charioteer and the archer. One soldier drove while the other shot arrows. Can you fire arrows from the back of this bike?"

Jerry walked up beside them.

"I think so." Chrissy cocked her head. "But how do I hold on?"

"With your knees."

The camp stilled. Chrissy blushed crimson. Pizzaboy guffawed.

Her husband puffed up his chest. "See, all those sasquatch-hunts will come in handy after all."

Glynn covered his face with his hands and then shook with laughter.

"Hunter, bring me a quiver!" Chrissy grabbed her braid.

As she mounted behind Glynn, he said, "The Philistines had battle braids, too."

The first time she drew her bow, she clobbered Glynn on the back of his head with her elbow. They tried shooting starboard and port; always her elbow fought his back or skull. She even tried facing backwards on the bike, but fell off once too often.

Watching from the edge of the field, Pizzaboy told Jerry, "I have an idea, but I don't think you'll like it."

"My wife is riding in the bitch seat of the colonel's bike, honing her archery skills so she can blow aliens to hell. What's not to like?"

"If she sits in front of him, he maneuvers the bike from behind her, she'll have elbow room and he'll be able to balance them both."

"If she sits in front of him. In his arms." Jerry's face darkened.

"See, stupid idea. Sorry I mentioned it."

Jerry put his hand out. "No, the skittle-shine was a stupid idea. We're never going to let you forget it. But this one is good. This one will give us a way to sting and fly without getting singed. You're brilliant, Joe."

Pizzaboy beamed.

Jerry whistled and waved for Glynn to come to him.

"Get off the bike and switch places," he ordered, helping his wife stand.

"My archery skills are crap, and she can't drive well enough," Glynn argued.

Jerry held up a silencing hand. "Put your quiver in front of your chest, dropped down across your thigh. You, Colonel, sit behind her and drive."

With Glynn's long legs stretching from the backseat, he actually felt more in control. Chrissy straddled the bike and tried shooting from a seated position but almost immediately discovered she could crouch to almost standing with Glynn's arms bracketing her waist. Her aim with the long bow improved and her range grew to almost three hundred feet.

By the third pass-by, Chrissy had turned so she faced right but still straddled the bike. Her bow in her right arm, fletching arm and elbow were clear over the handlebars of the bike. Glynn's arms reached around her trim stomach and hips with ease. They got the bike up to forty-five miles per hour without wobbling and Chrissy hit her target four out of six times.

"Once you hit the mark, drop your arms and hold on. I'll punch it to sixty and we'll be out of range before the alien explodes." Glynn made a circle back toward the target.

"Sixty?"

"Trust me, Battle Braid." He smiled.

"Easy peasy, History Channel." She looked terrified.

It worked well. They made some adjustments as to where to store her bow and quiver as she cowered in front of him and he naturally leaned forward as the bike roared at sixty-five mph. They finally agreed on strapping her quiver to the outside of her left calf and laying her bow across her right thigh, parallel with the bike, with her hands gripping the manifold between her thighs, allowing Glynn to maneuver the bike with ease.

They rode back to the crowd of Troughtons amidst cheers.

"Can I offer you supper, Glynn?" Jerry helped his wife to stand.

"I wouldn't say no, except to your wine." He kicked the bike to stand.

"It's a little too early for wine," Chrissy shook her shoulders. "It won't be ready for two more weeks."

"Jailbird found some early dandelions last week." Jerry pointed the colonel toward the campfire. "Hunter, go fetch Shayla and get your quiver. She drives, you shoot."

"That's my bike," Glynn stopped.

Jerry stared, "And once my people learn how to shoot and ride with Philistine precision, we'll sit down to barter about ownership of three of them."

Glynn rolled his eyes.

"Jailbird and Angel, you're next. Then Preacher and Smartboard."

"Hooyah!" Pizzaboy shouted.

11
NOW RUN!

The 74th had eight bikes and were not willing to part with them. However, they did agree to lease them out to the Troughtons for practice time and as needed to sting the mechmons. They siphoned gas any chance they got and rigged a workhorse for additional practice and training. By April 15, the Troughtons had blown up twelve mechmons without an injury. Where they were awed before, they were legends now.

By the first of May, they were training the other legions' best archers. The 74th, on scouting trips for additional bikes, had found and acquired six more.

The column also picked up another two hundred survivors. Some were assigned to a specific legion because of their skills, or lack thereof, but most took less than a week to befriend like-minded people.

Two hundred and sixty miles from St. Louis, they came upon three hibernating CE just south of Memphis. Their gills were covered with faceplates, their appendages around each edge were sealed behind the mandibles. They usually stayed twelve miles apart in the direction they were traveling. These three were almost clumped together, one mile apart each way. They didn't move.

"Maybe they're full," Pizzaboy suggested.

"Full?" Jerry prodded. Glynn came closer to listen.

"Sure. We've always wondered why they just stop and hibernate like this. They consume everything and poop out everything but metal. They don't procreate by fission or fusion, at least, not that we've observed in almost two years. They don't grow in size. There's only so much metal a thing can consume. It has finite space. So, what does it do when it gets full?"

"Hibernates," Glynn repeated.

Hunter spoke everyone's thought out loud. "What will it be when it wakes up?"

Chrissy pointed. "It still has gills. If we tape them all, maybe it will suffocate in its sleep."

Glynn turned to Mickey. "Go up to the 74th. Tell Captain Dilts to requisition ten rolls of tape and thirty-six soldiers. Metal-free before they get near here. Take my bike."

Mickey launched himself east. The 74th's headquarters was the first unit in the procession; Troughtons were second in line.

"Song and Dance," Jerry shouted. "Run back to the Cherokee Nation. Tell them to hold up where they are and to pass the word west. We hold until the CEs are taped and secure."

The men saluted and began to run.

"Twelve men per CE," Glynn spoke calmly. "Plus six Troughtons – two per CE."

"To make sure your boys don't mess up," Jerry gloated.

"To observe and advise – only. Once you climb up onto the CE, keep your eyes peeled for roadsters and mechmons. They're always near a CE."

"Maybe they're hibernating, too."

"I doubt it. From what we've seen, their primary purpose is to serve as replacement parts when CE's need a new unit."

"Secondary purpose – search and locate metal deposits to lead the CEs to. Like worker bees to a hive." Chrissy held Jerry's hand and leaned against his shoulder. "I don't like this, Love."

Jerry cupped her cheek and kissed her tenderly while Glynn stared off into the distance.

Jerry called out, "Pizzaboy, Peggy; you take the middle CE. Preacher and Smartboard, the closest. Hunter, feel like going for a walk with your old man?"

"Always!" he replied.

"Let's gather weapons and pack a lunch. God knows when the 74th will finally get here." Jerry grinned at Glynn.

It was a gorgeous day. Eighty degrees with a cool breeze. Clouds like white mountains banked across pure blue skies. The smell of new grasses and blossoming flowers enlivened them as they walked across buffalo grass toward the sleeping giants.

They stopped a quarter mile from Preacher's and Smartboard's CE and sat down for a picnic.

"They were headed south, so if we climb up and tape east to west and west to east, we can jump off without being near the mandibles," Belly suggested.

"When we've taped awake CEs, they take about ten minutes before their exhaust becomes toxic. You jump down and run back to the line. You can make it in ten to fifteen minutes, easy," Jerry said. "Might as well let the 74ths tag along. We'll have a huge cookout tonight. Dancing, singing."

"Sasquatch-hunting!" the Troughtons shouted together.

Jerry handed Glynn a chicken breast. "Why don't you bring that major with you tonight? She's a little prickly around us Troughtons, but maybe after some dandelion wine, she might have talents we've never seen."

"Yeah," Jailbird grinned. "Maybe she sings."

Glynn snorted, "She'd never relax, dandelion wine or not. I think her uniform's stapled on."

"Best not let her near the CEs, then," Smartboard laughed.

"Seriously," Jerry swatted Glynn's knee. "You need to get married again. I would never have survived without my wife. And Hunter. I can't imagine fighting this war alone."

"Margaret's been dead a year and a half, but sometimes, I think she's just out on a call. She was a doctor. She's just at the hospital and will be back any minute now." He stared at the CE. "Our kids don't even know she's gone."

"They're in South America," Chrissy supplied to the Troughtons.

"Well, it's about damn time," Glynn stood up, shading his eyes as eight double-loaded bikers rode toward them. Another twenty soldiers ran behind them.

"Might as well sit back down and finish eating," Hunter did so.

Glynn went out to greet them.

"How should we work this?" Jerry asked Pizzaboy.

"Since we don't know what they'll do once we tape them, I think we should do them at the same time. That way, if this wakes them up, they're too close and likely to start going after each other."

"With us as horse devours if we're not all clear," Belly added.

"Did you mean *hors d'oeuvres*?" Smartboard titled her head.

Belly nodded, "That's what I said – horse devours."

Smartboard took a deep breath and then continued, "We'll need a signal, once everyone's in place."

"Where's the triangle?" Jerry asked.

"Back at camp. Sorry."

"Not a problem. CEs are not much more than giant kettle drums. Once we get to the farthest one, we'll beat out a rhythm. You hear it, Jailbird, you pound on the sides until Preacher hears it. He beats out something and when we hear the third set, we count to five and then tape the gills. Fifteen minutes to do that, then look – that rise to the east, about mile and a half. We all meet there."

"Those of you not stinging today might as well go back to camp. We're going to have three dozen hungry soldiers to feed," Chrissy's voice carried.

"You go, too."

"I'm not. I'm going with you and Hunter."

"No, wife. This is just a routine duct-hunt."

She pulled him against her. "How can we sing ballads about your great and daring deeds if you don't let us come watch?"

He smooched her lips. "I love you, wife."

"I love you, husband."

"Colonel Glynn, I'll ask you to accompany the middle team. Belly, you head up the first team. Battle Braid here will escort my team."

"Let's go sting them where it hurts!" Chrissy shouted.

The Troughtons responded as they ran, "Troughton Company is here. Mechmons best be a'feared!"

Snow, wind and rain had caused sand and vegetation to drift up against the south side of the third CE, making an easy access-ramp up onto the beast. Jerry and Hunter stood side-by-side at the center of the twelve by twelve grid. The soldiers, six on the east and six on the west, stood ready with rolls of already spliced duct-tape shoved up their arms like bizarre bracelets.

Jerry raised his staff and then pummeled the metal plate at his feet. It was the Troughton Cadence. Chrissy cheered from her observation post one hundred yards away. In the distance, they heard it repeated once, and then again. "On my mark! Three, two, NOW!"

Fifteen minutes was a good estimate. The CE was taped on each four sides of the one-hundred-forty-four gills.

They leaped off the east and west sides. Hunter and Jerry were the last to abandon the deck. The sand drift made the metal slippery. With an undignified grunt, Hunter found himself belly down and rolling towards the southern edge.

"Dad!"

Jerry turned back immediately and helped him to his feet. The sand shifted and Jerry's face paled. He dug his fingers into Hunter's shoulders. "You're the finest person I've ever met, and I thank God every day that you are my son. Now run."

Tiny black hairs spread like tendrils and rivulets just beneath the surface of Jerry's skin. Hunter screamed, but the net nozzle had already absorbed Jerry's body before his scream ended.

The CE lurched beneath him and nozzles flailed around his feet, legs and shoulders. He heard Chrissy screaming, but only his father's echoed *now run* registered. He ran north and soared off the back end of the CE as it lumbered south.

As Hunter ran around to the west side of the beast, he saw Chrissy, bow in hand, arrows flying as she ran straight at the southern edge which was now writhing with three dozen black tentacles. He yelled, but he didn't remember what, and ran toward her.

Bikers appeared, Mickey on one, Glynn on the other. They raced past the fleeing soldiers and snatched up Hunter and Chrissy. He saw her screaming and beating Glynn around the shoulders, trying to fire her arrows at the CE, but the bikers sped beyond the murderous beasts to the rendezvous on the rise.

Hunter climbed off Mickey's bike and went to Chrissy. He threw his arms around her and she clung to him. He heard sobbing; knew everyone around them were crying and screaming and wailing.

"Oh Chrissy, I'm so sorry." Hunter looked sideways at Angel. It was the first time he'd ever heard her speak. He reached out and drew her into their embrace.

Monstrous crunching sounded behind them as the third CE attached the second. Then the sealed gills began to trouble it. They could see the waves of built up exhaust rippling above the top deck.

Chrissy reached into her quiver and pulled out three fiber-wrapped arrows. She straddled the bike and pulled Glynn on behind her. "Light it," she held them out to him.

"You're too close, Chrissy," Belly warned.

"We're only three miles from the column," Jailbird cautioned.

She glared directly at Glynn. He had his arms around her

waist, hands on the throttle, but it was all he could do to keep himself from pulling her into him.

"I'm sorry, Chris. I won't."

Her breath came in jagged sobs and she began to shake, but she held the arrows in her fist still.

Glynn stepped off the bike. "Hunter, drive your mom to the camp. We'll be there within the hour. Jailbird, I hope your dandelion wine is worse than the sweet potato was."

He nodded.

"You and Angel go with them."

Hunter got behind Chrissy. Glynn took the arrows and quiver from her. He wanted to light the arrows and stab them into the heart of the beast below, but he had almost four thousand people to take care of. He couldn't afford to succumb to his desires, not of revenge for Jerry, and not of longing for Chris.

Glynn's voice cleared away some of the madness. "74th! We'll stand watch here. If anything breaks off, we'll torch it. Otherwise, we'll observe from here until they stop moving again. Peggy, Preacher, take the Troughtons back to the camp. They'll need you. We'll be there after dark."

The Troughtons wrapped arms around each other and walked away.

"Mickey, ride west and spread word of what happened today. Flags at half-mast across the column. Tomorrow morning, we head to Jackson double-speed. We put this hell-hole behind us."

For the next week, everyone went out of their way to be quiet, but eventually, normalcy returned and the Troughtons adapted and adjusted to life without Jerry. They cried and held each other and made sure Chrissy and Hunter stayed fed and comforted. Shayla rarely left Hunter's side; Glynn rarely came near, but he watched and guarded from afar.

They planned to hold a memorial service for Jerry and other civies and soldiers who had died along the trail once they all reached Jackson. In the meantime, they dealt with a dozen other hibernating triplets of CE, two dozen active roadsters and they blew up each and every mechmon they came upon. Chrissy and Glynn became experts at it; it was the only time they spent together, the only time they touched, but it was enough.

12
HURRICANES AND DRY SOCKS

June had been extremely dry. July was usually wet and humid, so the Troughtons were delighted as they watched huge mountainous black clouds build in the northeastern horizon. They usually marched until around eight o'clock, giving themselves an hour before sunset to pitch camp and cook a decent meal. On the second of July, the 74th sent runners through the column around five-thirty to settle in before the storm clouds reached them. It was the Troughton's turn to play host to the 74th's commanding officers: Glynn, Major Crumbley and Captain Dilts. Each night the officers ate with a different legion, showing support with equanimity and listening to ideas, complaints, and building camaraderie and respect. It had been Chris' idea, but she presented it as if it had originally come from Jerry.

The Troughtons did themselves proud: stick biscuits made from cattail pollen, pouched fish, wild sweet potatoes (or possibly tame from an abandoned farm along the Alabama trail) served on a bed of steamed dandelion and cattail leaves.

"I always love it when we get to eat with the Troughtons," Dilts pulled a fishbone out of her mouth and tossed it towards the flames. "Thanks, Chris."

She smiled. Somewhere along the way, just after Jerry's death, people had begun to call her Chris rather than Chrissy. She liked it, but it saddened her, too. It marked the passage of her innocence with the death of her Love. She grew up. Chrissy was now Chris. Like a Troughton nickname, it was adopted and used by all without question.

Their usual joviality was overshadowed by the approaching front. Children hovered near the adults, who cast fearful glances towards the north.

Finally, Chris stood and addressed them, "That's not a normal storm."

Glynn stood, too, and nodded. "Reminds me of the History Channel specials about the Dust Bowl. The farmers tilled up the buffalo turf and then they had a ten-year drought. Wind picked up soil along the way with nothing to stop it."

Belly pointed, "You think that's a dust storm?"

"We'll know soon enough."

"How?" Chris faced him.

"Static electrical charges preceded each storm. I've got to get back to the 74th." He reached out to his bike. There was a blast of light and Glynn found himself on his back eight feet away.

"Like that?" Chris helped him to his feet.

He nodded, not yet able to speak with dignity.

"CE's have stripped all the soil and cities between here and the Atlantic," Mickey cautioned. "There's been nothing to stop that storm. It's going to barrel over us and keep going until it hits the Gulf."

"Tents aren't going to hold against the wind." Daisy-Mae's words were accompanied by the flapping of the tents against the guide wires.

Chris, still holding Glynn's hand, asked, "What you got, Pizzaboy?"

He wiped sweet potato from his scraggly sasquatchd and stood.

Behind him, the children giggled. Glynn fretted his eyebrows. Chris leaned in and whispered, "Inside joke. The kids have noticed

Pizzaboy stands when he's got a brilliant idea. Like the phrase – it only stands to reason."

Glynn clamped his mouth shut – pursed lips refusing to allow the hysterical giggle trying to force its way up his throat.

"I got it – we'll be Arabian Nights. Everybody – dump dirt around the outsides of your tents, so the wind can't get underneath and fling them. Then we douse all the tents with water, get inside, and use our duct tape to seal the doors."

"Wrap wet handkerchiefs or shirts over your mouth and nose, especially the children. Major, Captain, mount up!" Glynn walked back to his bike and gently tapped the back of his hand against the metal. Electricity arched; he grimaced, but it dissipated with each tap. His officers realized what he was doing and did the same to their bikes.

"We've got to warn the legions." He mounted and Chris grabbed his elbow.

"If you're caught out in this – you'll suffocate."

He rubbed her hand, "Would you mind taking your time taping up your tent?"

Her grasp tightened. "It'll take you an hour to reach the last legion. The storm will be on us by then."

"Hey," he squeezed her hand. "I didn't make colonel because of my good looks. I go back to the 74th and volunteer eight bikers to warn one legion each. Then I'll come back here. Major!" he hollered, "Captain! You two ride to the Maliziars and Zielinskis. Warn them about the storm and tell them how to fix their tents and then hunker down with them. You stay put until the storm passes, then provide what aid you can and meet back at headquarters as soon as."

They kicked their pigs and roared off. He turned back to Chris, still clutching her hand against his elbow. "Just so I don't upset the neighbors, which one's your tent?"

She snorted and pointed. "That one there, with the buffalo painted on it."

"That's a buffalo?"

She stepped back, "You better hurry, Colonel."

He saluted her and roared off.

"OK. Bucket brigade – those of you who have laundry duty this week. Use the tubs. Bachelors and orphans, divide up between the tents. I want the children inside tents immediately. Bachelors, secure the food. Women's tent – you're the medics tonight. Listen out, but we come to you; you stay put. Hicks, you're closest to the water. Tie ropes between the tents. Yours to Pizzaboy's to Jailbird's to Preachers, to the women's, to mine. Andrews, tie a line to Preacher's tent. Sally, tie yours to Jailbirds. Wrencrest, tie up to Andrews' and Sally's. If your tent collapses, chose a direction and follow the rope. I've seen the same History Channel films the colonel spoke of. If this is an Okey Duster, we won't be able to see our hands in front of our faces before too long."

"Fill up all canteens and bladder bags with water," Preacher shouted because the wind had begun to howl.

Gristly sand and pieces of vegetation stung the Troughtons as they prepared their camp. Within the hour, it seemed night had fallen, thick and blinding. Electricity snaked in shattered bolts along the ground, dancing like wraiths along the tent spikes and poles.

Chris surveyed her camp. The tent sides were dug in up to a foot, the door flaps were sealed. Hunter and Shayla stood inside the buffalo tent, holding each other tight.

"Momma, come inside," Hunter shouted.

She shook her head, scanning the distance up the road. She'd heard the eight bikers go past forty-five minutes earlier. He should be here by now, damn him.

"There," Shayla pointed. A solitary torch bounced toward them, the sound muffled to silence by the edge of the storm. He laid the bike down and ran toward her.

She choked back a sob and sealed the door flap behind him.

"What took you so long?" Hunter asked.

"The armory. All that metal. I had to make sure it wouldn't ignite in the electrical storm." Glynn took his helmet off and shook the dust off of him.

"Should we douse the lights?" Shayla's voice trembled.

"Put on your handkerchiefs," Chris demonstrated. "Let's just sit down and try to relax. Hunter, get out that pack of cards. Everyone know how to play Hearts?"

Shayla, Hunter, two orphans and a bachelor, Chris and Glynn sat and leaned against each other, trying to find a comfortable position to wait out the storm.

Despite the wet canvas and duct tape, dust and fine black sand began to sift down on them from above and through the canvas walls. The weight of the growing sand dune pitched against the north wall of their tent grew to fourth feet above the ground in thirty minutes, pressing that side in, threatening to buckle the integrity of the sides. They propped their belongings against the weight of the sand.

"Will we have enough oxygen?" Daniel the bachelor whispered.

The wind made a sound unlike anything they'd ever heard before. It was indescribable and it smelled of mold and rot and death.

They all held hands or clung to each other through the five hours of relentless wind. By the third hour, the tent was under ground on the north and east sides. They had begun pressing the built-up silt against the tent walls on the inside, too, forming a short foot tall wall by the end of the storm.

It was sometime after midnight. They had each fallen into a tormented slumber when Chris realized the wind had ceased to howl. Hunter and Shayla were slumbering in front of her, Glynn was pressed behind her, his strong arms wrapping her in his protective embrace. The oxygen in the tent was thin, her chest labored to suck molecules of O_2 through her dust-coated bandana. She stirred, awakening Glynn. He tightened his embrace.

127

"The storm's over. We've got to get air inside here." She gently and reluctantly pushed out of his arms. He sat up and helped her unseal the door. They all gasped as fresh air filled the enclosure.

"Momma?" Hunter sat up.

"Wait here. Glynn and I will check on the other tents. Don't leave this tent."

"Yes, ma'am," Shayla pulled the t-shirt off her face and coughed.

"Got a lantern?" Glynn asked.

"Did." She blinked at the thick layer of dirt inside her tent.

"It's OK. Stars are out now." Her peered out. "The ropes between the tents was a good idea."

"Little House on the Prairie," she smiled.

He laughed and took her hand.

The column faced two more dust storms as July rolled into August. They survived, but most of the children developed a deep-seated cough, as did the eldest survivors. Glynn sat out each storm in the Troughton's buffalo tent, with Chris lying in his arms. It seemed incongruous, but those were the only nights he remembered sleeping deep, dreamless sleeps. He awoke aroused; she knew he was, she could feel his every inch pressed against her, but she never acknowledged it. She still grieved for Jerry, but she never dreamed of him.

The second week of July, the column bid farewell to the Maliziar Legion. The next fifty miles belonged to them. Each week thereafter, they left a legion behind on the new territories they had each claimed. As the column grew shorter by about four hundred people each week, the mood and steps lightened. They made better time, sometimes crossing twenty miles each day, but dust storms, starvation and persistent dysentery plagued them.

Glynn stroked and prodded and cajoled his legions along. The sight of him racing toward a lagging legion brought hope to each countenance. The reserve he showed as death claimed one of his people gave them all the courage to pick up their belongings and move beyond the pitiful graves. He contained his passion for battles when Chris was in his arms and they slew the metallic dragons together. They raced in close to the deadly tentacles, fired burning volleys into the tender mandibles and roared away as flames and explosions shattered the beasts.

The Troughtons were the elite of the 74th. An entity under Chris' Presidency, they worked as soldiers – the best – of the 74th. They developed specific routines – Philistine chariots for mechmons, duct and runs for city eaters, and a combination for roadsters. Pizzaboy and Peggy had worked it out – tape the outer eight units of a roadster and then ignite the center one by using a long fuse made up of braided rags stuffed into the gills. Since energy was repelled by the mechmon units in equal amounts in the exact opposite direction, the explosion of the central unit caused an equal and opposite reaction – resulting in an implosion of all nine units and a crater one-half mile deep three miles wide. Shrapnel and heat extended another mile in each direction, reigning death out and down. It was dangerous, fool hardy, and exciting as hell.

They found deserted towns and abandoned subdivisions along the way, so as a hurricane loomed toward them from the Gulf, the last week of August, the two thousand people making up seven legions and the three-hundred fifty soldiers of the 74th sought shelter in cement walls of a little village called Eufaula along the Alabama and Georgia line. There, they scavenged food, candles, beds and clean clothes. The Troughtons chose five ranch style houses with connecting back yards to occupy. They tied ropes between them and divided their membership between the houses. The rest of the legions did likewise: ten or twelve people to each house. By the time the winds hit ninety mph, everyone was safe inside a building. They sat out the gale force winds and rain, enjoyed but were not fooled by the eye's reprieve, and then waited out the fierce backside of the hurricane. Trees crashed, roofs blew off, walls crumbled, but the legions regrouped as needed and survived. They rested in the village another day, allowing the waters to recede from the rain-soaked trail and the sleep-deprived columnists to relax in what little comfort they had found.

Glynn stopped by the Troughton quarters late afternoon of the day of rest.

"You look like crap," Hunter greeted him at the door.

"Thanks, kid. Is your mom home?"

Hunter stepped back and hollered, "Hey mom, some door-to-door salesman wants to show you a vacuum cleaner."

"I'm in the kitchen!"

Glynn followed the sound of her voice.

"No, the pastas are moldy, just pack all the cans. And be sure to wrap all the soap bars in the plastic sandwich bags." Chris commanded her team from a ladder-back throne at the wooden table. "Hey Colonel, welcome to the Troughton ambassadorial suite. Want some coffee?"

"Real coffee?" he swayed. They thought he was fooling around, but then his eyes rolled and his face turned gray.

Chris jumped up and grabbed his left arm while Angel grabbed his right. "Get him to the master bedroom."

They propelled him through the dining room and into a plush bedroom with soppy wet carpeting and a queen-sized bed.

"Let go of me," Glynn growled, but was unable to persuade them.

They sat him on the mattress and Chris asked Angel, "Bring him some coffee and a fish pie."

Angel departed and Chris knelt down and began unlacing Glynn's boots.

"Stop. Stop, Chris." His hand rested on her hair. "I can't rest yet. Too much to do."

"Of course there is. I just thought you'd like some clean socks – there's a drawer full – and you can't put on new socks until you take off your boots."

"About the socks, and the canned food and bars of soap," his fingers combed through her hair. "You've washed your hair."

"With real shampoo. And there was some deodorant."

His boots removed, Chris stood and firmly pressed Glynn backwards onto the bed.

"I don't need to lay down to put on clean socks," he protested, but didn't rise.

"Of course you do. If you stayed seated, your feet would get wet from the carpeting. Rainwater flooded in under the back door."

He sighed, fighting to keep his eyes open. "This is the Nguyen Territory. They came to me during the eye of the storm and claimed all houses and their contents belong to them. You can't take anything you find in here, including the socks. Everything stays in the houses when we set off tomorrow morning."

"I see," Chris drew a light blanket over him.

"Don't let me go to sleep."

"Just rest your eyes while we heat up the coffee." She smoothed back his jet-black hair and watched his eyes close as he succumbed to exhaustion. She guessed he hadn't slept since the day before the hurricane hit. She smelled coffee and turned to find Angel at the door. Chris put a finger to her lips and walked with Angel back to the kitchen.

"Pack everything. Linens, towels, soap, razors, pots and pans, books, jewelry. Everything." Chris tugged at her braid. "The Nguyen think everything on their land belongs to them. Well, these five houses are the embassy of the Troughton nation while we're here, and as such, Troughton soil. Everything belongs to us, and we're taking it with us as we go."

"Won't the colonel notice?" Sally asked.

Mickey opened his mouth but Preacher nudged his arm. "This is women-folk business. Household items and food – women's domain. We'll do well to butt out."

"We can't carry all of this," Mickey countered.

Chris pointed, "Drapery rods. Solid wood. We'll loop the

canvas shopping bags through it and carry them between two people on their shoulders."

"Like an African safari," Shayla grinned.

"Shower curtain rods – in all five houses," Peggy ventured. "They'd work, too."

"If we tied the sheets like papooses, we could slide them onto the rods and carry larger items in them." Daisy-Mae suggested.

Mickey put his hands on his hips, "The colonel said no."

Chris tugged her braid and glared.

"Wait," Hunter put up his hand just like Jerry used to do. "The colonel said nothing could be removed from the houses when we leave tomorrow morning, right?"

Chris nodded.

"So," Hunter grinned. "We strip the houses tonight and march ahead of the column so - legally – nothing will be removed from the houses as the column leaves as per the colonel's orders."

"The letter of the law," Preacher intoned.

"Can we do it?" Smartboard looked at Chris. "Can we strip all five houses and leave without anyone raising the alarm?"

"Yes. Oh yes!" Chris beamed. "Hunter, get your dad's maps and find us a rendezvous spot. Belly, you and the kids spread the word to the other houses. Adam, you and Jailbird choose the porters once you count all the rods. Daisy-Mae, give the children all the pillowcases. Stuff them with all the useable clothing but don't go into the master bedroom. We don't want to wake History Channel."

"There are wheelbarrows in the garages," Preacher added.

"They'll do nicely for the heavier canned goods and pots and pans. Thanks for being in charge of those."

"Anything for Troughtonia, Madame President."

Five households – divided between fifty-six adults and a dozen children plus what the Troughtons brought with them was a massive amount of portage. Everyone was burdened with sacks, makeshift quilt-wrapped or sheet-enclosed bundles, and Samsonite ensembles. The Troughtons waited until dark and quietly followed the trail Hunter had chosen for them.

Glynn awoke with the dawn around four-thirty to find a thin white blanket covered him. He rolled over and blinked. His boots were on the bedside table along with a balled pair of socks. The room was barren of everything except furniture. Glynn slipped on his boots and fingered the socks, but left them there. He went to the bathroom, enjoying the novelty of a commode and then noticed that the cabinet was almost empty: a dozen squares were left on a thin roll of toilet paper, but that was it. He wandered through the house. Of linens, towels, knick-knacks, food, kitchen utensils and the cushions from each chair and sofa, nothing remained.

Glynn returned to the bedroom and fingered the ball of socks again. He took a deep breath and pocketed them. He glanced down at the bed, thought a moment, then snatched up the blanket and wrapped it around his shoulder.

The column trailed behind the Troughtons for three days. Glynn eventually and intentionally caught up with them at the border dividing the Nguyen Territory and that of the Shepherds. Most of the legions had stripped the houses, too, so when he got off his bike and faced Chris – her hands gripping her battle braid, her legs braced, her mouth set – he grabbed her braid and tugged it. "You owe me a cup of coffee."

She smiled, so he tugged her braid again.

Six more weeks, six less legions later, they left Jackson and headed north east to Rome, Ga. For two weeks, they took their time traveling and hunted and gathered all the bounty autumn had to offer them along the way. At the end of October, the column breasted a hill and looked at the college spread below them. Dirt dunes covered the northern walls up to the eaves of single story buildings and the roof was off of what looked to have been the gymnasium. But other than that, it was a welcome sight.

As they made their way into the valley, the black heads of a dust storm rolled over the top of the hills from the north and tumbled down towards the college.

The two legions and the 74th took refuge in the dormitories and the classroom, relishing the feel of solid walls and floors holding back the feral winds. The Troughtons claimed the bottom floor of Jefferson Hall and as was becoming habit, Glynn rode out the storm with them.

"What would you think about everyone staying here for the winter?" Glynn spoke softly. He and Chris sat against the wall on a twin-sized bed. Hunter and Shayla slept together on the matching bed across the dorm room. "It would give the 74th time to establish this place as a permanent headquarters. Let the legions rest up."

Chris wiggled, trying to get comfortable. "The Rutherfords are anxious to press on. They're just fifty miles from their border."

"Yeah, but if we let them cross into their land before us," he tugged off his boots. "I don't trust them. I would hate to find they've instigated a toll or some such on our trail. Or flat out deny us passage."

"Us?" She kicked off her moccasins and stood. "You're already home."

"What are you doing?"

"This bra is killing me. I cried when my last bra dissolved into tatters in April. I found this one during the hurricane. It's got underwires. What moron invented underwires!?" With her back to him, she quickly removed her shirt, unsnapped her bra and flung it across the room and then started to put her shirt back on.

His hands cupped her breasts from behind. His thumbs flicked her nipples erect and he pressed his lips against her shoulders.

She moaned.

He slid one hand down her stomach and pulled her back against him onto the bed. His lips traveled to her neck; she turned her head and nuzzled against him.

Gently, he lowered her onto the mattress and lay next to her. The candle light flickered as dust sparkled around the room. He kissed her. She wrapped her arms around his neck and kissed him back.

"Slow down," he pulled back and began unbuttoning his tunic.

"I make a lot of noise," she worried.

"Promise?" he grinned and kissed her again.

She fumbled with his buttons. "I've never slept with anyone else."

He cupped her cheek and waited.

"I've never kissed anyone else either, except you."

"Chris, do you want me?"

She nodded.

"Do you love me?"

Chris hesitated.

Glynn's lips twisted in a bitter smile. He leaned over and blew out the candle. "Turn over with your back to my chest. Go to sleep."

She obeyed him. "I'm sorry," she whispered.

"Don't be. I'm patient. And I can't afford to love you either. Not right now. We both have too many people depending on us. We have to be leaders first. Maybe later, we can be lovers."

He felt her sobbing, but rather than weakening his resolve, it strengthened it. He remembered the six months after his wife died. Chris had been widowed less than six months. He realized his crush on her had deepened into great affection, but she was still in love with Jerry. He'd never had an affair and he never would.

As the storm passed, Glynn felt Chris breathing deep in slumber. He gently crawled out of bed and went in search of a cold shower.

13
MILITARY HEADQUARTERS

"So, what do you think?"

Chris looked around what used to be the President of Kendrick College's office. A mahogany desk and leather chair faced the double doors. A small sofa in flowered chintz graced the wall next to the door. Behind the desk was a panoramic view of the eastern campus. Duct tape zigzagged across the glass repairing a crack in the pane.

Glynn opened a door next to the sofa. "Large bathroom replete with shower, commode and sink."

"Very nice," she peaked in. "I understand two of your sergeants are working on getting the water running."

"And on the other side," he crossed the office to the solid oak door there.

"Wow!" A queen-sized bed, a six-foot chest-of-drawers and an armchair vied for space.

"This used to be the board room." He led her inside.

"Pretty nice for the provisional governor of the New United States."

"Well, Madame President of Troughtonia, it's secluded, and big enough to do what one needs to do in a bedroom."

She perched on the bed and bounced the mattress. "Doesn't squeak."

"Even if it did, doesn't matter." He closed the door behind

him. "You could make as much noise as you wanted. Here."

She drew a quick breath. "What about the whole – leaders versus lovers thing?"

He knelt in front of her. "For everything there is a season."

She leaned forward and pressed her lips to his forehead. His fingers found her buttons and slowly opened her blouse.

He laughed, "No bra."

"Damn underwires."

He kissed her breasts and felt her surrender.

The door flew open and Crumbley shouted, "Colonel! City Eaters!" She saw what she was interrupting. "Oh Snap!"

Glynn stood and faced his major. "Report."

"You ever heard of knocking?" Chris buttoned her blouse, her face was a livid red.

"Who the hell has sex at ten o'clock in the morning?" Crumbley snarled.

"Obviously no one today!" Chris snarled back and stood.

"Major," Colonel reminded both women he was in the room. "What city eaters?"

Crumbley glared at Glynn, intently ignoring Chris. "The watch in the bell tower just saw a CE cresting the hill about ten miles north-north-east from here. We can't see a trail anywhere farther east, so we think it's the first of a triplet. It's heading south with a trajectory putting it eight to ten miles from the college in five hours."

"That means the second one is headed straight at the college in eleven hours." Chris grabbed her braid.

"We assume the secondary CE is on a course perpendicular to the Headquarters, yes," Crumbley corrected Chris.

"Well," Chris gently pushed around Glynn. "Let's saddle up and go take a look-see."

The major blocked her exit. "May I remind you, Madame President, you are a civilian guest on a military installation? You don't give the orders here."

"What were you before the war, a book keeper?" Chris advanced. "A desk jockey? When you can ride or shoot with the Philistines, I'll take notice that your lips are flapping. Until then, get the hell out of my way."

"Or what?"

"Stand down, Major." Glynn's voice brooked no argument. He and Chris pushed past her and ran to gather the Troughtons for a reconnaissance mission.

"It's not going anywhere," Preacher handed the binoculars back to Hunter.

"Maybe it's full, like the others," Jailbird suggested.

"No. Look," Hunter put down the glasses and pointed. "It's flanked by three roadsters on each side, and there's a line of mechmons in front of them. It's like they're trying to find a way down the slope."

They watched in shock as the massive CE slipped sideways. The sound of twisting metal was horrendous as the echoes bounced back and forth against the mountainsides. The CE righted itself again to face due south and then slipped and slid and plummeted down the face of the mountain, crushing trees and dislodging boulders, leaving a scraped path behind it.

As the air cleared, the Troughtons and 74thers saw something they'd never seen before: the undersides of a CE.

Hunter clutched the binoculars to his eyes. "Tractor belt feet. Like a bulldozer or a tank. That's why they can't turn. They're black, rubbery tractor feet, like their tentacles."

"The tentacles explode," Chris had a death grip on her braid.

"You're not going down there," Glynn ordered.

"We wouldn't have to get close, just above so we could shoot some arrows and lobby a torch or two into the escaping gasses," Pizzaboy surmised.

"Do it," Chris commanded. "Hunter and Shayla, Angel and Jailbird, History Channel and me. We ride down that road there, shoot our flaming arrows up and while they're falling onto the CE's tootsies, we ride back here, out of range of the explosion."

"No." Glynn crossed his arms.

"No? What do you mean *No*?"

"No, Madame President."

She grabbed his upper arm and yanked herself up to his face, nearly nose to nose. "Do we need to go have a private talk, sweetie?"

"Sweetie?" Glynn growled.

"OHMYGOD!" Shayla squeaked and giggled.

Pizzaboy turned to Preacher. "Did you know they were sweeties?"

"This is why you don't boink the natives," Crumbley sneered.

In two seconds, Chris let go of Glynn and threw a sucker punch at the Major, knocking her on her butt.

"Look at that," Hunter, eyes still to the binoculars, pointed. "What the crap are those things?"

"You bitch! We're under martial law. I have the right to shoot you." Crumbley stood up and wiped blood from her lips.

"Stand down, Major or I'll put you on report. Calm down, Chris or I'll – I don't know. I'll spank you."

"OHMYGOD!" Shayla squealed again.

"Can we watch?" Pizzaboy laughed.

"Shut up all of you!" Hunter yelled. "Look! Look at their backs. Look at their gill plates. Here!" He shoved the binoculars at Glynn.

"What the?"

"Looks like spikes."

"Yeah, could be." Glynn handed the glasses back to Hunter. "Jailbird, let's go take a look." He jutted a finger at Chris. "You stay here."

"I'm your partner. You're not leaving me behind."

Glynn raised an eyebrow and then hopped on his bike without her.

The Troughtons watched the two bikes snake down the mountainside and stop. Glynn and Jailbird ran toward a solitary mechmon and jumped onto it. They bent over the gill plate and then ran back to their bikes and within ten minutes were back with the team.

"Like razorwire, all along the edge of the gill plates," Jailbird explained.

"No way to adhere tape to it. Not anywhere," Glynn concluded.

"They've adapted again. Dad said they would. I'm surprised it didn't happen sooner."

Chris looked at Hunter. "How do we stop them now?"

"They're still vulnerable to flaming arrows."

"Not unless they've built up their exhaust gasses. Not really." Pizzaboy corrected.

Chris pointed, "Right now, that CE's gills are stuck in the dirt. It's belly-up and helpless. We've never had an opportunity like this before. We may never have one again. We've always worried about the devastation from flaming a CE. Here's our chance. It's contained in that valley, so the explosion will be contained, too. The college and the column – OK, Major – the Military Headquarters and the Legions – are on the other side of this mountain, protected from the blast."

"I hate to agree with your girlfriend," Crumbley frowned, "but she's right. I said it months ago – we've got to see for ourselves what a CE does when it explodes."

"We're not protected from the blast," Shayla spoke softly.

"Head back now. All of you. You'll be over the top and down the other side in no time." Chris tugged her braid.

Hunter faced his people, "Do as she says. Go back to the college and wait. Warn the legions and soldiers to prepare for ground shocks – broken windows, roofs, that sort of thing."

"Like an earthquake," Preacher nodded.

"And be ready for the other two CEs heading this way."

The Troughtons looked between Hunter and Chris, unable to disobey them, but unable to leave them, either.

Jailbird stepped forward. "No."

Hunter and Chris both blinked.

Preacher, Angel and Pizzaboy stepped forward and said together, "No."

Shayla's voice shook, but she said, "We're Troughtons. We stay with you."

The major sniggered, "Troughtons to the rescue again, huh? You're not in charge here. Go back down and do some sasquatch-hunting and leave this to the professionals."

Shayla straightened her five-foot-three frame and growled, "We are Troughtons, and we have been together from hell and back, and we have saved your professional butt more times than we care to remember. So we have the right to make this decision. And if you don't like the decision, keep your fruiting mouth shut!"

Crumbley stepped back from the girl's vehemence and stood silently brooding with her arms crossed over her chest.

Shayla looked at Hunter, "Don't tell my mom I said fruiting."

Chris stepped closer to Colonel Glynn and lowered her voice, "You'll need someone to toast the CE, while it's still contained and vulnerable."

He reluctantly nodded.

"You'll need the Troughtons to do it."

He looked at her in that way he did, weighing her soul against his needs. She stood still, trying not to lose herself in his eyes.

He kept his voice quiet, "I've lost too many people since they landed. My wife. Your husband. I can't risk losing the Troughtons. I can't lose you."

"You'll lose all of us – the legions, the soldiers – all of us if those CEs make it over the mountains. We just need to blow this CE at the right time."

"Anyone who is on this side of the mountain will die."

"No sir. Your slow-assed soldiers might die. But we're

Troughtons."

He stared at her, grinding his teeth, but schooling his features to remain calm. He stepped closer to her and lowered his voice to a whisper. "Mrs. Troughton. Chris. Battle Braid, it's suicide."

Her gaze fell to the lips she had so enjoyed. Her nostrils flared and she breathed in his scent. Her voice carried boldly. "When I come back, I want to go sasquatch-hunting with you."

"Sasquatch-hunting!" he roared.

"Yeppers!" Pizzaboy got elbowed by Preacher.

"Well, it's not like you can pin a medal on my chest; all the medal factories have been destroyed."

"Do you honestly believe you can destroy the CE and get back to the college side of the mountain?"

"Me and mine; yes."

"You'd best make damn sure you come back."

President Chris Troughton saluted Colonel Peter Glynn and he returned it.

"Pizzaboy, what will we need?" Chris released her braid and turned to her people.

He stood still, peering down into the valley. His head tilted up and his gaze followed the bald trail caused by the CE's tumble down the mountain. He pointed below them, "Hunter, is that a house down there?"

Hunter used his binoculars. "Yeah, a little cabin. Looks to be stone and logs."

"Okeydokey." Pizzaboy turned to Glynn. "Does the army still have condoms?"

Glynn choked. The major answered, "About a gross of them."

"Does that bazooka Edwards keeps boasting about – could it carry a line with it, you know, if we shoot it across that gap below? Like a whaler's harpoon."

"Could be. If we rigged a harness type – we'll get someone on it. It'll work." Crumbley bounced.

"How about circus performers? Got any tight-rope walkers in

the legions?"

Glynn blinked. Shayla answered, "No."

"Snap." Pizzaboy perched on his heels and stroked his beard. "Thank God we've got lots of rope and those curtain rods."

14
GOING WELL, CONSIDERING

The night was spent filling condoms with gasoline and/or rendered lard. Anyone who had a crochet hook and knew how to use it was given yarn and fishing nets to weave together until they had net approximately eighty feet wide and long. Twelve strong strands of nylon rope were tied at even spaces to the top edge of the net and twelve more to the bottom edge. Each of the strands was fifty feet long. In the center of the net, they tied one gross of filled condoms and gingerly rolled the edges toward the center until they had a very long sausage made of fish netting and rubbers. It took twelve men to carry the sausage up the mountain and down to the cabin, where the adapted bazooka was being mounted to the roof. The cabin had a gloriously clear view of the valley below; the vista had been cleared of trees years before.

"Lay the sausage out like a spear pointing to the other side," Pizzaboy directed.

They used one wooden curtain rod to girth hitch the outgoing ropes and a metal shower curtain rod on which to girth hitch the ropes that were closest to the cabin. Onto each rod was tied a longer rope; one was anchored to the cabin's stone foundation with a retraced figure 8, the other was firmly secured into niches whittled along the shaft of a nine-foot-long wooden curtain rod which would serve as the harpoon; its outward end had been sharpened to a viscous point.

Hunter, Shayla and Jailbird began pouring gasoline trails from twelve evenly spaced piles of debris they had built fifty yards down the hill from the cabin. They let the petrol find its level as it raced in thin streams down through the leafy loam of the forest into the valley below. Since they were metal-free, no mechmons came their way. The mechmons and roadsters were in fact surrounding the CE, patting it along the edges with their spatula-like appendages.

An hour after dawn, the Troughtons met with Glynn and his small team of volunteers on the front porch of the cabin. Hunter faced them. "It is all a question of timing. The gasoline trails will act as fuses. The valley below is full of mech-thane. Once the lit fuses hit the gas, well."

"Big boom," Chris smiled.

"Yeah. What Mom said."

They all laughed.

"It all depends on the net and how far it will be launched across the valley and if it will stick into the cleared soil on the other side."

"It'll work, Hunter." Pizzaboy was serious.

The young man nodded. "So. Launch the harpoon, which drags the rolled-up net across the valley and anchors itself in the other side. The net unfurls. Archers shooting from the roof of this cabin ignite the brush piles and then everyone takes off up and over the mountainside. The gas fuses set off the mech-thane and fills the valley. The individual units of the CE begin to explode up. The flames hit the net and the tiny rubbers melt and drop flaming oil and gas down on top of the CE. So it's going to think the energy is coming from above it, not from down the sides of the mountain. It expends equal and opposite force up and not out."

"Yep," Pizzaboy nodded. "That's about it."

Glynn nodded, too. "All non-essential personnel, head up and over the mountain top. Now."

The Troughtons blinked at him. No one moved.

Chris stood beside Glynn. "You heard the colonel, all non-essential personnel. That means you and yours, History Channel. Pizzaboy gets to shoot the bazooka, that's only fair. Hunter, Shayla and I are the archers. And Jailbird watches our backs."

"We have bikes waiting for you on the ridge," Glynn was calm. He opened his mouth to say something else.

"We're losing daylight, Colonel." Chris tugged on her braid.

He looked down at his feet, clenching his jaw.

"Troughtons to the roof." Hunter took his mother's arm and led her down the steps and over to the ladder leading up.

Glynn nodded to his team and watched as they scrambled up the slope to the road.

"What's it doing?" Glynn heard Jailbird's voice from above.

"It's breaking apart. Look, those three over there are flipping over." Shayla cried.

"OK, Watch your feet, step back away from the bazooka. If you get caught in the rope, you'll sail with it," Pizzaboy cautioned.

Glynn stepped back inside the cabin, away from all the ropes, and waited.

Chris's voice sounded calm. "We launch the harpoon first and make sure it hits and sticks. They we light them up, hit our piles of debris, and run like the wind."

"Don't look back. Just run." Hunter confirmed.

"Mr. Joe Lloyd," Chris called to Pizzaboy. "Take your shot."

There was a thump, a whoosh, and a zinging sound as the curtain-rod-harpoon sailed off the roof and across the yard, trailing the heavy netting and oil-filled condoms. Glynn couldn't follow it from inside the cabin, so he walked back onto the porch as the lines grew taut above his head. There was a resounding crack and the cabin jolted under his feet, knocking him to the floor. He looked up and watched the column of the cabin's foundation follow behind the ropes as they continued their flight behind the harpoon.

Into the resounding silence, Pizzaboy stated, "Oh. I didn't

think of that."

As Glynn crawled back to his feet, the floor began to tremble and everything on the shelves crashed around him. The cabin was moving down the mountain.

"Light them up!" Chris screamed. "Shoot the piles as we go past them!"

"And then jump off!" Glynn hollered to them as he crawled up the porch railings and onto the roof.

"Shoot! Just shoot!" Jailbird was yelling.

Flaming arrows pierced the sky and fell haphazardly on and near the gas-soaked brush – behind them. The cabin was picking up speed.

"Troughtons, JUMP!" Glynn grabbed Jailbird and Pizzaboy and flung them from the roof. Hunter and Shayla were already rolling behind the descending cabin. He held out his hand and Chris flew into his arms and they landed painfully.

As they rolled, flaming trails of gas seemed to dance down toward the shifting metal monsters. The stench of mech-thane was choking. They grabbed each other's hands and struggled up to where the cabin had once stood. The others were ahead of them.

"The basement!" Chris screamed up at her people. "Get in the basement of the cabin!"

Hunter and Shayla reached it first and tumbled down into the gaping hole. Jailbird yanked Pizzaboy in his wake. Pizzaboy was looking back over his shoulder, trying to see what had become of the net. Glynn shoved them down and Chris jumped in beside them all. They could hear the rush of ignited gas as it swept through the valley.

Glynn sounded so calm. "Crouch down against the wall closest to the valley. Cover your ears. Close your eyes. Open your mouth."

The ground rumbled with the familiar sound of moving mechmons. The six humans clung to each other, trying to press as closely to the inside wall as possible.

Pizzaboy stood up and climbed up the wall to peek over the foundation. "That's impossible."

He dropped back down and looked at them.

"What?" they all asked.

"It should have worked. I'm sorry." Tears streamed down his face as he whispered to Chris.

There was a crunching sound, granite stone against stainless steel, then the screaming of children which indicated a breach in the mechmon mandibles.

Jailbird grabbed Pizzaboy and they flung themselves to the ground as a wave of fire blanketed the mouth of the cellar. The earth lurched around them as rocks and soil jarred up from beneath them and pelted down on them in equal measure. Around them, trees shattered as sap boiled, and the face of the mountain slipped down toward the valley. The landslide slipped over the top of the cellar like the skin of an onion, covering them with dark loamy soil, which actually protected them from the flames.

All in all, Chris thought things were going well, considering.

Hunter was walking through a field of wheat. The stalks were taller than his head and the world smelled rich and bountiful. Sunshine dappled his skin and glinted off of something just beyond the field. Hunter walked toward the shiny material. It was the roof of a huge farm house. The tin roof caught and reflected the blazing light, so it was a moment before Hunter noticed there was somebody walking beside him.

He looked at the man and smiled. "Hi, Dad."

"Hey, son."

"You're dead, Dad. Am I dead, too?"

Jerry shook his head, "Not here. Not in Montana."

"You made it. You made it to Montana!"

Jerry shook his head again, sadly this time. "Only in your dreams. But you'll come here. You'll lead them home, son. Just look for the tin roof."

Hunter looked up where his dad was pointing. The light hurt his eyes.

"I love you, son. Now run."

Hunter tried to sit up, but Jailbird was sprawled against him. Shayla was crumpled beneath him, close to the brick wall. His ears rang and his head hurt. His mouth tasted like he'd bitten into a rotten egg.

Run, he heard Jerry's word again.

"Get up! Get up! Troughtons! We've got to get out of here!" He shook Shayla and pushed Jailbird away. "Mom!"

Chris moaned and then was awake. Glynn's face was bleeding and his arm looked bent at the wrong places. "Where's Pizzaboy?"

A hand clawed up from beneath the soil behind them. They pulled him out of the dirt and helped thump his lungs clear.

"Listen. We've got to get out of here now. Trust me." Hunter shoved Shayla up toward the surface where the cabin had once stood.

She screamed. A black spatula on a hose swiped at her, knocking her back into the cellar. Three sides of the cellar edge above them were lined with mechmons.

"What are they doing? There's no metal here!" Jailbird yelled.

Hunter pointed. "That way. Run and don't look back."

Shayla obeyed, quickly followed by the Troughton men. Hunter helped Chris get Glynn to his feet and then they followed just as the mechmons converged on the other side of the cellar.

Hunter shoved Glynn's weight onto his mom's side and turned. "Hello. My name is Hunter Troughton. You killed my father, prepare to die!" It was a revision his favorite line from his favorite movie. It had never been more appropriate. He kicked at the closest mechmon, shoving it just enough over the edge to make it lose its footing. It fell with a crash onto the cellar floor and the smell of mech-thane rushed up at him. Hunter ran as far as he knew his shooting range was and turned to face the cellar.

Thinking of the tin roof on the farm house and the warmth of being at his dad's side again, Doug "Hunter" Troughton lit and fired an arrow into the air. He watched it curve gracefully up and then down. As the shaft disappeared into the cellar, Hunter smiled and ran.

Mickey was waiting at the ridge of the mountain road with six bikes. Chris helped load Glynn behind Mickey and then each of the Troughtons got on with the waiting soldiers and were driven back to camp.

The college looked like a war zone. Walls were cracked, roofs had collapsed, and there was shattered glass everywhere. People were running back and forth, some carrying injured to a place, others away from a place. The seventy-fourthers ran here and there and the sound was deafening, even to Chris' numbed ears.

Mickey drove straight to the infirmary, so the others followed. Glynn was rushed inside and the Troughtons found themselves in a sea of bleeding hysterical civies.

"Shut up!" Shayla hollered. The room stilled.

"Thank you," Hunter said softly.

Jailbird giggled. Mickey laughed. Chris shook her head and they all hugged each other.

Glynn's arm had been dislocated and was reset. His forehead bore a gash that would leave a scar. The Troughtons were covered with abrasions and swollen bruises and just walked away when the doctors insisted they spend the night for observation as Glynn was being forced to do.

From scouts, they learned that the CE heading directly toward the college seemed to watch the first CE's plight from the ridge of the mountain and then turned and headed west, as did the third one. They never returned.

The Troughtons had a private celebration that night, but discovered that several people from the Rutherford legion and a contingency from the 74th had left gifts of food and shine. They ate, drank and slept well that night and rested the next day.

As evening fell, the Rutherfords decided to hold an old-fashioned hoe-down, but Chris had other plans on her mind. She bathed and dressed in a purple nylon gown Mickey's wife had loaned her. The gown wasn't Chris' style – it was slinky and cut on the bias. Chris preferred one-hundred percent cotton but hadn't owned a night gown since she fled her home in Orlando two months after the aliens arrived. So, Mickey's wife to the rescue for tonight's long-awaited assignation with Colonel Peter Glynn would have to begin in a dime store nylon negligee. It didn't matter; Chris didn't plan to keep it on for very long. She stuck her feet inside her worn moccasins and covered herself in a trench coat in order to make her way from her quarters to his without too much notice. At Glynn's door, she paused. She tapped lightly and heard him, "Come in."

He was working at his desk, the lantern light pooled in circles around his maps. His arm was in a sling and his head bandaged. He looked up at her and swallowed. He stood and poured two drinks from his whiskey bottle – real whiskey – Glynn had found it in the desk's bottom drawer.

She knew he was in his mid-forties, a decade older than her. After what they'd been through, not just on the mountainside, but throughout their journey, age no longer mattered. Glynn looked like he had the whole world on his shoulders, and quite honestly, he did. His black hair and blue eyes softened his thick body and ferocious nature. She remembered the first time she'd seen him – and the first time she'd kissed him - and her heart skipped a beat in anticipation of tonight.

Taking the glass from his hand, she allowed her trench coat to fall open.

He eyed her gown and sipped his whiskey.

The silence stretched and she frowned.

"You're my best soldier," he toasted her.

She swallowed in one gulp and put her glass on the desk. When she turned back to face him, he looked embarrassed.

"I didn't expect you to survive."

She froze.

"I'm glad you did, Mrs. Troughton, don't misunderstand me." Glynn held out a hand. "What you did was incredible. We're safe for now, unless other CEs can find a way over the mountains."

She looked at his open hand and then back up at his face.

"When my wife died, I didn't even realize it. I didn't know she'd died, not for two days. Matthews told me. *So sorry for your loss, sir.* He thought I already knew." He tilted his head and winced as his arm ached. "She was a doctor. That was her life. Margaret was a doctor first and foremost, and then she was a mother, and sometimes, when she remembered, she was a wife. She enjoyed being a wife. But she was a doctor."

"And I'm a soldier, is that it?"

He didn't answer her.

"I'm not a soldier because I want to be one. I'm a soldier because I have to be one. I have to fight. I have to make sure the aliens don't win." She tried to not yell. She whispered, "You're a soldier, too."

He winced again. "And what are you first and foremost? Before the soldier? Before the woman? What are you?"

"What do you want me to be?"

"My wife. I want you to be my wife. But even if you were, you would be a Troughton first and foremost."

Her hands left her hips and reached for her missing battle braid. She had her waist-length hair unbound for what she thought they'd agreed would happen between them.

"Oh, Battle Braid, I love your hair down like that." He came around the desk and combed his fingers through her tresses. She leaned into him and remembered how she'd felt when he first kissed her. "Stay with me."

"Yes," she whispered.

"No, Chris. I mean stay with me. Marry me."

"I've got to take the Troughtons to our land."

He stepped back. "See?"

"Come with me. Marry me and come with me to our thousand-square."

He spoke slowly as if the air were thick, "I can't. And you can't. So, we can't."

"And that's it? I don't follow your orders so you don't want me? I don't want to abandon my duties to my people and play house with you, so that's all? All or nothing?"

"You're not making sense, Chris."

"I promised you that I would make it back from the mountain, and I did. I wouldn't have if you hadn't been there. So now I'm here. And I just want –"

"What? To reward me for my bravery? Take the boy sasquatch-hunting because there are no more medals to pin to his chest? Is that what you want?"

She swiped at the tears on her cheeks. "Yes. Yes, that's what I want. I want to make love to you, because you were brave and saved my life in so many ways this last year. And I love you. And I was brave and I saved your life and what else is there in life? We love. And then we die. That's all. Isn't that enough?"

It wasn't. It wasn't enough and he knew it. But she was his Battle Braid and he was her History Channel.

Chris was right; the gown didn't stay on very long.

15
MOVING DAY

Five days after what would ever hereafter be referred to as Big Boom Day, a contingency of the Rutherford legion came to the Troughton quarters. It was midmorning, so the slop buckets had been dumped, breakfast had been shared and cleaned up, and a poker game, begun three days earlier, was being continued.

Chris had spent each night in Glynn's room, relishing the ability to make love in a soft bed within safe walls and in the arms of a man she loved. But she always returned to her people before breakfast and was crocheting a pair of baby booties for Sally. She had found a skein of camo-colored yarn and bartered a pair of jeans for it. She had long ago grown too thin for the jeans, and by the time she realized they were too small for Hunter, she had grown used to carrying them around. But as trade goods for the camo yarn, they were worth it.

Hunter came into the common room of Parker Hall. "Mom, we've got visitors."

Four people accompanied President Rutherford and sat down. Chris smiled and laid aside her crochet. She glanced between them, waiting for Beverly to speak. Chris knew Beverly would be the one to speak for the others. She was incredible – brave, cunning, and cut to the point but in a diplomatic way.

Chris was right. The sixty-three year old woman spoke, "I think the 74th is settled in nicely."

"Soft beds and strong walls will do that to people," Chris nodded.

"We're looking forward to finding soft beds and strong walls of our own."

President Rutherford butted in, "Before winter sets in."

"Yeah," Gabby added. "This college is not built for this many of us. We're getting on each other's nerves."

"I heard that," Chris laughed. "We've gotten used to having a mile or so between our legions."

Hunter stood behind her, "Soft trails and the safety of family is worth more – to my way of bartering."

The Rutherford delegation nodded.

"We want to be on our lands by Thanksgiving."

"I agree. The fields between here and there are ripe with grains and we'll have a lot to eat along the road, just by gleaning what's at hand."

Hunter pointed, "Mr. McNally, I believe you have a plan for gathering crop seeds along the way, to begin next year's plantings. I know Preacher and Andrews were excited about it."

McNally nodded, "Can't gather if we aren't walking."

Rutherford countered, "Can't walk if we get eaten by mechmons at every turn."

Beverly had the situation now set up. She played her card. "We need the Troughtons to guard us. You be our warriors and help lead us home. We'll make it worth your while."

Chris grinned up over her shoulder at Hunter. He came around the couch and sat beside her. She knew she'd leave the bartering up to him. She reached down and picked up her crochet.

After two hours of negotiations, Hunter closed the deal with a hand-shake and an offer to share lunch. As warriors for the East Legions (as they now referred to themselves), the Troughtons were allowed to hunt mammals, fowl and fish along the trail for free. Plus, the Rutherford legion would allow them to glean bushels of crop seeds from fields along the paths. That would give them about four bushels of starter seeds when they got to their own lands and full stomachs and dried meats along the way.

"The only thing left to set is moving day." Chris stretched. "When do we leave?"

Gabby grinned. "We've been packing all week. You just tell us when you're set and we'll line up in formation within the hour."

Hunter and Chris exchanged glances. He answered, "Let us get back to you on that. We'll have your answer by supper time."

Beverly reached a hand out and touched the booties. "These are adorable. When are you due?"

"Oh no, Jerry can't have children." Chris blushed, "Jerry couldn't have…"

The delegation paused in awkward surprise.

"I'm sorry," Beverly's expression showed no remorse. "I had just assumed, since you and the colonel are such good friends."

Chris grabbed her braid, "Well, don't assume."

She didn't join the Troughtons for lunch. She went to the small dormitory she'd moved to, to give Shayla and Hunter privacy, and began to pack. There really wasn't much to pack; the habits of being a nomad had left very little room for non-utilitarian items in her life. Three blouses, four jeans, two bras (she'd removed the underwires), seven balls of socks, a hand-crocheted sweater, a bar of soap in a plastic bag, a few towels that served all sorts of purposes, and in the very bottom, rolled up and wrapped in a pillow case – a blah-grey oxford shirt that used to be blue and still smelled of Jerry's sweat. She pressed it to her face and sobbed.

The all-call triangle clanged as soon as the Rutherfords left after lunch. Those not on duty – which was pretty much everyone since as had been pointed out – there wasn't much to do inside the campus – all crowded into the common room and settled down.

Hunter stood and addressed his people.

"Those of you who have been Troughtons from the beginning, and those of you who joined us over the last two years, know without a doubt that we are searching for our Montana. It may not be the state so named on the US map, but it is the Montana Jerry could see. His vision was for rich farmland and houses that we could turn into homes. He saw children and grandchildren for all of us, and he never let us forget, no matter how hard the trail or how dangerous the situation, that he loved us. We are Troughtons."

He waited for the fifty-some-odd Troughtons to stop cheering.

"During our last daring deed – and if you haven't heard about it yet you could probably coerce someone to tell you about it." They all chuckled. "Anyway, during that event, when we were trapped in the cellar, covered with dirt and flames eating up every lick of vegetation above us." Hunter's voice quivered, "I had a dream. Jerry was there. We were in a wheat field. The most beautiful field I've ever seen. Above the field, on a hill, was a huge farmhouse. You know, the kind that's three stories high and goes on and on with porches around every side. It had a brilliant tin roof. The sunlight reflecting off that tin roof was blinding. He told me to look for that tin roof; because then we'd find our Montana."

The crowd was still with concern tempered by faith.

"We've cut a deal with the Rutherford Legion, to protect and preserve them until they get to their land. Then we go on to ours. I made this deal on the Troughton's behalf, but I didn't let you vote on it. So, before we set a moving day, I need to see a show of hands who wants to keep going."

Not every hand was raised, but at least forty were.

Instead of looking to the back of the room where the hands had stayed down, Hunter turned to Chris. "I understand how things change and how important relationships and responsibilities are. If you decide to stay, for no matter what reason, I'll understand. No one has to go with me to Montana. No one will blame you if you stay behind, or decide to go somewhere else."

Chris furrowed her eyebrows and fingered her braid.

Billy Junior stood up. "Can we bring others with us? From other legions, if they want to come?"

Belly was rocking Georgia in his arms, but his voice sounded fierce, "Who you got in mind, son?"

"Becky Cardinal of the Rutherfords." Billy Junior's cheeks were red.

Belly turned to his wife and whispered, "Thunder Thighs?"

She smacked the top of his head.

Chris grinned and waved for him to sit down. "The law as was set up at our one and only legislative meeting in March stated that inter-legion marriages and transfers had to meet the approval of the 74th's Commanding Officer. I think we ought to have both of the Eastern Legions gather a list of perspective changes in citizenship – you know, names, from and to, and make sure each person requesting the change has a sponsor from the legion they are joining – I'll give it to the Commanding Officer as soon as it's ready. Once he approves or denies it, we'll make the changes."

"Is your name going on the list?"

Chris glared at Shayla and took a deep breath. Everyone looked at their feet or up in the air, but each Troughton silently awaited her response.

"No. And Glynn's name won't be on any list, either. As he has so recently reminded me, I'm a Troughton, first and foremost. I have fought too hard to get us to Jerry's Montana and sacrificed too much to turn back now."

She found herself wrapped up in Hunter's arms. She hugged him back while the Troughtons chanted, "Troughton Company is here, Mechmon best be a'feared!"

Moving Day was set for three days from that day. She planned to tell Glynn before they went to bed, but he met her at the door and they were wrestling and kissing and consumed with each other before she could say a word. Later, she lay in his arms and made sure that the first non-sasquatch-hunting phrase out of her mouth was, "The Eastern Legions are moving on in three days. The Troughtons will act as warriors."

"I know."

She peered up at his face.

He shrugged, "Matthews told me. He's sweet on a girl in Rutherford's legion. He's going with them."

"There will be a lot of transfers. I've told them to put everyone on a list and you can approve or disapprove of them and give us word back."

"Us."

"Yes. Us."

"I'm not going to beg you to stay."

"Good. Because I'm not staying. And I won't beg you to go with me."

"Good. Because I won't go."

"Fine."

"So this is goodbye."

"No. No, Peter. We have two more nights. I love you and I love being with you. If this were any other world, any other part of history, I would never leave your side."

He huffed out a breath.

She ran her hand over his chest and up to his face. "You know it's true."

He nodded and swallowed. "Yeah."

"So, History Channel," She crawled on top of him and began kissing his neck. "To my way of thinking, we have twenty years' worth of love-making we need to fit into these last nights together."

"Oh, Battle Braid!"

16
MARCH OF THE EASTERN LEGIONS

The Eastern Legions began their march at dawn.

Of the seven-hundred fifty soldiers in the 74th Cavalry at the beginning of the journey, a dozen or so had stayed behind with each Western Legion. About the same number marched forward with the Eastern. However, almost one hundred civilians remained behind at Kendrick College.

The Eastern Legions walked east and skirted around what used to be Atlanta. When the aliens came, they headed south and finally got to it January two years ago. This would have been a month after Glynn's wife and most of the population had died of cholera and the 74th had been forced to flee north to Virginia. Their huge machines scooped up mile-wide portions of Atlanta – they did the same of every metropolis. They sifted through the pieces, keeping metals and spewing out everything else through their gills. In one week, Atlanta was gobbled up and reformed as seventeen large piles of non-metallic rubble. Chris had heard it took the aliens three weeks before Manhattan and Long Island were piles of everything except metal.

So, they had a wide-open road before them, marked only by the occasional massive alien scat along the way.

The Troughtons rode ahead of the column and behind it. Plus, Chris sent out scouts in all directions and Hunter kept track of the maps. As they entered the Rutherford territory, a cheer rolled through the legions. They camped and walked, camped and walked for three more days and came at last to the center of the Rutherford lands. There, they spent two days, washing clothes and getting drunk. There was a lot of sasquatch-hunting between the legions, but that was only natural.

Chris walked point as often as she could. She tried not to think about all the things she had left behind her. She thought of what lay ahead. She clung to those thoughts. When the legions were drinking and celebrating, Chris stood guard against all the horrors that might lay in wait for them in the darkness.

Of the three dozen CEs they came across over the four-hundred miles, none were awake. Few had the razor wire adaptations. The Troughtons made a big deal about going on duct-hunts, but the most dangerous things they came across were wild boars and sand storms.

When the Troughtons left the Rutherfords behind, the last of their Legion neighbors, they fell silent and marched swiftly toward the boundary that marked their land.

Hunter raised his hand; the Troughtons stopped. "This is it. This is where our land begins."

Their people hooted and danced.

"We'll walk three more miles today, and then pitch camp."

They began walking, and within a quarter hour, they were running and jumping and laughing. Hunter stopped them in a meadow surrounded by oak trees and within walking distance of a clear-running stream. He looked happy. He felt happy. His people were home.

He put his arms around his wife and mother, "Now we look for the tin roof."

The next morning, when most people clung to their skulls and complained bitterly about the raging sun, Chris discovered that her toothpaste had gone rancid. She threw up and heaved and felt woozy for most of the morning. She hadn't had a drink since she'd left Glynn, but most people thought she suffered as they did from a hang-over.

That evening, she took Hunter aside. "I think we need to scout ahead, take a look at our land and see where we could best settle."

"I agree. I thought I'd send the bachelors out and bring them back in a week."

"I think that's a good idea, and since I'm a bachelorette now, I'll go too."

Hunter scowled, "I need you here."

"I can't be here right now."

"Mom, you've been through a lot, more than most. You need to rest up and eat more. What are you – skin and bones now?"

"I need time alone. You need time to be in charge. They look to you. You're the natural heir to the throne. Jerry would be so proud of you."

"What about you?"

"Oh yes! I'm so proud of you, too."

Hunter laughed and lowered his head. "I meant, are you OK? If you want to go back to Glynn, I'll send someone with you. To keep you safe."

"Hunter, I don't want to go back. I want to go forward. I want to run and run and run and find that tin roof you saw in your dreams. I want to find Jerry's Montana. I can't sit here and wait for," she licked her lips and drew a shaky breath as tears filled her eyes. "I can't sit here and wait for someone to show up, because that's not going to happen. Jerry's gone. Glynn's behind me doing what he needs to do. You're here in charge of the Troughtons, just as Jerry always seemed to know you would be. I've got to go out there. I've got to find who I'm supposed to be."

He wrapped his arms around her as she cried. The next morning, she was gone.

Six hours beyond Macon got her to Andersonville and the famous Civil War Memorial park. The statues were gone, gobbled up by the mechmons, as was the museum and most of the picnic area. She stretched and sniffed the air for fresh scat. The air was sweet, with just a hint of mountain laurel. She and Jerry had come here one vacation. They'd wandered around, watched the movie, listened to the audios beside each museum artifact. But her favorite place was where he'd given her the news that he'd been promoted and they could start looking for a house. She remembered it was where the icy cold water boiled up in the center of a small lake. She went to find the spring. The sun was setting as she refilled her water bottles. Down the stream, she set fishing lines made from bamboo rods, string, and bone hooks. She kept those in her survival kit no matter where she went, along with a wooden and rope drill to start fires, a dagger with a bone handle and flint blade, a first aid kit made up of gauze, thin plastic needles, thread, plastic tubes and ointments, and small plastic sugar tongs: nothing metal. Plastic, bone, glass, stone, wood; the human race survived only because they were willing to forgo metals.

She set her fish lines and then found a safe burrow back from the river where she stretched out and slept.

She awoke around dawn and lay there, listening and sniffing the air. No smell of fresh scat, no crunching sound of anything being pulverized. No motors. She crept out from under the shading branches and stretched. She was a damn fool and felt it. She'd left everything and everyone behind because of her pride.

She couldn't go back. There was nothing to be done but to go forward. She retrieved her trout lines and ate well before getting the maps out of her backpack.

She tamped down her fire and headed southeast.

The aliens tended to leave the little towns and farms alone and unless the CE's were on a direct course through one, they survived – little suburban islands between huge swatches of plowed and chomped ribbons of land. The CE's glutted on the cities and highways, perhaps leaving the smaller places for desert.

She checked her maps again, tested her balance under the strain of the heavy load, and began marching. She kept her eyes open for abandoned houses and stores where the Troughtons could get supplies.

Just outside of where Cordele used to be, Chris was set upon by a pack of dogs. She used her walking stick to intimidate the largest two, but the three tiny terriers were bent on stripping the flesh from her bones. She loved dogs, but she couldn't think of these as pets. She took out her dagger, intending to do harm.

"Don't you hurt Mr. Tilly Willy!"

Chris heard the strange command right before something hard connected with her skull.

17
MR. TILLY WILLY

"You can't go around hitting people on the head, June."

"But she was going to hurt Mr. Tilly Willy."

Chris' head throbbed. The light was dim and the room filled with the thick smell of wood smoke and melting wax. She squinted her eyes open and looked around the bedroom. On the right side, Barbie dolls and cheerleader pompoms lined the top shelf, while photographs and dust collectors lined the two beneath it. Past the foot of her bed was a closet and a door opened to what looked like a hallway. On her left were two people: an old man sitting beside her and an old woman standing.

"Now, just lie still, young lady," the man patted Chris' arm. "You've got a concussion. I put three stitches in the back of your head. You've been asleep off and one for almost twenty-four hours. So just be still now. No one's going to harm you."

"You mean – again. Or do you mean, no one except that lady?"

"I couldn't let you hurt Mr. Tilly Willy."

"You looked at my ankles, ma'am? Mr. Tilly Willy was holding his own." She sat up and then wished she hadn't. "Where am I?"

"How could you not know where you are?"

"June, maybe our guest would like some tea."

Chris glared at the old woman who glared back.

"We're the Arnolds. I'm Dennis and this is my wife, June. "

"I'm Chris Troughton of the Eastern Legions of the 74th Cavalry." She hoped it sounded impressive rather than pretentious.

"Cavalry?" He raised a disbelieving brow.

"Where's your horse?" June asked.

"Your dog ate it."

"Mr. Tilly Willy did not!"

"Ms. Troughton, forgive me, but where's your uniform?"

"Mr. Arnold, no offense, but we don't wear uniforms unless we're regular army, and there hasn't been a regular army in almost two years."

"I was a medic in Viet Nam." Dennis turned to his wife, "Tea would be really nice, darling."

"I'll be right back."

"No," Chris stood, careful of her head. "I need to be on my way."

"Take it easy. It's about dark. We don't open the doors after dark. I couldn't drag your pack; it's still outside."

Chris thought about the likelihood of her food bag still being intact after twenty-four hours with those dogs around. "I need my pack. Would you take me there?"

"It's just a few houses away. I brought your bow; I thought you might need it."

She entered the kitchen and found June boiling water in a Corning ware coffee pot on a gas stove. The table was set with three cups and saucers in a pretty floral and fruit pattern. One teabag – well-used and thin – rested on a tea strainer, ready for the boiling water.

The sun was setting and Chris could hear the dogs baying and fighting somewhere in the distance.

"See your pack over in that yard?" He pointed out the screen door.

"I'll be right back, if that's alright?"

"More than welcome, Chris." He opened the door for her while handing her the unstrung bow.

The dogs hadn't returned; her food supply was untouched. Keeping watch while she returned, Chris counted three very healthy deer and a dozen fat rabbits munching in the surrounding overgrown yards. The houses were similar: small, two to three bedrooms, ranch style cement block, single story. Each had one large picture window and a single-car garage attached. The main difference was the Arnold's yard was manicured while the others were overgrown and thatched, and there was a light shining dimly through the picture window.

He let her back in and said she could leave her pack in the same bedroom where she'd been – his daughter Emily's room. When he said it, "my daughter Emily's room," Chris heard that unmistakable sound of unrequited grief and sorrow. Somewhere along his lifetime, his Emily had died. After two years of death-by-aliens, and death-by-accident, and death-by-starvation, Chris acknowledged the gentleman's loss with an empathetic nod of her head.

"Bathroom's to your right. But the lavatory is out back. We use the one in the shed. I think we're having English peas and carrots for supper. Join us once you've washed up."

She couldn't see the bandage on the back of her head when she looked into the mirror over the sink. She could feel it, though, and the stitches. She didn't know how she'd be able to keep a wound clean that she couldn't see. Her Troughtons would have been watching out for her, but she'd left them behind. The books she'd been reading for the last decade suggested lard and honey, spread over a wound, sealing it until it healed.

These people hadn't seen a decent meal in months. There was no protective layer of fat under their skin, just flesh and bones, and if the solitary tea bag was any indication, they hadn't replenished their pantry in a while. She dug into her food bag and pulled out dried meat and a still-sealed plastic bag of Uncle Ben's finest.

At the kitchen door, Chris paused. June was tending to a Pyrex pot of carrots as if it were a turkey dinner. Her smile of domestic bliss was jarringly out of place in this post-apocalypse, but it gave her a beauty, a sense of belonging.

"Mrs. Arnold," Chris stepped inside.

"Who are you?" The woman put her hand to her throat, startled.

"I'm Chris Troughton." Chris' heart pounded. "I'm Chris. You invited me to dinner."

"Chris?"

"Yes ma'am. I have rice and venison. If you'd allow me to share."

Dennis came in from the backyard, holding onto two cans of garbanzo beans. He eyed the rice and jerky and smiled. "Looks like Thanksgiving."

While Mrs. Arnold boiled the rice and venison in one glass pot and added the cans of beans to her carrots, Chris set the table.

"You keep your cans in the shed?" she asked, looking at the empty cabinet shelves.

"Safer that way," he replied.

"But – your oven. That much steel, pretty risky."

"Worth the risk." He didn't look like he believed himself. Chris waited.

"We have a huge stone barbeque pit out back. But she insists on staying in the kitchen to cook."

"Are you a friend of Emily's?" June turned and smiled.

"No ma'am. I've never met your daughter."

"Dennis, did you remember to pick up biscuits when you went to the store?"

"I haven't been to the store today. I'll get it tomorrow."

"The store?" Chris' eyes lit up.

Dennis gave a slight shake with his head.

"May I use your lavatory?"

"I'll take you out back. We can talk there." Dennis kissed his wife's cheek. "We won't be long, darling. Just got to feed the sows."

There was a picnic bench in the back, next to a beauty of a stone grill.

"This is incredible. You did this yourself?"

"I had three heart attacks about eight years ago. I had to retire, but I needed a hobby."

Chris explored the facets – dutch ovens, grill, smoking area – of the stoneworks. "You could preserve an entire deer on this."

"Could, if I could kill one."

"I could."

"With that bow? We don't allow firearms of any type here. We'll not risk the mechmons after surviving this long."

"I could take a deer down with my bow, and then dispatch it with mercy with my blade. I've done so many times."

"Dispatch it with mercy?"

Chris blushed.

He chuckled, "Don't mind me, Chris. It just had a nice ring to it."

"One or two deer would keep you through the winter. I'd love to see your store."

Dennis raised his hands to the houses around them. "The Stevens loved English peas. The Wilkins kept a fine stock of brandy. McGregors over there had more tuna than sense – to my way of thinking, but June loves to make tuna casserole. So, we did well for most of this year, after Cordele disappeared."

"From what I've seen, most households keep a year's supply of canned goods. There must be twenty-five houses in this subdivision. Why are you starving?"

"Two months back, a wagon load of people came through. They had children with them, so we let down our guard. On closer inspection, the children were tied to the wagon. They scavenged all the homes on Delaney Avenue and killed the few neighbors who protested. Yes," he nodded. "There are six families left here. But we keep to ourselves mostly. I tend them when they're sick, but we're all just – we're just old and waiting."

"You're a doctor?"

"A surgeon specializing in obstetrics and gynecology. Until my hands palsied with the coronaries."

"We could use a doctor. We had about thirty medics and doctors in the column, but they all divided up between the legions and the Troughtons were so busy fighting, I guess we forgot to get us any. You and June would be welcomed to join us."

"You speak of columns and legions and cavalries. So how come you're all alone?"

Chris took a deep breath and didn't want to answer. But she did. "This is Troughton land now. We call it Troughtonia. One hundred miles east to west by one hundred miles north to south, all the way to the Piedmont Plateau. There are ten more legions of the same size stretching west to the Mississippi, plus the Military Headquarters in Kendrick College. My people are resting up; I'm scouting ahead. I'm not alone."

"We couldn't travel now. June's not well."

"The books I read said it was best to keep patients with senile dementia in familiar surroundings."

"Are you a doctor?"

"No," she scoffed. "I'm a Troughton. Now a days, that means I'm part of an elite fighting force, we destroy mechmons, roadsters, and one very irritating city-eater. Might have felt an earthquake about six weeks ago. That was us. But I used to be a secret shopper for three department stores."

He blinked without responding.

"My husband's mother suffered a minor stroke when she was fifty, but three years later, she began the symptoms of senile dementia. Because of the previous damage, her progression was swift. She lasted only two years."

"June started to drift away two months ago."

"Those raiders? Did they hurt her?"

"No. Well, yes. They killed Mr. Tilly Willy and two dozen other dogs. Maybe she'd been slipping into dementia before then – I mean – these last two years, we all were partially insane – but something broke inside her two months ago."

Chris didn't say anything; she reached out and grasped the doctor's hand.

Chris awoke early, her back ached from sleeping on a real mattress again and her stomach felt queasy. She dressed and took up her bow and quiver and slipped out of the house.

The deer were congregating by the fountain at the end of Delaney Avenue. Chris observed them and picked two doe she thought looked healthy. If she missed one, she would try for the second.

The stag stood on top of a burnt-out car, eyeing the terrain around his harem. Chris was careful to keep downwind from him. She relaxed and set her bow. She aimed for the throat, centered herself and released the arrow. Fluidly, before the arrow had hit its mark, Chris set another arrow up and let it fly at the second doe. The herd scattered; the stag reared and then bounded away. Two bodies writhed on the ground as the fountain clouded with blood.

"God, grant this creature sweet release." She slit its throat and did the same for the other doe. She was used to doing this, but suddenly, the smell of the fresh blood overwhelmed her. She took four steps off to the side and vomited. She heaved again and sobbed. Then she stood straight and went back to the carcasses.

She felt like she was being watched, so she notched an arrow, but held it loosely in one hand and stood. The woman observing her from between the houses put a hand to her throat, terrified.

After a minute of silence Chris grinned, "Good morning."

The woman screeched and ran back between the houses.

Chris tied the does' legs and slipped her bow between them.

They were forty to fifty pounds each and Chris wasn't sure she could lift them both over her shoulders, but she didn't want to leave one behind. As she pondered her dilemma, the woman returned with another woman and a man.

"Put down your weapon," the man demanded. He held a musket to his shoulder. It was an ancient as the man, but Chris paused.

"I'm not here to harm you. I'm just taking the deer to my friends, Doctor and Missus Arnold. Do you know them? Dennis and June. I'm staying with them."

"Did you kill the Arnolds?"

"She did not." Dennis' voice carried across the yards. "Put down your musket, Carlos. Help us get the carcasses to my shed and we'll have a feast tonight."

As they walked back, Dennis kept glancing at her.

"What?" Chris snapped.

"You seemed to be a little ill back there. You threw up."

She sighed and shrugged. "I think my toothpaste has gone rancid. I didn't know that could happen, but maybe after it expires, it goes bad."

"You brush your teeth in the morning."

"Most mornings. When I can."

"You didn't brush your teeth this morning. I'm a light sleeper."

Chris remained silent.

"Remember me saying I'm an OB-GYN? I can't help but wonder what you're doing out here all alone, without your Fighting Troughtons, because to be quite honest, dear, there's nothing wrong with the toothpaste."

Seven couples and three single women joined the Arnolds that evening. They ate roasted venison and shared hoarded vegetables and home-made moonshine. She took special pleasure in cooking her favorite dish – sautéed deer heart. Joan had a bottle of olive oil, and the rest of the neighbors brought onions, carrots, and a bottle of Worcestershire sauce. Chris sautéed the one-inch cubes of heart with the oil, and then added the vegetables and the sauce. The two hearts were only large enough for each person to have a small serving, but they all agreed with her; it was delicious.

Chris stayed with them for one more day and left them with sheds filled with dried venison and rabbit. They discussed going northwest and joining the Troughtons, but voted against it. Where two years ago they had been solitary families, each poorly fending for themselves, they were now a democratic group of survivors, banded together, helping each other: starting again.

Dr. Arnold walked with her to the edge of the subdivision. "I wish you wouldn't leave."

She smiled and shrugged.

"Why did you leave the father of your child?"

"Pride. My late husband entrusted me with the safe-keeping of his people. I need to get us all to the place Jerry dreamed about. So, it's a good kind of pride, but I felt I couldn't stay behind."

"I'm so sorry for your loss. It will be hard to raise a child alone in this world."

Chris opened her mouth to speak and then closed it. "Jerry's not this baby's father. Jerry was killed last spring. I know it seems unchristian to have taken a lover before my widow-year was up. But things work differently now in the world."

"Do you think he'll come looking for you?"

"No." She made a face. "He's got eleven legions and about seven hundred soldiers to take care of. His name is Colonel Peter Glynn – the commanding officer of the 74th Cavalry and the Provisional Governor of the New United States."

"When you get your people to their lands, why don't you go back? You don't strike me as a woman who gives up easily."

She re-adjusted the straps on her shoulder. "We have a preacher in the Troughtons. He often says, *for everything there is a season*. I've got to find a place for my people before winter sets in. History Channel will just have to wait for his season."

"What does TV have to do with this?"

Chris grinned. "It's his nickname. He's History Channel, because he's always quoting famous battles to the 74th. And I'm Battle Braid, because of this," she flipped her braid up and wiggled it.

"And what season will your little one be born?"

"June or July. Summer. That will be nice – the season of new beginnings."

The doctor hugged her and kissed her cheek and watched her until she was out of sight.

At the end of their first week in Troughtonia, when the scouts returned with their marked maps and tales of adventure, Chris didn't show up. However, Glynn did.

The sound of a motorcycle growled its way toward the Troughton's camp just as Smartboard rang the triangle for an all-call to discuss what to do about their missing leader.

"Maybe that's her," Peggy said hopefully.

"Not likely. Chris went southeast. Biker's coming from the west."

"From the 74th," Belly added.

It came into view.

Preacher stood up, "Well if it ain't John Wayne on a Harley."

"John Wayne?" Shayla asked. "Wasn't he with one of the Western Legions?"

Preacher groaned.

"Showing your age, dear one," Smartboard commiserated.

Glynn swirled the bike with a flourish and came to a revved stop. "Howdy, Troughtons."

"See, substitute Pilgrims for Troughtons; John Wayne," Preacher stepped forward to shake the colonel's hand.

Glynn grinned and greeted everyone. Hunter hung back but

Glynn came to him and gave him a hug and a thump on the back. "So, you made it. How do you like your piece of Montana?"

"We just got here. Well, a week ago. We're resting up before spreading out."

"Good. Good." Glynn nodded absently, searching the camp for Chris' face.

The crowd grew expectantly silent.

"I know it's been six weeks since you left the 74th, but by bike, it took me three days to drive. It would have been shorter, but every settlement of the Rutherford legion wanted me to stay a while with them. At least for a meal." Glynn turned around, searching the empty lands behind him.

He turned back and faced Hunter, keeping the panic out of his voice with great effort. "Where is she?"

"We don't know."

Glynn shuddered. Hunter continued, "She went out to scout ahead for one week, along with six other Troughtons. She headed southeast and was supposed to be back here yesterday. Everyone else returned."

Glynn clenched his teeth and leapt back onto his bike. Hunter grabbed it from in front and shouted over the roar of the engines. "Stop. Wait for us. We've got the maps and I know where she was headed."

"Where?"

"The Civil War Memorial just east of Andersonville."

"That's only twenty miles from here. She should have been back in two days."

"Then she was going on; we're meeting tonight to –"

"Damn your Troughton Town Hall meetings. Get out of my way."

"Listen to me, Glynn."

The rest of the Troughtons formed a circle around them. Glynn cut the engines and glowered.

"You ride ahead, ten miles at a time. Then circle back and

report to us. We'll take only the fastest runners and follow. But you circle around in ten mile chunks and report to us each time."

Glynn nodded. "Now get out of my way."

"You need food and water and gas to fill the tank."

"Carry it with you; I'll refuel when I meet with you. I don't need any food."

"The food and water's not for you. It's for Chris if you find her. Do you have a med-kit?"

Glynn stared at Hunter in disbelief. "What kind of moron would head out without one?"

"One that's thinking with his heart and not his head."

Daisy-Mae thrust a sack into Glynn's arms. "Here! Food and an extra blanket. Nights are getting cold."

"We'll meet you at the Memorial, just inside the main gates."

"What road are you taking?"

Hunter pulled a worn map out of his pouch and opened it. "Look, she was taking the old highway 128 to the memorial and then follow 280 to Cordele. It should have taken her two more days. After that, she was supposed to head north on 41 to join back with us here. Seven days max. Steve ran across three roadsters outside of Hawkinsville."

"Toasted Roadsters," Steve supplied.

"And Vanessa came across a bunch of refugees that had taken over a shopping mall outside of Warner Robins."

"They weren't real friendly," she said.

"So there are still pockets of people around the area. We already figured that." Glynn nodded.

Hunter looked at him, "Are you armed?"

Glynn gritted his teeth again, "What kind of moron -" He whipped it out.

Pizzaboy moaned. "Springfield Military Special autoload, .45 ACP caliber and five-inch barrel weighing about 39 ounces. Cocobolo grips. Fixed sights combat three-dot. Single-action, parkerized, stainless finish, 7-shot mag capacity."

Glynn blinked and slowly holstered his handgun. "Anything else?"

Pizzaboy nodded, "Sells for about $770 to 840."

"Man knows his weapons," Preacher praised.

"Yes, he does," Pizzaboy's wife boasted.

Glynn blinked again.

Hunter interrupted. "I was just asking. There's safety in numbers, and I realize now that the legions were insulated from the rougher parts of humanity by its size."

"And by the 74th."

"Hoyah!" Mickey grunted. It helped break the tension and everyone laughed.

"Who are you taking with you?" Glynn calmed somewhat.

"We were about to call for volunteers."

Fifty hands shot up into the air.

"You'll need fighters to go with you, and fighters to stay to protect your people."

"I know who I'll take. You just be where I told you to meet us."

"I can make the loop in six hours."

Hunter glanced at his people. "Do it. Ride the loop backwards, down state road 41 and then onto 280. If you find her, bring her back to camp, if you can. If you don't find her, meet us at the memorial and we'll spread out in an organized search grid from there."

The Troughtons watched as Glynn roared off into the distance. Then they turned around and faced Hunter, waiting. "I'm going to ask Belly, Pizzaboy and Peggy, Angel and Jailbird, Preacher and Smartboard, and Mickey to go with me."

The rest of them grumbled with disappointment. Hunter held up one hand and they grew silent.

"I chose these Troughtons because we've been together the longest. Daisy-Mae and the other Hicks were there at the beginning, too, but Daisy-Mae's got little Georgia to nurse, and

Billy Junior just got married and Shayla will be filling in as nurse what with Peggy going with us."

"What about me?" Tim Hicks asked.

"Tim, you've got the best aim with a sling shot I've ever seen. I need you to stay here to help protect the Troughton camp. You heard the scouts, there are still mechmons out there, and worse, there are humans out there who don't remember what it was like to be civilized. We're counting on coming back to you, and once everyone is back, we'll move on."

Mickey spoke up, "We'll need to pack light but carry extra water. We'll be running most of the way, so if you have an extra pair of socks, I'm sure we'd appreciate them."

"We leave in thirty minutes. Any questions?"

They shook their heads and quickly dispersed to help the search team pack.

Hunter turned to Shayla and spoke softly, "If we don't come back within two weeks, you have to lead them on. Go east, but don't follow our trail. Keep going until you find the tin roof."

"I can't lead the Troughtons!" she squeaked.

Hunter touched her shoulder, "Of course you can. You're carrying Jerry's grandchild. I know you'll find the way."

"I know you damn well better come back! But don't tell my mom I said damn."

18
REPUBLIC OF DELANEY

The search team traveled faster and rested in shorter bursts
than Chris had. They were confident that they'd left the legion in
safe hands, so they could turn their attention to the task of tracking
Chris and they easily found her signs. The scouts had been out
beyond the highways, and they spent the last two days transferring
information from their maps onto Hunter's. The search team now
compared Hunter's marked maps with the war-torn terrain: a star
for schools, smiley face for stores with stock, frowny face for
empty stores, crosses for churches, a square with a triangle on top
meant housing developments, same sign with an X in it meant the
houses had been pillaged already, backwards triangle on a stick
mean gas stations, Xed out – empty ones. They had shaded out the
areas destroyed by mechmons – useless territory for survivors.

Glynn was waiting at the memorial, a large swath of stomped
grass testament to his agitation.

Hunter and Glynn faced each other while the others settled
down to rest.

"She didn't make the turn onto the state road."

"How do you know?"

Glynn shook his head, "Because the 41 north of Cordele is
gone. Gobbled up along with most of Cordele. And there were no
footprints along the sand, just animal tracks. No one's been that
way in months."

Hunter held out a piece of braided grass. "Have you seen any of these along the way?"

"Markers?"

"Sort of. Chris had a habit of braiding grass as she walked, to help pass the time, I guess. We collected one every other mile up to here."

Glynn took the one and pocketed it. "Would've been nice if you'd told me. I would have been on the lookout."

"You spent as much time with her as anyone. Didn't you notice?"

"The time I spent with Battle Braid, she usually had her hands full of flaming arrows."

"Anything interesting between here and the state road?"

Glynn shook his head, "Fallow fields, an occasional shanty and graveyard, and a sign pointing down a side road for a deserted subdivision. You know, one of those fifty-five and older age-restricted communities set bum-fruit in the middle of nowhere."

"You sure it was deserted?"

"No," Glynn sat down and drank from his plastic canteen. "It was about ten miles north of the road. I was just doing a dry run around her planned positions. But I think it's worth exploring, now that we know she went off of her planned route."

"Well imagine that, Chris not following procedure," Belly laughed.

"Rest up ten more minutes, then we run for another hour."

No one groaned; they all wanted to find Chris alive and well.

Mickey came back from point and spoke to Hunter. Whatever he said excited the president; he held up his hand and the Troughtons came to a stop. Mickey pointed back the way he'd come.

"Mr. President," Mickey saluted. "See the oak tree at two o'clock behind me?"

Hunter nodded. The Troughtons circled and – though vigilant

– became even more alert.

"There's an old woman up there, in a tree house, with binoculars."

Hunter peered over the soldier's shoulder. A dinner bell sounded, like the triangle hanging from Smartboard's tent back at camp.

"Wait for it," Hunter sounded confident. This was the first sign of life he'd seen in two days. "They know we're here. Let's hope they are reasonable and friendly."

It didn't take long to find out.

"Troughtons of the 74th Cavalry?" a voice called to them from a hidden location.

"You know us, sir?"

"I know of you. I've been led to understand that we are now part of Troughtonia. We figured you'd come to call."

"Is Battle Braid with you?" Mickey shouted.

"Who?" the voice asked him.

Mickey reddened and repeated, "Is Chris Troughton with you?"

"Depends," came the response.

"On what?" Belly growled.

"Silence," Hunter hissed. "To whom do I have the pleasure of speaking?"

"Doctor Dennis Arnold. And you?"

"My name's Hunter Troughton. We're looking for my mother, Chris."

"I'm Colonel Peter Glynn of the 74th Cavalry. We'd really like to speak with you face-to-face."

"Are you friend or foe?" a woman called.

"I don't understand. You know who we are. I assume our missing person gave you this information. So we're friends if she's been treated kindly. But we're foes if she's been harmed." Hunter led the initial contact.

"Damn straight," Belly affirmed.

"You misunderstand us. You are a friend if you're following her to Montana. But if you're lying to us, like those other people did, well," the doctor was interrupted.

"You better pray to whatever tin god you got, 'cause you'll be meeting him soon," a deeper voice assured them.

"Or her," the woman corrected.

"You better pray to whatever tin god you got, 'cause you'll be meeting him or her soon – just doesn't have the right sound," the deeper voice snarled.

"Tin god?" the doctor's voice was softer.

"Clint Eastwood," the deeper voice explained.

"That was John Wayne, you damn yankee," the woman scolded.

Mickey turned his back on the houses and spoke to his team. "I do believe we're being threatened by a band of geriatrics."

"Geriatrics!" Pizzaboy squeaked. "Where were they when we needed them to walk the tight rope over the belly-up city eater!"

"That's geriatrics, not gymnasts," Jailbird snorted and shook his head.

"We're waiting on your answer, Troughtons," Dennis shouted.

"Friends!" The Troughtons shouted together.

"Is my mom there? Is she alright?" Hunter took a step closer. A rock smacked the ground at his feet.

"Don't come any closer," the damn yankee warned.

"Do you have Chris or not?" Glynn yelled.

"Don't misunderstand us. We liked Chris. And if you're the Troughtons and her colonel, then you're welcomed as all get out. But who's to say you didn't find her along the way and torture her into revealing our location." The woman shouted down to them.

Glynn turned his back on the geriatrics and hissed, "We can take them. They threw a rock at us; that means no artillery. If we rush the gate, and I take out anyone standing in the way."

"No." Hunter was firm. "We know she was here. They just

told us she left them. She's not here anymore. I'm not starting our life in Troughtonia by murdering old folks."

Hunter turned back and raised his voice. "We understand your concern. I just need to know what direction she took and how long ago she left."

The Troughtons could hear the people speaking, but not the words themselves other than, "Put it to a vote."

"The ayes have it. Troughtons, how do you like your steak?"

"Take your pick of any of the empty houses," Stacy announced. She had introduced herself as the Republic of Delaney's Goodwill Ambassador. She was in her late seventies and used a walker to get around.

Jailbird smiled at her, "The abandoned houses would be those with unkempt yards."

"Why, yes," Stacy smiled and then frowned.

"How do you keep your yards mowed and," Preacher held out his plate, "May I have some more fried rabbit?"

"Jim Easton has a push mower, the old-fashioned kind. He charges one meal each time he mows a lawn."

"And once Chris taught us how to make snares and skin rabbits, some of us," Stacy nodded her head to the two unmarried women, "have a lot of yard work done."

Mickey sat down next to the colonel. "Martha and George over there tell me the Republic of Delaney was hit by a band of pirates – their word, not mine – two or three months ago. Killed the dogs and a few of their neighbors. Kind of got them banded together."

"The Republic of Delaney?"

Mickey pointed to a nearby street sign, "Delaney Avenue."

Glynn sipped from his tea cup and glowered.

"My point is," Mickey stopped talking when Glynn held up his hand.

"I know the point. She's alone out there. I should have never let her leave. I should have forced her to stay with me when I had the chance. If she dies out here, it'll be all my fault. Is there anything I've left out?"

Mickey cocked his head and bit his lip. "You might want to ease up on that moonshine."

"What moonshine?" Glynn took another sip from his cup.

"Would you like some more tea, Colonel Glynn?" June glided toward the table, teapot in hand.

"Yes'm. That'd be mighty nice. It has a real nice twang to it, sort of lemony."

Mickey took the pot, "The colonel doesn't need any more tea, thank you, Mrs. Arnold."

"May I ask you something, Mr. Mickey?"

"Yes ma'am," he poured some shine into his plastic cup.

"Are you a black man?"

"My father was."

"But your mother, she was a white girl?"

"Yes ma'am."

"I think you have the prettiest eyes. And just think, if your parents had been the same race, your eyes would be so – so –"

"Blue?"

"Yes. Blue."

"Mrs. Arnold. Do you drink a lot of this tea?"

"Yes Mr. Mickey. Why?"

"Did Chris taste any of this while she was here?"

"No, I don't believe she did. She told Stacey's husband how to brew it before she left, but the tea wasn't ready yet. Is it important to the mission?"

"Not a bit, ma'am."

"You do have the prettiest eyes, Mickey," the colonel declared. "I never noticed that before."

"Oh hallelujah," he muttered. I am surrounded by drunk white people who think my eyes are pretty."

"Hey Mickey," Jailbird called from across the back yard. "Miss Rosa here says you got the prettiest eyes she's ever seen."

"My wife – my pregnant wife – thinks so, too." Mickey left them behind and bivouacked in a house three doors down.

The Troughtons stayed in the Republic of Delaney until noon the next day in order to mow and trim all the yards.

During the morning, the colonel was called to the doctor's home and met with him privately in his study. Glynn and Dennis sat in leather armchairs and smoked very fine cigars. They sipped at small sniffers of brandy. Finally, Dennis spoke.

"I lost my daughter to pride."

Glynn sighed and gritted his teeth. "There's a difference between pride and responsibility."

"I'm sure there is," he held up a mollifying hand. "I'm not comparing myself to you. Chris said, and I hope I'm not breaching some confidence, but she said you two couldn't be together, because of pride."

Glynn tried to cover his surprise, but wasn't able to. "She told you about us?"

"Beautiful woman, alone in a world set on the edge of hell, I couldn't help wondering about her."

"She was out here alone because she's a Troughton first and foremost and doesn't realize she's a woman and there are things in this world she can't shoot with her flaming arrows."

"So, we both know why she left and kept going. I now would like to know, why did you let her go?"

"I didn't." Glynn blinked. "Well, I did. But once I figured they'd gotten to their land, I came after her. See. She's done what she needed to do – led her people to the promised land. So then, she'd fulfilled her responsibility to her late husband and her people and she could come back with me."

"So, you love her."

Glynn smirked and sat forward, "The Troughtons have a saying – abso-fruiting-lutely. Yes, I love her."

"She asked me to go with the Troughtons. I can't right now, because of my wife. But, come get me around June. I think you'll need a good doctor by then."

"You'd be welcomed anytime."

19

HORSE

To the east, she could see a rooftop above the rows of wheat and smiled. The roof looked black in the late morning sun and meant an intact shelter and maybe food. She gathered wheat heads and munched them as she walked. Their nutty flavor was sometimes spiced by mildew and ants, but she enjoyed every mouth full. They also calmed her stomach and seemed to settle her bout of morning sickness. As she crested the rise, the farmhouse came into view. However, a stench hovered in the air, and Chris paused.

The scent was old, past the smell blowflies render to dead meat, but not to the burnt-bacon-smell stage of desiccating flesh. Three weeks' maximum. If she were smelling three-week-old mechmon scat, why was the roof intact?

She thought of poor Mr. Tilly Willy. Marauders. She snuck off the road and into the amber waves of grain.

The farmhouse had an abandoned look, but that's where marauders would most likely hunker down if they were still here. Chris worked her way to the barn where the stench was strongest.

The bodies of two men – one in overalls, the other in jeans and a t shirt, lay on the barn floor. The man in overalls had been shot in the chest. Impossible to tell by his features, but Chris guessed he was well into his senior years because his hair was white. The other one - younger by a half a century - still had the business end of a pitchfork sticking in him. There was no rifle in his arms or near him, indicating that there had been at least three people in the barn. It hadn't taken long for the human race to turn on itself.

A strange noise terrified her. She had her arrow already notched; she drew the bow and aimed it at the stall. A thin nose with soulful brown eyes peered at her. The horse shivered and blew out a breath again.

Chris swallowed and lowered her bow. She had a pocket full of wheat. She held out her hand, offering it to the animal. As the horse took the grains, Chris looked into the stall. Full of manure and flies, the stall had been bolted shut. The water trough was nearly empty, as was the grain bin. The horse was in horrible shape.

"Why did they leave you?" she asked gently as she held out more grain. She unbolted the stall and the horse wobbled out. She led him to the trough outside and pumped it until fresh water flowed. The horse moaned and lowered his head, like a parishioner in prayer.

Chris looked up at the farmhouse. If the horse was here, maybe the marauders were, too. Or would be coming back…

Her exploration of the house revealed a sad tale. The jewelry and money and guns – had there been any – were gone. Clothing - men's only - was strewn about the largest of the eight bedrooms and the bed sheets were soiled and stained. The other bedrooms were devoid of personal items, but Chris had the feeling that they had been unoccupied for a while. The kitchen larders were empty except for one can of black olives.

Chris tried not to wonder what bizarre sin black olives had committed to be left behind by such horrible creatures. Dirty plates and pots filled the kitchen table and counters, but not many. The marauders had stayed less than twenty-four hours if there were a half-dozen of them; less time if there were more of them. That meant they'd been gone about three weeks and hadn't returned. Leaving the house stripped clean, they had no reason to return here.

Chris used the sheets off the beds to shroud the bodies. When she removed the pitchfork, she had to step aside and throw up. She thought very seriously about burning the barn, but the horse whinnied from beyond the doors as if to say, *it is a very nice barn, and my master deserves a better resting place than where he was murdered.*

"Alright horse, you'll have to help me, then."

She opened the barn doors wide, trying to clear the stench and wound a shirt over her nose and mouth. Over the last two years, Chris had learned how to tie many types of knots to serve all sorts of purposes. She used an overhand follow through knot to attach a rope to the shrouds and put a plow harness over the horse, giving thanks to Michael Landon and her years spent watching Little House on the Prairie when she was a little girl. In place of a plow, Chris hitched the two shrouds and used the reins to direct horse out of the barn and up behind the house to a family cemetery.

She knew she could not dig large enough holes to decently bury these two large men. She unhitched the horse and led it back into the barn where she removed the plow harness and then patted its neck. It leaned into her affectionately and then turned and headed for the wheat fields. As she headed back up to the small cemetery, she gathered an armload of brush. She glanced around at the two dozen markers and wondered about who they had been. The dates ranged from 1823 up to one only three years ago. Nathalie de la Boise had been born before WWII and was the beloved wife of Yves de la Boise. Yves' stone was not there. She stood and spoke softly, "Yves, I believe you lost your life to a marauder. I'm not able to bury you beside Nathalie, but you'll be near her. I'm so sorry. I bet you missed her when she died, but maybe it was better that she didn't have to live through these last two years. Maybe losing her was a mercy."

Chris let the tears fall for a moment, and then headed out of the simple stonewall enclosure. Ten trips around the barn-side of the house, she gathered enough brush and bramble to set a good blaze for a funeral pyre. She used her drill to start the fire and then stood back and made sure it caught well before she turned and left the flames to finish turning dust into dust. She didn't fear that the smoke or flames would attract anyone; fires ignited with regularity where fuel tanks leaked and buildings were neglected. If anything, it might indicate that there was now nothing left to retrieve.

She hoped so.

But just in case the fire did the opposite, Chris slept out in the wheat field that night.

She awoke to a warm kiss. The horse, now well fed on fresh grains, found her. She sat up and rubbed his nose.

"So, what do you think, horse? How's Montana sound to you?"

It snorted and shook its head as if saying *No*.

Standing up, she ran her hands over his ribs. "You're not strong enough yet, are you, Horse? You'll need some time to heal." She rolled up her bedding and tucked it into her pack. Hoisting it firmly onto her back, she continued addressing the horse. "Well, I've got to head back to my people. You are more than welcome to come with me. If you don't mind, I might ride on your back."

The horse shook its head. It moved around her and butted its head against her shoulder, pushing her toward the house.

"Hey! I can't stay here, Horse! I have people who need me."

It shoved her again and she stumbled forward. "OK, I'll make a deal with you. I'm actually a little lost. And they won't mind if I'm a little late. If I let you take a few days to build your strength up, will you go with me back to get the Troughtons?"

It blew out a breath and nudged her gently.

"It's really a beautiful place you've got here, Horse." Chris looked up at the house. The rising sun on the other side cast a black shadow over the roof. "Three stories, four bedrooms on each of the top two. Kitchen big enough to feed an army, dining room, living room and – what would you call it? – a parlor downstairs. Nice fireplaces. But if we're going to stay here, we'll need to fortify it somehow."

The horse accompanied her to the front porch and circled the house with her. The windows were double-hung sashed panes, bright and welcoming. The house itself was wood frame with overlapping boards and gingerbread decorating the eaves. It was on a raised foundation with crawl space underneath. The foundation of the huge hearth-stone fireplaces was built up from beneath the ground. It looked like an original wall of a previous building – perhaps an ancient homestead – because it ran the entire width of the house underneath.

"Easily breached. Easily fire-bombed. Or smoked out, if the purpose was requisitions."

The horse nodded.

"Is there a cellar?"

The horse lost interest and wandered away.

Just right of the back porch, hidden by the summer-blasted shrubs, were two wooden doors slightly raised and inclined from the ground. The marauders had missed it. She carefully lifted one side with the door between her and the basement, just in case the farmer had thought to booby trap it.

Nothing exploded.

The horse returned, its nostrils flaring with anticipation.

"Horse, you smell apples, too?"

It whinnied.

Sitting on the far end of the top step was a glass oil lamp. It was an antique, but the pack of kitchen matches next to it proved it was still working. Lamp in one hand, dagger in the other, Chris descended into the cellar.

There were bins half-full of apples, potatoes, ears of corn and gourd squash. Garlic and dried peppers dangled from strings along the shelves above the bins. The shelves held a strange accumulation of hand-thrown pottery and rocks. On closer examination, Chris discovered the rocks were actually stone chips, predominantly black flint, but also granite and marble. They were not naturally found in this part of Georgia, so Chris assumed there were some tables and counters missing their marble or granite tops. The pieces ranged in size from tiny arrow tips to massive axe blades. Some were sharp, but most were still blunt cut. She found a grinding wheel and a pottery wheel on the other side of the central chimenea. A squat square table sat between them. Chris cocked her head. There were two thick ropes tied to its sides and looped under the table top. She lifted the top cautiously and drew up one of the ropes. It was heavy and attached to a dripping bucket filled with fresh water: a cistern.

"Oh my God!" Chris looked around the fortification. One side of the cellar was the continuation of the stone wall she'd viewed from above. A double-bed filled one corner, and enzyme-self-contained toilet waited behind a screen on the other side of the cellar. Oil lamps sat on every bench, table and shelf. Three armchairs in a half-circle around the chimenea were flanked by a braided rug. Behind the chimenea was a spiral staircase which stopped at the ceiling. Both the clay piping of the chimenea and the stairs butted the stone wall.

"Why were they killed?" she said out loud. "They had everything here they'd need to survive. Why would they have left the safety of this cellar?"

The horse whinnied from above ground and she heard it galloping across the yard toward the house. It stopped at the cellar doors and sounded again. "OK, Horse, I'm coming up."

After moving her pack into the cellar, but keeping her bow and quiver on her shoulder, Chris carefully closed and camouflaged the cellar's opening.

Between the house and the barn was a massive stone kiln.

Shards of pottery and half-burnt kindling were scattered around the open end. One side was shaped like a counter top. A glass skillet and corning ware coffee pot – the collectible kind with the blue cornflower on it – made Chris assume that, when the kiln was fired up, this counter served as a stove. Three compartments above the stove served as individual ovens. One held the remains of three-week-old, dehydrated casserole.

There were a lot of foot prints on the dry ground, too many for just two people. Had the marauders come up on Yves and his son or maybe grandson here? Overwhelmed them here? Dragged the men into the barn?

The horse pressed its nose against her shoulder blade. She pulled an apple out of her pocket and gave it to him.

The first night Chris spent bolted inside the cellar, with a full stomach, bathed body, clean clothes and a soft mattress, she dreamed. When she awoke twelve hours later, she didn't remember the dreams, but her pillow was wet with salty tears.

She wandered the farm, gathering wheat into a sack she'd found in the barn, setting snares, and enjoying the feel of the land. There was something very homey about this place. She knew she should head back to the Troughtons today at the latest and even then, she would probably be a day late, because she should check back with the Delaney Republic, but she lingered.

Chickens roamed freely, so she gathered eggs and rebuilt the coop inside the barn. She fed the hens and the newly hatched chicks wheat and what vegetables had rotted in the bins. She found a large mortar and pestle in the kitchen and ground two cups of grain. For late lunch, early dinner, she baked a squash and rabbit quiche. Then she molded a dozen biscuits and baked them in the kiln's retaining heat.

Down in the cellar, she picked through four dozen *Mother Earth News* magazines and found one that interested her. "Good night, Horse," she called as she bolted herself inside and snuggled into the bed to read.

She awoke to find the landscape covered in fairy frost. A flock of hens were roosting on the kiln ledge and roof; its heat keeping them warm. She went to the barn and found horse surrounded by warmth-seeking chickens. She lit a fire in the stone fire pit in the barn and the one in the adjacent bunk house. The horse came back into the barn while she was stoking the fires and nodded his head as if in approval. Then she went and built up the fire in the kiln. She knew it wasn't too early for frost, but she wasn't sure about snow. People in the legions had been talking about the effects of the aliens on the environment. She'd seen the sandstorms and the hurricane and felt it wouldn't surprise her if the devastated continent might face an ice-age in the coming decade. She was cold and she was tired.

She should have been back to camp yesterday morning. She was at least four days' walk from there. She should feel some urgency to return; her people would be worried about her. Instead, she spent the day washing her clothes and two quilts she'd found in the cellar-hide-away and hung them on the lines out back. She settled down in the comfy bed and napped the afternoon away.

The sun was setting when Chris was satisfied that her clothes were dry, but the quilts were still damp, so she left them hanging. She was hungry. She fried a three-egg omelet for dinner, rode Horse around the surrounding area checking for any possible dangers, and then led him back inside his stall in the warm barn. Horse snorted and then stomped.

"Good night, Horse," she said. "We have to head back to my people tomorrow."

It burbled a soft reply.

The next morning, she spoke softly to Horse before rebuilding the fire. He greeted her with a warm kiss and eagerly accepted the apple she had for him. Chickens cackled around Horse's feet. Three rabbits peered out from a hole they'd excavated during the night just beside the bunk house door. The stall was warm and smelled like cowgirl heaven.

After a wheat patties and scrambled eggs breakfast, Chris filled the wheel barrow with last night's muck and rolled it around the barn to the compost heap.

She spoke to the horse as she worked, "No sense in leaving a mess for the next person who comes here. And honestly, it may be the Troughtons who come here. I love it here." She dumped the wheelbarrow and then threw up. "Damn it, how long does morning sickness last?"

Horse just shook his head. He snorted and shook his head more fiercely, in defiance of the drops of ice cold rain which began to fall. Chris hadn't noticed the heavy black clouds; she'd been so engrossed in the contents of her wheel barrow. She dashed the barrow back into the barn and stood shivering by the fire pit. Horse joined her and again pressed his nose against her. She hugged his neck. "I do love it here. The Troughtons will love it, too. And you'll love them. Eight bedrooms in the farmhouse, plus there's room for two dozen in the bunk house. That leaves only about a dozen more to find beds for. We could build makeshift dorms inside the extra stalls, at least until spring."

Chris peered out of the barn at the torrential rain and hail. She spent the afternoon exploring the barn, cleaning the stalls and sweeping the bunkhouse. When the rain finally stopped, she headed back to her hidden cellar and took a long hot bath before crawling once again into the comfort of the bed. She slept, and if she dreamt, it was of wheat fields and safety.

As she was heading out of the barn the next morning, the horse trotted up to her and pushed her shoulders. His eyes were glazed in fear. Horse was trying to push her back into the barn.

"What is it, Horse?" Then she heard what he'd tried to warn her about – the sound of a motorcycle.

"Hup!" she commanded, leaping onto Horse's back. They

quickly disappeared into the wheat fields and watched the biker's cautious approach to the house.

Horse snickered and shook his head.

"It's OK. He can't see us here." She patted his neck and got down. She heard the motor slow and then idle just in front of the house. The biker looked over his shoulder at the squad of people running up the road toward him. Chris blinked in surprise.

"It's just like I left it last night. Looks to be abandoned but it would be a great safe-place if she got this far."

Chris stopped breathing. She'd recognize Glynn's voice anywhere. She giggled and buried her face in her horse's mane. "Friends," she sighed, releasing her terror. "They're Troughtons, Horse."

Her son's voice broke through the crisp morning air, "Spread out. Jailbird, you and Pizzaboy check out the barn. Preacher and Smartboard – circle the house, look for tracks. Belly, I smell wood smoke. Find it."

"Hey, Hunter!" Pizzaboy shouted. "The barn's warm and we found eggs! Real eggs!"

"Shut up!" Glynn growled. "You trying to get yourself killed?"

"Killed? Marauders!" her warning came out a whisper. Were the marauders behind them?

Horse stomped as if in frustration.

"Hunter," Preacher called. "There's skeletons back here. Looks like a funeral pyre. Done all proper-like."

"Who?" Glynn snapped.

"What do I look like – a medical examiner? I just pray over them, I don't dissect them."

Smartboard answered, "From their skulls, looks like two men. A week or more old."

Mickey and the colonel exchanged glances. "Sergeant, check out the house."

"Yes sir." Mickey took a side-winding approach and flanked

the front door before dashing inside.

She wasn't sure why she stood there, still hidden in the wheat, but she did. She watched as they discovered her kiln. They discussed the deplorable condition of the house but the immaculate barn.

"There's obviously a horse here, and moccasin tracks all over the back yard, fresh snares, and two clean quilts on the wash line."

"So, where are the people?"

"Oven has fresh wood in it; manure on the compost is still steaming," Smartboard commented.

"How come the house is trashed? Someone's living here, but not in the house." Pizzaboy noted.

Glynn answered, "Cause she's smart. Scavengers will hit the house and maybe take a look at the barn. You know Battle Braid. She couldn't fortify the house – too open – so she left it looking deserted and of no value." He turned full circle, scanning the farm. When he saw her, he blinked. She stood at the edge of the wheat field just behind his bike, one hand gripped her braid, the other caressed the nose of a horse.

Something that had died inside Glynn came to life again, and he blew out a deep sigh.

She watched his face and saw his relief. Horse snorted and pushed her shoulder towards the Troughtons. "You know," she shouted, walking past the bike. "Ya'll have got to be the stupidest bastards I have ever laid eyes on. There you stand, clustered together in the middle of a wide-open space. Your bike out of running range, gabbing like a bunch of third graders beside a house that was obviously ransacked by bad guys."

They beamed in delight.

"And you, Pizzaboy. Those are my eggs! Damn well use a skillet and wash up afterwards."

"Ma'am yes ma'am!" He saluted, cracking an egg open against his scalp.

Angel flew into her arms and held her, sobbing. Chris kissed her forehead and hugged her fiercely. Then she hugged and kissed the rest of the Troughtons, laughing and crying. Horse went over to the Colonel, who held up a hand and stroked his nuzzle.

The Troughtons stilled, waiting for Glynn to acknowledge Chris or for her to greet him. He ignored her, enraptured as he was by the horse.

"Get the colonel's bike into the barn. The trough by the barn pumps clean. There's a bathtub in the bunk house, and soap. Towels are upstairs of the main house. Bad guys didn't mess with them."

"You telling us to bathe, Mom?"

"Well, Hunter. Ya'll smell like you've been rode hard and put up wet. I thought you might like to wash up some before we eat."

"It's a might chilly. We'll catch our death," Smartboard complained.

"Potbelly stove in the bunkhouse works just fine. Kindling is stacked in the last stall."

They blinked at her.

"Belly, I don't suppose you've got a jar of honey on you."

"Yes ma'am."

Chris smiled, "Well, hurry up. Bring your mess kits up when you're clean. I should have a stack of pancakes ready by then."

"Pancakes?" Preacher drooled.

Pizzaboy began running to the barn.

Glynn remained, still stroking the horse. Chris took a deep breath and went to her cellar doors. When she came back with a bowl of flour and a bucket of water, she was amazed to see Glynn racing across the fields on Horse's back.

"Well," Hunter joined her. "He is in the cavalry."

"Hunter, tell me flat out, before the others come back. Why is Glynn here?"

"Don't be stupid. Speaking of stupid, though, where the hell have you been?"

"Here. I've been here. It's like something inside of me kept me walking and led me straight here. And I can't seem to leave."

She poured a ladle of water into the flour and stirred while she was talking. She added more and more water until the flour was a thick paste. Using clean hands, she dropped one scoop of dough at a time onto the griddle and waited for bubbles to appear on the surface. "I don't have any platters. Clean off that end of the stove and we'll stack the cakes there."

"Dr. Arnold says hello."

"Oh God, what else did he say?" she paled.

"Nothing, why?"

She shook her head and handed him the spatula. "Don't flip them until they stop bubbling."

"Where are you going?"

She shook her head and ran to the backside of the house. She threw up as quietly as possible.

20
COME JUNE

After a very lengthy brunch, she showed them her cellar by opening the double-doors and letting them glance inside. "It can be barricaded from within and there's an escape path up the spiral stairs into the side of the fireplace in the parlor above."

"A little snug, but looks safe," Hunter helped her close the doors.

Chris led them around to the back. "There's a washer on the back porch. Old fashioned barrel, like a butter churn, only huge. I guess the laundry soap got taken by the marauders, but I shaved up a bar of soap and used a handful each load. Clothes line needs to be pulled taught, but it's strong."

"All the comforts of home," Glynn surmised.

"Yes," she stated.

Jailbird whispered to Angel, "Is she crying?"

Angel nodded.

"I'd like us to live here. You could go back and get the Troughtons. They could be here in just over a week. By then, I'll have the bedrooms cleaned and ready. I've already started on the bunkhouse."

"This sounds like a Troughton all-call," Glynn spoke without harshness. "I'll go ride the horse again; you Troughtons talk. But then, if you'll allow me, I'd like to speak with Mrs. Troughton alone."

Chris nodded and gave him a tight smile. "Before we make a decision, let me finish showing you around the place. You've just glanced at the house. It's wonderful."

"Can't be defended easily."

"I know, Jailbird. But," she grinned, "the barn can. Come on."

An old rung ladder led from the barn floor up into a wide and deep loft. Things scurried away from the humans but Chris led them sure-footedly across the straw-covered planks to a side-wall. Wider rungs were set into the wall. Chris grinned at them and ascended, pushing a door up and open above her head. Sunlight pierced the shadowy loft and they all climbed up.

"It's a widow's walk, like you'd see on houses by the ocean. Look," Chris pointed. "You can see every direction from here."

A short guard-rail surrounded the deck which ran all around the lower portion of the barn roof. An ancient ship's bell swung from one arm of a post, while an old mariner's lantern hung from the other arm.

"From here, we could warn of danger, or do an all-call," Smartboard began.

"And guide the way home," Preacher finished.

"There's a well beneath the house, in the hidden cellar. And a secret passageway from inside the house down into the cellar."

"Like a priest's hole?" Glynn stuck his head up onto the widow's walk.

"No," Chris smiled at him. "Ya'll didn't get a chance to really explore it. It's huge. It's wider and longer than the house above. We could all live down there if need be. It has all sorts of little side halls and doors, some of them are locked but I didn't look for a key."

"Dungeons?" Pizzaboy shivered.

Chris paled. "I didn't think about that."

The wind kicked up and they all shivered.

"You'd have to dress warmly, to be on guard duty here." Belly headed for the trap door.

"Look, over there." Peggy pointed. "Is that a house?"

Smoke curled up from a patch of woods about five miles distant.

"Neighbors!" Jailbird smiled.

"Or marauders," Chris cautioned.

"Pirates," Hunter nodded. "That's what the Delaney's called them."

"I really liked the Delaney's," Chris headed toward the trap door, too.

"Well, they really liked Mickey," Jailbird teased.

"What's not to like?" Mickey volleyed back at him.

Glynn stepped aside to let Chris step onto the ladder. "I really liked the doctor."

Chris slipped on the rung and Glynn grabbed her wrist.

"What did the doctor say?"

"About what?"

"Nothing."

As they all got to the bottom of the steps on the loft, the Troughtons exchanged looks behind Chris and Glynn's backs.

"There's about one hundred acres here. Most of it wheat, but some is soybeans and beets, I think."

"One hundred acres would feed a lot of people." Hunter took her arm at the top of the ladder. "Let me go in front of you."

Chris paled. Hunter winked and kissed her cheek.

"Land looks rich – plenty of wild game. I like your chickens. The land's cleared enough for three or four cottages without losing any fields," Preacher added.

"Oh, look, rabbits," Peggy said. The so-mentioned creatures bounced into holes along the barn walls.

"Oh, look, rain," Glynn groused.

"Sleet, by the look of it." Smartboard added. "It's too early for that, isn't it?"

"I would imagine this winter is going to be tougher than last, after the sandstorms all spring and summer." They nodded at Belly's sage opinion and headed to the double doors.

"The house has radiators in every room. I think there's hot water flowing once you get the fireplaces blazing."

They blinked at Glynn.

"I was here last night, remember? I looked around. Except, I didn't find you."

"You didn't make a sound. Why didn't you call out?"

"What kind of moron shouts out from inside a ransacked house?"

"Right," Chris pursed her lips.

"Anyway," Hunter glared at Glynn. "We won't get too wet if we race across to the farm house. A hot shower sounds like something out of a science fiction novel right now. Is there kindling?"

Chris nodded. "A pile in each room, and a crib out behind the back."

"Is there anything in the kitchen?" Pizzaboy hoped.

"A can of black olives," Glynn laughed. "That's it."

"Gather all the eggs in the barn. I don't suppose you've got onions? I've got dried peppers and potatoes. Belly, do you mind checking my snares back beyond the house? There are eight of them. There are several rain coats hanging from the bunkhouse. When it stops raining, you can tack the hides to the barn, unless it's a rat."

"Waste not, want not," Belly stated as he headed out back.

Chris continued, "There's plenty of other foods down in the cellar. Use the secret door behind the fireplace in the parlor so you don't get wet."

The Troughtons glanced at each other and realized Glynn and Chris wanted to remain alone in the barn.

"Stay warm," Preacher said over his shoulder as they all dashed out across the yard.

Glynn had her in his arms and pressed against his chest before she could think. They whispered endearments and startled the hell out of a nesting chicken as they began rolling on the straw. She had planned to tell him to wait, to slow down, but then she became other-wise occupied and they had finished the first round before the thought connected with her lips.

"Wait," she whispered huskily.

"Too late for that," he pulled her close to his side and tried to catch his breath. "God, I love you. I've missed you."

"I missed you, too."

"Oh, Dr. Arnold said hello."

She stiffened. "You spoke with him."

"Yeah, really nice man. He called me into his office and offered me a Cuban cigar. He said he'd join the Troughtons, but not until around June."

"He told you – June?"

"Yeah, he said he figured we might need him and that he'd come when he could. But, yeah, June was what he was aiming for. You know, his wife isn't well."

"So, you're ok with – him coming in June?"

"I hope he plans on staying a long while," Glynn rolled on top of her again. "Because I have a feeling we could use a man like him around."

"Really?"

"Oh Chris," he mumbled against her neck.

"Glynn!"

"What?"

"Are you happy?"

"I'm ecstatic. Now let me concentrate."

They spent another hour in the barn.

They shared a meal of omelets and fried hare which they cooked in the fireplace of the kitchen. They sat together at the table (they had all pitched in and cleaned it while waiting their turns at a hot shower) and swapped tales about what the other scouts had discovered.

"They're right about the crops in the area. We need to harvest as much as possible before too much longer. Once it snows, I think the wheat will begin to rot. I'm not a wheat expert, but citrus and strawberries can't abide freezing temperatures."

"You just amaze me, Mrs. Troughton," Mickey reached for another biscuit and Preacher pushed the honey jar in his direction. "I didn't know secret shoppers grew strawberries."

They quipped and joked with each other, eating relentlessly until all the food was gone and found they'd talked their way past dusk.

Horse whinnied from just outside the kitchen door. Chris laughed, "He wants me to go tuck him in."

Glynn stood. "We need to set four-hour watches up on the walk. I'll take the first. Mickey, relieve me about midnight. Then Belly and then Preacher."

The Troughtons bit their lips and looked at Hunter. The young man drew a calming breathe. "We'll handle the watches, Colonel. And we'll watch in pairs. Angel and Jailbird, Preacher and Smartboard, Pizzaboy and Peggy. Then Belly and I will take the watch until dawn."

Glynn frowned and then looked at his feet, relinquishing control reluctantly.

"You can each take a bedroom on the second floor. There's linens in the closets. Toilets flush from inside the house since it has running water, too." Chris stood up. "I'm going to put my horse in the barn. I'll see you all in the morning."

"May I join you?"

"I'd be delighted, History Channel."

Behind them, they heard Hunter say, "Give them a moment to put the horse up. It'll give us a moment to talk."

Chris reached up and stroked horse's nose. Glynn rubbed down horse's neck. They walked together to the barn.

"Night, Horse," she whispered. She turned to face Glynn and

they stared silently at each other.

"What do you suppose they're talking about?"

"I would imagine it's about staying here. About bringing the Troughtons here to settle."

Glynn stroked the horse's neck again. "Nice quarter horse. Good stamina, well-trained."

"Loyal, too. He stays close to the house."

"You've taken good care of him. I didn't know you'd been around horses."

"I've never been around horses. Not much room for horses in a condominium. But I've read Louis L'Amour and Mother Earth News and Horse just sort of tells me what he needs."

"I was raised on a horse ranch," he stared at her, "In Montana."

"No!"

He laughed. "No. In Texas."

She shook her head.

Glynn turned around looking beyond the barn walls. "This is an incredible place. It's perfect. Everything a man would need to survive and build a future."

"Do you mean that?"

He turned back to her and then hung his head. "You know I can't stay."

A wind ripped through the barn, carrying the smell of fresh rain.

"May I offer you a warm bed to spend the night, Colonel?"

"It would be my pleasure, ma'am." He followed her into the cellar and watched as she bolted it shut.

"Have a seat," she pointed to the arm chairs.

"Can I help?" He took off his boots.

"Yes, stoke up the fire. I'll be right back."

She went into one of the side rooms and returned with a bottle. "I warn you," she uncorked it and poured it into one tumbler. "It smells like it's about one hundred proof."

"Not unlike Mrs. Arnold's tea."

"Oh God, did they actually get the still to work?"

"I still have the hangover."

They smiled tentatively as she handed him the glass.

He gasped and tried not to swallow. "Are you sure this is wine?"

"Wine, whiskey or horse liniment. The bottles aren't marked, but they're set up in a room on racks, like a wine cellar."

"Snap!" he took another sip and closed one eye, then the other. "Nope. I haven't gone blind yet."

She laughed. He smiled, that languorous smile he had when all was right with the world. "You're not having any?"

She allowed her smile to fade and tried not to show her confusion. "Well, no. I haven't been drinking for a while, now."

"Any particular reason?"

"Yes." She huffed, then figured he was teasing her. "Once you've blown up a city-eater, nothing else gets your blood racing."

"Not even me?" He put the glass aside and pulled her close.

"I don't know. You'll have to allow me to compare. Do you have any specialties?"

"Vixen," he lifted her in his arms and carried her to the bed.

Around midnight, they heard Preacher and Smartboard stomp out of the house and five minutes later, Angel and Jailbird stomping into the house. The light from the chimenea bathed the ceiling with fairy light.

"Look," Glynn pointed at a beam above their heads. "Yves loves Nathali, 1946."

The carved words were encircled within a heart.

"I believe Yves was the man I found in the barn. And Nathalie is the name on a grave stone back in the cemetery."

"Why would you live in a cellar when you had that whole house above you?"

"It's not just a cellar. It's a bomb shelter. A place to survive. 1946, they knew what an atomic bomb could do. Maybe because the house above and the lands were filled with people they loved, they built this to shelter them. Just in case."

"My grandparents built a bomb shelter in the early sixties, right after Kennedy was assassinated. We used to play hide and seek there when we were kids. God, I hadn't thought about that in years."

"Look around you, Peter. These people had everything they needed to survive – self-contained water source, food, tools, they had a damn widow's walk around their barn. I can't understand how Yves and his grandson could have been so vulnerable – so trusting."

"Steady, Chris."

Chris took a deep breath and rolled off of his chest and onto her back. "I love this place. It was made with love, with caring hands and with foresight."

"Chris," Glynn sat up. "Two bodies, three chairs, one bed. Unless you rolled the mattresses up in the bunkhouse, there's no evidence of two people sleeping here on the farm."

"It's a big bed," she scooted up to him.

"No, it's not a big bed," he crawled back under the comforter and pulled her against him. "See? Just right for two. But, as much as I loved my Grandfather, I didn't sleep in the same bed as him."

"Maybe the younger man slept upstairs in the main house."

"Maybe he was a neighbor who dropped by for a visit now and then. Someone Yves trusted."

"There was someone else in the barn. Whoever had the shotgun killed them both."

"If the marauders had a shotgun, why would they have used a pitchfork?"

"Oh no, I put them together on the pyre. If pitchfork-guy betrayed Yves, I should have left his carcass to the wolves."

Glynn's grunt of agreement slid into a snore. They floated

into dreams and clung to each other all night.

He awoke to find his body was greatly in need of her. She awoke to find him staring at her with hunger in his eyes. She grabbed her battle braid and hissed, "I got to pee." He saw the honesty in her expression and came to his senses. He relaxed his grip on her buttocks and shoulder and pulled away.

She quickly jumped up and ran behind the curtain to the latrine.

"I like the bed. I love the bed, just, no more wine." He hung his feet over the side of the bed and grabbed his skull.

"I'm thinking it was horse liniment," she came back around and washed her face and hands in the porcelain bowl and pitcher standing by the screen.

"Laudanum? That's something these off-the-grid homesteaders would make, right?"

There was a polite tap on the door above the stairs and then Mickey stuck his head in. "We're setting down to breakfast. Thought you'd like to join us."

"We'll be right there," Chris shouted.

They dressed quickly and then went up the inside spiral staircase that opened into the parlor.

The Troughtons were congregated around the kitchen table; Pizzaboy and Belly were frying up rabbit and boiling beans they'd brought with them. Everyone greeted each other; the Troughtons looked much better for a night inside warm beds.

Chris sniffed and swallowed, "I'm not hungry, but thanks."

"You alright?" Peggy took her elbow.

"Sure. Yeah. No problems," sweat popped out along her upper lip. "I'll go get some more eggs." She fled out the back door and ran to the barn. She puked up just inside the wheelbarrow.

Horse came to her and pressed his lips along her shoulders in comfort.

"Thanks, Horse. I might as well muck out your stable while I'm here." She added the manure to her morning offering and hauled it all to the compost pile.

Pizzaboy greeted her as she returned the wheelbarrow to the barn. "You OK?"

"Sure."

"You look like crap."

"I think my toothpaste's gone bad."

"Ew."

"Yeah. Don't mention it, ok?"

"No. Sure. We were just wondering about the eggs. You didn't come back with them." Pizzaboy blinked. "You didn't come back at all."

"Eggs. Bring me that basket."

Pizzaboy helped her gather another eight eggs and when they brought them into the kitchen, he signaled to his wife to come outside. They whispered together while Chris tried desperately to stay inside the kitchen as the smell of fried eggs and rabbit fat choked her.

She looked sideways from her cup of coffee and found Hunter staring at her. She tried a wane smile. He looked furious.

Peggy bounced into the kitchen with egg baskets from the barn. "We ladies are going berry picking."

"We've got to pack up and get back to the Troughtons," Jailbird argued.

"No," Pizzaboy glared at him. "The women-folk are going berry picking. We can pack while they're gone."

Jailbird looked at Hunter, who was scowling. Belly burped a laugh and then covered his mouth. Jailbird turned back to Pizzaboy. "Sure. Yeah. Whatever. Angel loves berries."

Angel took a basket from Peggy, and Smartboard took Chris's arm. "*Vamanos*," Angel said sweetly.

"Let's grab our quivers as we go," Chris suggested. "You guys are eating me out of house and home!"

The women laughed and grabbed their weapons.

The men followed the women out into the back yard and

watched until they had disappeared into the thin woods. Then they returned to the kitchen to clean up and argued about whether they had time to wash their clothes or not. They were standing on the back porch, filling the wash tub and pinning clean clothes to the line when Peggy came running back and Pizzaboy met her in the yard. She whispered something to which he yelled, "hooyah!" He kissed her firmly and patted her butt as she turned and ran back into the woods. Pizzaboy went first to Hunter and then, the other Troughtons gathered around him, listening.

Hunter turned to face Glynn, glaring at him with anger suffusing his cheeks. Glynn walked down the steps to join the men.

"Is it my imagination," Glynn said to them all, "or were the women-folk acting a little strange before they went berry picking?"

"You son of a bitch. She's my mother!" Hunter decked him.

When Glynn picked himself up off the ground, the other men had stepped between he and Hunter and were babbling about various ways that each man should remain calm.

Glynn pressed a hand against his sore jaw and asked, "You just now noticed she and I were lovers?"

"Being her lover has nothing to do with this!" the young man retorted.

Pizzaboy stepped in, "Well, actually, it does, really."

Hunter brushed the other men away and faced Glynn. "What are your intentions for Chris Troughton?"

"I intend to marry her, if she'd stay still long enough."

Hunter blinked. "Seriously?"

"Fruiting yeah." Glynn looked at the men grinning in relief at him. "But she won't marry me. She has to get the Troughtons settled in Montana first. How is it you don't know this?"

Hunter turned to Pizzaboy. "What do you figure? How long?"

"June, July at the latest," he said firmly.

"June?" Glynn began brushing off his clothes. "Why is everyone so interested in June around here?"

"Well, duh!" Pizzaboy exclaimed.

"Chris told the women that you knew. About June." Hunter sucked on his busted knuckles.

"June. Yeah. Dr. Arnold said he was coming to join the Troughtons in June. Seemed to cheer Chris up. I think she really liked the old man."

The men blinked at him with open mouths.

"That's it? That's all you figured it meant?" Hunter asked.

"Isn't it?" Glynn looked at the men, trying to read their faces. "What am I missing?"

"God, you're a moron!"

"Alright now, Hunter, give the man a chance to speak," Preacher tempered.

"Why don't you Troughtons tell me what's going on."

"Did you notice that she has lost weight?" Jailbird started.

"And that her breasts are swollen?" Belly added.

"Throws up when in the presence of smelly food?" Pizzaboy continued.

Glynn shook his head. "She mentioned something about her toothpaste going rancid."

"Yep," Mickey nodded. "Same thing happened to Sally's toothpaste about six months ago."

"Really?" Glynn frowned. "Should we check all the expiration dates?"

Mickey grabbed his commanding officer by the arms and pushed him, ever so slightly, backward, as if in fun. "You're a fruiting moron, Glynn. It wasn't the toothpaste."

"What? Was she running a fever? My late wife said to watch for fevers; it meant the difference between upset stomach and real food poisoning."

Hunter puffed up again. "Chris told the women that she'd discussed it with you. And that you were ecstatic."

"About food poisoning?" Glynn looked as stupid as he sounded.

"Did you notice what kind of doctor Arnold was?" Jailbird

smiled.

"No. I wasn't thinking about that. I was worried about Chris."

Belly grumbled, "I need a drink. Is there anything remotely alcoholic around here?"

"Yeah. Wine. Or maybe horse liniment." Glynn motioned them to join him and headed to the outside cellar doors.

They spied the corked bottle on the work bench and Mickey made the decision. "Jailbird, you know more about it than the rest of us. Taste it."

"Don't take more than a mouthful. I swear, I haven't felt this bad since I tasted your sweet potato wine," Glynn warned.

They watched Jailbird sniff the bottle. He touched his tongue to the inside of the neck and squinted. He poured two fingers worth into the empty tumbler.

He sipped and tilted his head. He gulped and swished the brew through his teeth. He guzzled and gasped, wiping away blinding tears.

"Is it laudanum?" Glynn asked. "Or horse liniment?"

"Damn fine Blueberry Cordial. A little vinegary, but damn fine." He refilled the cup and handed it to Preacher.

"The blood of Christ," he took a gulp and handed it to Belly.

"Spit out your gum," he grinned and took a swig.

"To the father of my mother's child," Hunter held up the cup. Everyone else paused.

"Who? What?" Glynn blinked.

"To you." Hunter gulped the liquid without coughing.

"No." Glynn put his cup down. "Chris can't have children."

"Who told you that?" Hunter asked.

"Jerry did. Back at the Mississippi River camp. There had been a string of miscarriages in the camps, and Chris was upset. Jerry told me they couldn't have children."

Hunter shook his head. "Jerry couldn't have children. So Mr. and Mrs. Troughton didn't have children."

Glynn blinked and blinked again. Then he smiled and put

down his cup. "Jerry. Not Chris? She's pregnant?"

"He's a little slow, don't you think?" Pizzaboy asked.

"He's a moron," Hunter concluded.

Glynn hooted and declared, "I got to go find her."

Hunter nodded.

Each member of the Troughtons shared the bottle and spent the afternoon munching on cold lunch, opening another two bottles and snoozing in the safety of the underground cellar.

As evening approached, they were three sheets to the wind and didn't realize the berry pickers should have been back by then.

Smartboard reiterated the state of the Troughton Nation as the women filled baskets from a row of blueberry bushes. "So, Sally is due in February, Lovenia is due in March."

"Her husband said to expect twins. They run in his family." Peggy dropped a handful of berries into the basket at her feet. "Don't pick one at a time, Chris. Scoop them into the palms of your hands. They're ripe, should have been harvested in June, so they just fall off when you brush against them."

Smartboard continued, "Then you're due in June, along with Daisy-Mae."

"Again?" Chris squeaked.

The women shrugged.

She laughed, "It's Belly's damned decorum, I reckon."

Angel cleared her throat. The women looked at her. "Me, too. In May. Maybe earlier."

They embraced her.

"The safer we feel, the more likely we'll be to start having children. It's Nature's way."

"How about you, Smartboard? Did Preacher ever get up the nerve to go sasquatch-hunting with you?" Peggy teased.

Smartboard frowned and leaned closer to Chris, "We're being watched."

Chris fletched her bow immediately, as did the rest of the

women.

The bushes trembled and they heard the exhalation of a man's breath.

Chris turned and with a smooth movement sent an arrow at the sound. A man cursed. "I meant to miss you, Mister. But I won't the next time. Show yourself."

A man in what looked to be brand new jeans and a denim jacket stepped away from a cluster of trees with his hands up.

"All of you," Chris growled.

Three more men stepped in from right and left, forming a semi-circle around the women. They were not as nicely dressed. Torn and filthy hunting camouflage on one, the remnants of a mustard-yellow deacon suit on another, and baggy jeans and a ripped t-shirt on the third. They grinned with voracious expressions at the women.

21
CODY AND LITTLE SIS

Denim jacket guy stepped forward again. "We didn't mean to startle you. More likely, you four visions of beauty startled us. I thought we'd come upon forest nymphs." His smile didn't reach his eyes.

"That's close enough," Chris stated. "What do you want?"

Their eyes revealed exactly what they wanted, but the leader laughed, "I want a Big Mac and fries. And a chocolate milkshake. What would you like, little lady?"

As a whole, the women grimaced at his words *little lady*.

"Your name. The name of your affiliation. You're not part of the Eastern Legions. Where have you been for the last year?"

"I'm Beau Pellegrino. These are my brothers, Mason, Xander, and Stub. We live just over there. It's our farm."

"We've seen the smoke," Smartboard allowed.

"And now, may I have the pleasure of knowing your names?"

"We're the Troughtons."

He pursed his lips, not used to being vexed. "All of you?"

"Maybe you've heard of us."

He glanced at his men; they'd heard the name. He shook his head, "We've been so busy, and we try to keep pretty much to ourselves, ever since Atlanta fell."

Mason kept his eyes on Angel, but addressed Beau, "Maybe they'd like some food. We have food. Are you hungry?"

Beau glared viciously at Mason and then schooled his features. The lips-only smile returned, along with a glint in his eyes. "Of course, what was I thinking? Allow us to offer you a meal and a warm place to stay. We're just beyond the hill there."

Chris answered him, "Thank you for the invitation. Maybe we could all come for a visit – our husbands, too. We're taking over the de la Bois farmstead."

"Yves' place? That's a nice spread."

Stub's voice was surprisingly high for such a barrel of a man. "That'll be nice for the old man. He loves company."

"Shut up." It was a curt command one might give a dog. Stub hung his head and obeyed Beau.

"Yes, Yves loves to talk," Chris stared directly at Beau and saw the reaction she'd expected: he knew Yves was dead.

Beau glanced between Chris and Stub and his voice was too loud, "How is the old man? We've been gone – hunting the north woods, you know – about a month or more. Just got back a few days ago. We'd love to come see him. We'll bring some boar bacon, if you don't mind putting up with rough and rugged bachelors."

"I'm sorry to tell you," Glynn stepped into the space between the Troughtons and the men, holding Peggy's rifle to his shoulder. He heard sighs of relief from behind him and saw the eyes of the men tighten and their lips twist in disdain. "Yves and his grandson were murdered about three weeks back."

"Yves is dead?" Stub asked. "But he didn't have a grandson."

"Shut up," Beau snarled. To Glynn, he said, "Stub's a little slow, you know. He doesn't understand much more than a second-grader might."

"Stub may be right. It may not have been his grandson. Might have been one of the fruiting scum that killed the old man."

Beau relaxed his facial features and tried – but failed – to look sorrowful. "That's a damn shame. Pardon my language, ladies. I truly liked the old man. He had a way with growing things. The children will be so sad to hear of his passing."

"Children?" Smartboard asked.

"Cody and Little Sis. My children. They miss their momma something awful, you understand. She died year and a half ago, as we were making our way north from N'orleans." He saw the gleam of interest and compassion in Smartboard's eyes and continued. "Cody's a bright little man of fourteen. Smart as a whip. Sis is a little doll baby, just turned eight in June."

"Children," Chris said, smiling. "They make all the difference in the world, don't they? Where a band of adults might seem like fearsome strangers; kids make them seem safe and friendly."

Glynn's head nodded but he didn't take his eyes off the men.

Beau lowered his hands a little, "I hope you come to know us as safe and friendly. The offer of dinner is still open. You and your man could go back and get the rest of your people while the ladies accompany us to our cabin. They can be resting while we fix a huge meal."

"It seems we're going to have neighbors, sweetie." Glynn lowered the rifle to his hip. "But I'm afraid we'll have to take a rain-check on the invitation. Our women-folk have laundry and the like to do. House-keeping chores, you know. Women-folk stuff."

Beau licked his lips, all but drooling at Peggy. "I do indeed."

"Bye now," Chris kept her bow nocked.

Glynn said as they backed away, "You might want to sound out if you come onto the Troughton property. Our watchmen have rather twitchy fingers. They're young and might not realize that you come as friends. There's been marauders in the area. We're used to shooting first and asking questions later."

"Duly noted, Troughton."

"Bye, pretty ladies," Stub said.

"Shut up," Beau snarled.

They walked into the kitchen and put their baskets on the table. No one was around, so they went to the secret door and headed down into the basement.

"Are they dead?" Smartboard asked as they saw the men sprawled around on the floor and in the armchairs.

Belly farted.

"Oh, don't worry. If we're kidnapped by bad guys in the forest, our men will come save us!" Peggy shook Pizzaboy's arm. He snorted and mumbled something about wizards.

"Mine did." Chris looped her arm around Glynn's waist.

"Yep." He cupped her cheek. "That's what fathers do. You can defend yourself, but our baby needed protecting."

Hunter pushed himself up out of the chair. "Took him a while, but he finally figured it out. But he's still a moron. Is it dark outside already?"

"Who's on watch?" Glynn picked up an empty bottle and put it next to the others on the work bench.

Hunter made a face and squinted as he looked around him. "Hell if I know."

"We'll take watch, the four of us, in pairs." Chris got two blankets and handed one to Angel. "They're wasted."

"I don't think they'll come at us tonight," Peggy said. "They'll want to spy on us first, see how many fighting men we have."

"Yeah," Smartboard added. "They looked like bullies, and bullies only pick on the weak. They're cowards."

"And we're safe bolted in down here." Chris concluded.

They went upstairs to gather their bedrolls and bolted themselves in the bomb shelter for the night.

Mickey woke first, trying to remember where he was. He heard the sound again and whistled, "Pstt."

The Troughtons awoke immediately.

"Listen," he hissed.

Something tapped repeatedly against the stone of the fireplace above their heads.

"You don't know nothing, Sis," the voice of an adolescent male echoed through the chimenea.

"I do so! I know it's here. A secret door; Grandpa Yves said so," came the reply of a young girl.

"Secret door, my ass. Daddy's gonna whoop me if I don't find those people and make friends with them. And I want to bring back that horse."

"They got to be here. There are all those blueberries in the kitchen. Daddy Beau said they were nice ladies. He said one might sing real pretty, like your mamma did. Why do you suppose she went away?"

Silence followed tapping.

"Do you suppose she went away with Grandpa Yves?" the girl continued.

More tapping without a response.

"Where do you think the people have gone to?"

"Heaven."

"No, Cody, don't say that."

"Alright. I won't say it."

The Troughtons dressed and booted quickly. Glynn put a finger to his lips and then pointed two fingers to his ears and then at Hunter and from Hunter to the chimenea. He pointed at Smartboard and motioned her up the stairs. He put the palm of his hand to his ear. She nodded. She'd press her ear against the door.

"Come on, sis. There ain't nobody here. That horse can't have gone too far. Daddy Beau said," the boy's voice faded.

Hunter made walking legs out of two fingers, indicating the children were walking away from the fireplace.

They all heard the door of the farmhouse slam and the boy's shrill whistle. The Troughtons clustered by the spiral stairs. Smartboard stuck her head down. "They've gone outside. They'll see us if we open the double doors, but not if we go through this door into the house."

"Weapons notched. They're children. But they know about the horse and the man who lived here." Chris cautioned.

Belly growled, "How could any father send them here alone, knowing they might be in danger?"

"It must be Cody and Little Sis. That creep's kids." Peggy whispered.

"What creep?" Pizzaboy asked.

"While ya'll were guzzling up my fine stock of horse liniment," Chris held her nose and looked green. She gasped and ran to the commode behind the screen.

"We met the neighbors," Smartboard completed her sentence. "Beau, Mason, Xander and Stub."

"Stub?" Belly's eyebrows crinkled.

Chris returned, "Stub's the one to watch. He's dumb but honest. His face shows if the others are lying or not."

"Maybe the men are with them," Pizzaboy suggested.

"No. The boy said, 'Daddy's gonna whoop me if I don't find those people.' Daddy ain't here," Mickey concluded.

"The boy knew Yves had been killed. He said he'd gone to heaven," Hunter supplied.

"And make friends with them," Chris growled. "Those kids are being used by that creep to put us off our guard."

"We need to stay quiet," Glynn warned. "If we can hear them through the chimenea, chances are they can hear us."

"Up," Hunter commanded. "In twos. Observe. Reconnoiter. Rendezvous on the second floor, master bedroom. Deploy every ten second. On my mark. Now."

Within two minutes, they were all in the master bedroom staring out the windows at the children. Beau had said Cody was fourteen, but he looked more like twelve in overalls and a cowboy hat. The girl was in dirty khaki shorts and a blue polo shirt with a school badge on the left side.

"Shorts!" Smartboard huffed. "There's a layer of frost outside and that child is in shorts!"

Angel took Jailbird's elbow. She pointed out the window and then down the hall and then swooped her arms in an air hug. "I'll go and meet them."

"No," was all Jailbird said.

Angel cocked her head imploringly at Hunter.

Smartboard commented to no one in particular, "Seems like those two could use a good meal."

"And warmer clothing," Preacher concurred.

"Your house, your rules, Mom." Hunter acknowledged.

"You all stay here. I'll go out. If it's just the kids, I'll mention Christmas coming. You can all come out then and we'll have breakfast. I'll cook it on the outdoor kiln, to keep them out of the house and in the open."

"We already know it's just the kids. But that doesn't mean it's safe, Battle Braid." Glynn frowned.

"If I mention pecan pie, that means it's a trap. Shoot anyone taller than me from up here on the second floor. Windows open on all directions. Find the bad guys."

The Troughtons completed their motto, "Sting them where it hurts."

She stopped at the door and looked at Glynn. "You're so cute when you're worried. I like that in a husband."

"Get used to it," he nodded.

She blew him a kiss and tiptoed down the stairs.

They heard her call to the kids from the front porch. She walked out to them and moved with them until she was in plain view of the bedroom window.

"Hi, I'm Chris. I haven't seen too many people since I moved in! Do you live around here?"

"No," the boy replied, pushing the girl behind him.

"Where are you from?"

The girl pointed and the boy slapped her hand down.

"I'm Chris," she repeated, softening her approach. "What are your names?"

"I'm –"

"Shut up," the boy clapped a hand over the girl's mouth.

"Don't talk to strangers, is that it?"

The boy nodded.

"My son Hunter learned the same rule when he was growing up. Are you cold? I made a fire in that huge oven on the other side of the house. We could get warm there." Chris smiled. "There's a horse who stays nearby, too."

"The horse?" the boy asked.

"Yes. A horse. And chickens with eggs and rabbits. Are you hungry?"

The children looked at each other.

Upstairs, Glynn growled, "No, damn it, Chris! Don't take the combatants out of the line of sight."

"They're children, not combatants," Mickey countered. They raced around from window to window, trying to keep Chris in view.

Glynn puffed up. "Yves, the man the children mentioned, was shot to death in the barn. The men we met yesterday lied about it."

Hunter exclaimed, "Stay here. I look like a kid. They'll trust me."

Angel grabbed his shoulder. He nodded. The two of them dashed down the stairs.

"Mom?" Hunter yelled.

"Hunter?" Chris came around from beside the kiln.

"Mom!" He hugged her, as did Angel. "You were gone too long. We got worried, didn't we, Sis?"

Angel nodded.

"They call me Sis, too," the girl chirped.

"I'm called Hunter, what's your name?" he asked the boy.

"Cody. Cody Patterson. And this is little Sis, but she ain't really my sister."

"This is Angel. She's not really my sister either, but Mom

takes care of us both. You got a mom?"

The boy shook his head.

"Maybe you can join us. Mom's the best. She brought us here, you know, when the monsters came."

"You ain't been here since then."

"No, we've been traveling. You hungry? We caught us some rabbits with snares." Hunter was a natural leader. He grinned at the children. Cody stood up straighter and Li'l Sis reached across and took Hunter's hand.

"We saw you got blueberries in the house. Cody wouldn't let me eat any."

"It would have been stealing," the boy told her again.

"I won't steal, Cody. But I'm hungry," Sis answered. "I'm always hungry."

"Cody and Little Sis. Angel and I met your daddy yesterday. Beau Pellegrino and three of his brothers. Do you want your daddy to come eat with us, too? There's plenty."

"He's not here. He's at home." Cody eyed Hunter's quiver with admiration.

Chris stepped in. "How far away is your home? Maybe you could run get him and we'll all have breakfast together."

Cody and Sis exchanged glances. Sis supplied, "He couldn't get here by breakfast, but maybe by lunch."

"Well," Chris smiled. "It'll be just like Christmas!"

As the first round of rabbit and wheat cakes began sizzling on the stove, the Troughtons walked softly to the outdoor kitchen.

The boy jumped up and stood between the soldiers and his sister, a knife in his hands.

Glynn held up his open palms. "I'm Colonel Glynn of the 74th Cavalry, Provisional Governor of the New United States. You've met Chris and Hunter Troughton, and Angel. This is Sergeant Mickey, Preacher, Smartboard, Belly, Pizzaboy and his wife Peggy. Your name's Cody, is that right, son?"

He nodded.

"And Little Sis, there, nice to meet you." Glynn saluted her.

The boy shifted, uncertain, instinctively trusting the colonel but habitually expectant of a beating in exchange of misplaced trust.

"Go on, boy," Belly encouraged, handing Chris a basket of berries. "Eat up. There's plenty. Wouldn't mind some of that myself."

"Coming right up," Chris smiled. "Pizzaboy, go check my snares, would you? We got hungry children to feed."

"Preacher and I will check the barn. Check for eggs in the barn." Smartboard took his arm. Preacher looked unhappy about the prospects.

They returned from the barn separately and silently. Preacher sat beside the children and Smartboard headed into the house.

Smartboard came back with a blanket and a sewing basket. In no time, she had cut and stitched a poncho for the girl, who gratefully accepted it.

They ate a wholesome breakfast and the children began to relax.

"Do you live in the house?" the boy finally asked.

"We live nearby, but the house, barn and lands belong to us," Chris told him.

"It used to belong to Grandpa Yves," Sis piped. "If you see Grandpa Yves, tell him I said hi. Tell him I miss him."

Chris glanced at the Troughtons and they nodded their support. "Your brother was right, Sis. Grandpa Yves is in heaven. He was dead when I got here."

Sis looked up at Cody. He shrugged and put his arm around her. "People die. That's the way of it."

"Like your mamma died?"

"Yeah."

"Why'd you tell me she went away? Why'd you lie to me, Cody?"

"He didn't lie," Preacher said gently. "They did go away.

They went to heaven."

Cody's bitterness had etched ancient wrinkles around his young eyes, but he looked at Preacher with hope and gratefulness.

"I'll tell Daddy this land belongs to you," he nodded up at Glynn. "Come on, Sis. We got to be home before noon."

"Are you safe? Do you want us to go with you?" Smartboard suggested.

"No, don't come with us!" the girl panicked.

"We'll tell Daddy to come meet with you. Watch out for him. I mean, be looking for him. OK?"

It was a strange way to state that; the Troughtons glanced at each other.

After the children left, Pizzaboy followed surreptitiously behind them, tracking their path.

As soon as the children and Pizzaboy were out of sight, the horse returned and greeted first Chris and then Glynn with a kiss.

"Trust a horse," Glynn said. "Don't trust anyone the horse distrusts."

"Oh yeah. Horse doesn't like the kids. We got that," Hunter piped.

Angel nodded emphatically.

Chris sighed. "How much wheat can you carry back to the Delaney Republic?"

"In what?" Jailbird asked.

"I found burlap sacks in the barn. They're probably chewed through in a few places, but if you could fill and carry at least one of them, it would help them through the winter."

"We don't have time to harvest wheat if we are heading out today," Peggy pointed out.

"I don't think we can leave, not until we've dealt with Daddy Beau and his bros," Glynn stated.

"What if we divided up – half go to get the Troughtons, the other half stay here to hold the land," Chris suggested.

"We haven't decided to take this land," Hunter reminded

them.

"Whether we live here or not, it's still part of our thousand square miles," Angel said softly. "I don't like the idea of men like them living in Troughtonia."

"People are innocent unless proved guilty," Preacher held up a hand.

"That man is as guilty as sin," Smartboard argued. "I can still feel his murderous soul looking at me through those eyes of his."

"Preacher's right," Glynn stepped into the fray. "But any inter-legion criminal cases need to be presented to the Military Tribunal back at Headquarters."

"We're not hauling their asses four hundred miles west just so we can hang them for murder," Hunter faced Glynn.

"We're not hanging anyone!" Belly jumped in.

"That's right," Preacher nodded. "We can't continue the barbaric policy of the death penalty in our new world."

"What?" Belly looked at him. "Fruit that! I meant hanging's too good for them, and would take too long. A bullet between the peepers would do just fine for the likes of those murdering scum."

"Troughtons!" Chris bellowed. They stilled. "Take the wheelbarrow. Go out into the fields. Snap off as many heads of wheat as will fill one of those bags. Do it."

Hunter exhaled a deep sigh and said, "Come on. The Delaney's can use it to make whiskey or beer if we're lucky."

Once they'd walked to the barn, Glynn turned to Chris. "Stalling tactics?"

She nodded. "Until Pizzaboy comes back and he tells us what kind of forces we're facing."

"Chris, the Troughton main camp is only a day's ride on my Harley. It'll take them a week or more to get here, if here is where they decide to come. I could be there and back in no time. Well, time enough to face the Pellegrino brothers. Together."

"Why do you think I sent them to the barn? They'll see your bike. They'll remember that we were once a race of faster than the speed limit drivers. And they'll come back from harvesting wheat with a brilliant idea all their very own."

"To send me to the Troughton camp and head them this way?"

She smiled sheepishly. "Do you mind not being given credit for the idea?"

"I'd like to add to the idea, but I'm afraid Beau's group will attack before I get back. I'd like to ride to the Troughtons and head them this way, and then keep going back to Headquarters."

"You're going back."

"I have to, Battle Braid" He yanked the braid and laughed at her furious expression. "I can't exactly mail in my letter of resignation."

"You're going to resign your commission?"

He turned and looked around the farm. "My first memory was of riding a horse. I want our child to experience that wonder, too."

"So, you're marrying me for my horse."

"I think," he pulled her into his arms. "You've married beneath you."

"I like you being beneath me."

"Do we have time for a demonstration?"

"No. We've got to come up with some battle strategies to defend this property."

"If we could force them between the house and the barn, it forms a funnel, much like Boadicea and the Romans, only we'll be the Romans."

"Well, History Channel. I was thinking more like shooting fish in a barrel."

"Yeah, it really turned out to be just like that."

"Let's head up to the widow's walk. We can survey the land and develop various scenarios from there."

"Do I get to kiss you while we're up there?"

She walked backwards, pulling him along. "I might even let you clang the bell."

22
THE NEIGHBORS

Pizzaboy came back late that afternoon. He found the Troughtons in the farmhouse kitchen, taking turns at a hot shower after a hard day of harvesting wheat. They shared a pot of hot coffee, working on putting together the next meal and pausing to hear Pizzaboy's report.

"They went straight home, about two hours' walk. It's a farm house, like this one, but raggedy with junk all in the yard. Four men, no women, only the two kids. One man grabbed the boy – yelling about taking too much time bringing him information. He hit him – just once. The little girl ran up and kicked the crap out of the man's leg, saying something about she wouldn't play anymore if he hurt Cody. They went inside and I took a quick look around. Barn is full of commodities – food mostly – cans and boxes, and two gas generators, a wagon with two scrawny horses. But, they have cases of liquor – whiskey, tequila, bourbon, scotch, vodka. Then I came home."

Chris smiled. "Home."

Pizzaboy nodded. "So, what did I miss? Looks like someone took a bite out of the wheat field."

"We've been talking; spouting out one idea after another."

Smartboard glanced at Preacher and looked down and away.

"Arguing is more like it." Preacher glared at the top of her head.

"Arguing?" Pizzaboy looked at his wife. She shook her head and he pursed his lips.

"What we need is a hog," Belly said as he stuck two chickens in the oven.

"We've got a hog in the barn," Pizzaboy watched with delight as his wife rolled out the wheat mush on a baking stone.

"You're an idiot."

"Why?"

"I meant pigs. We need grease – lard – you know. And pork chops and bacon and pork rinds."

While Peggy gently sculpted the edges of her flatbread, Pizzaboy said, "You know - pigs are actually very intelligent and loving. Just like dogs but without a snout."

"Why do you have to say stuff like that?" Belly put his hands on his hips. "All I want is some deep-fried chicken that doesn't taste like it's been soaked in engine oil and you tell me, 'don't hurt the cute little piggy wiggies.'"

"Well, I happen to think that – this being our second chance of setting the Earth right, we should be cognizant of the moral issues when it comes to sentient creatures."

"Scented creatures? What are you, King of Stupidia? You think we should only kill and eat nice–smelling critters?"

"Sentient, you moron! Not scented."

"That's what I said."

"Shut up, the both of you." Chris spoke softly, but she was obeyed.

"Yes ma'am." Aside to Belly, "I bet you don't buy dolphin-free tuna."

"So, when are we heading back?" Chris tried to change the subject.

"Do you want to leave?" Hunter asked.

"No. I don't. But if those bad men are just sitting out there, feeding off of innocent women and children, and they have a mind to take this land – so much so that they murdered sweet Grandpa Yves in cold blood, what can we do?"

"I tell you what we don't do," Preacher stood. "We don't hang them. We don't put a bullet to their brains. We don't execute them with arrows."

Smartboard stood and put her hands on her hips. "You are so full of *don'ts* aren't you, Ned Chesterfield. Don't do this. Don't do that. Forget that I have stayed by your side every moment since the first time we met, DON'T TAKE THE SCHOOL MARM SASQUATCH-HUNTING!"

The Troughtons clamped their lips together and watched this finally unfold.

"I'm never going to get pregnant, am I? Everyone else around us is pregnant. But you've claimed me – no other man in the Troughton Legion will look at me because it's Preacher and Teacher. But you won't – nope – I'll put it into your words, you DON'T. You just don't."

"You want to get pregnant, is that it? You don't give a hoot in hell that I'm twice your age and white up here?" He waved his hand at his hair.

"Excuse me?" Mickey intervened.

"Oh, I see. I'm not good enough for the white preacher."

"That's not what I said."

"We all heard you," Jailbird took sides.

"I've got white hair. I'm old. I'm twice your age, Jessica. What the hell do you want with an old man like me?"

"Sasquatch-hunting, you old fart! I want to get pregnant."

"I thought we were friends. Is that all you wanted from me? To get you pregnant?" he growled.

She put her fists onto the table between them. "That wasn't the first thing on my mind, but now that you mention it – yes – I want to get pregnant. That's what happens when two people love each other – they have babies."

He grabbed the top of a ladder-back chair. "You don't love me."

Nose to nose, "I know what I know. I love you, you stupid old goat. I think you are the only one in this room who doesn't know that. But whether you love me back or not, I want to get pregnant. I want children."

"I will not impregnate you like I'm some type of a stud horse!"

"I wouldn't have your sperm if you offered it to me on a twelve inch-"

"OK NOW!" Hunter stood – arms stretched out. "That's enough! We'll all just sit down and stop talking about making babies."

"Good evening."

Everyone jumped up and pointed weapons at the well-dressed man standing at the kitchen door. "I knocked – several times – but I don't think you heard me."

"Where the fruit did you come from?" Hunter's voice cracked.

The stranger frowned, "I don't believe children should cuss, Hunter."

"I don't know you, and I ain't a kid."

"You told my boy you were, I believe," he pointed at Chris. "This woman's son."

"You're Cody's dad. Beau Pellegrino. This is one of the men we met in the forest." Chris put the bow down and took out the arrow. She walked to the man and stuck out her hand. "You'll have to forgive us. But I'm sure you understand our vigilance."

He shook her hand in both of his, eyeing her body with approval. "These are dark times. Trust is hard to come by. For those of your men who haven't met me, my name is Beau Pellegrino. My brothers and I run a farm about five miles north of here."

Peggy stepped up. "Can we offer you some coffee and

biscuits?"

"Yes. Yes, ma'am, you can." He followed her to the stove.

"Have you lived here long, Mr. Pellegrino?" Mickey stood and offered the stranger his chair.

"No, less than a year, but longer than you have been here. Are you just traveling through?"

Pizzaboy passed him the plate of biscuits. "We were just getting to discussing that. You know, winter's coming in and we've got dozens of mouths to feed."

"Dozens? I see only a handful."

"We keep ourselves spread out. We're warriors. I know you've heard of us," Chris refused to be charmed by him.

"What about you, Mrs. Troughton? Are your boy and your girl," his eyes lingered on Angel. Jailbird took his knife back out and thumbed the blade. "And your man," he nodded at Glynn, "Staying?"

"It's currently being discussed," Glynn answered in her stead.

"I had wondered if you were a single mother. Actually, and I hope I'm not crossing a line with you, sir, but I had hoped Mrs. Troughton was single. So many widows and widowers about since – well – since this time two years ago. I'm looking for a wife myself; children need a mother."

The Troughtons exchanged squeamish looks. To cover their discomfort, several members of the team got up to continue dinner preparations.

"I'm glad you're fixing up this house. I was so sorry to hear that Yves died. He had very nice wine, and Little Sister adored him. She misses her mother, you understand. I don't have time for her and even if I did, she longs for female companionship."

"Yves was murdered," Chris walked behind Glynn and placed her hands casually on the back of his chair. "The man who lived here was murdered, along with another person."

"Indeed. Such dark times. I know you and the ladies here are relieved to have such strong men to protect you."

"Strong men. Strong weapons." Belly rumbled.

"Well," Pellegrino stood. "It's nice to have well-rounded neighbors: Beauty and Brawn. If you'd like to barter anything – like coffee or those biscuits, I have a few things that might interest you."

"Thank you, Mr. Pellegrino. It was nice of you to come visit us. And tell your children they are welcome anytime," Smartboard escorted him to the door and shut it behind him.

"You were mighty friendly with the creepy guy."

Smartboard held up one finger and pointed it at Preacher.

"Don't start," Chris commanded. They glared at each other and then ignored each other.

She continued, "Well, I'll probably freeze, but I think I need to go up to the widow's walk for three hours. Colonel, if you'd relieve me at midnight, and then Smartboard relieves you at three a.m., we'll break dawn with Jailbird taking the walk. We're most likely being watched by Creepy Dad, so we don't use the outer doors to the cellar. And we keep the drapes in the parlor drawn – day and night – so no one sees the hidden door. Those not assigned to night watch have kitchen duty."

The Troughtons glanced at each other, but complied.

Glynn met her on the widow's walk at midnight. "You are relieved, Battle Braid. Stand down. There's hot coffee on the stove. I'll watch you until you get into the house."

"Good night, Colonel." She kissed him tenderly, enjoying his warmth.

At fifteen after three, he slid in beside her. He was still freezing but he'd removed all of his clothes except long johns and a T. She sighed and wrapped him around her back, pressing her warmth into his abdomen, knowing that this was the most vulnerable place humans lose body temperature. His arms held her close and snuggled into the downy mattress and comforter.

Around six, she heard Jailbird get dressed and try to step lightly on the stairs. She stretched and rolled. Glynn was awake –

in more ways than one. Without speaking, he cupped her face and kissed her. They explored each other's lips tenderly and cautiously. Her hands slid from his chest to his shoulders and then around his neck. She moaned and his embrace became more demanding. As they rolled so that she was on her back and he was on top of her, they hesitated.

The sound of a ship's bell broke the silence.

"On your feet, Troughtons! Proximity alert!" Chris shoved Glynn off of her and grabbed her bow.

The Troughtons, trained on the teeth of the apocalypse, were dressed and armed and roaring up the stairs in thirty seconds.

"Take your points," she ordered. They ran to the appropriate windows on the ground floor and raised the windows.

"Hello the house," a voice called from the edge of the wheat field.

"Identify yourself," Chris shouted.

"It's Beau. Beau Pellegrino, your neighbor." He shoved the two children in front of him. Two men flanked his sides. No weapons were visible on any of them.

Glynn stood beside Chris by the open front door. "It's a might early to be calling on the neighbors, Beau."

"Well," Beau looked around the yard. "We found some boar tracks nearby and thought your men might could help us. We'd share the meat fifty-fifty. Three of your men and the three of us – make a nice day of hunting and sure to have a pig roast tonight."

Chris glanced at Glynn. They agreed silently; she'd go out to talk. "It's not Christmas yet, hold your positions."

The neighbors walked across the road and up to the front yard where Chris met them – in plain sight of her marksmen at the windows.

"Good morning, Mrs. Troughton."

"Good morning, Mr. Pellegrino."

"You remember my brothers, Mason and Xander. And of course, you know the children."

The children looked exhausted and frozen. The men looked hard and hungry. She nodded at them from a distance wide enough to twang her bow if necessary.

"I recall you had another brother, Stub. I hope he's well."

"He's staying down the trail, keeping watch on the boar."

She nodded but didn't smile.

"I was wondering if the children could stay with you while we hunt. You don't need to feed them, but the world being the way it is, I don't like the idea of them sitting alone while we're away. As a mother, I know you'll understand."

She glanced at the boy and girl. They refused to look at her. "You look half-frozen. Go on into the house. Smartboard will find you a blanket." Chris didn't turn her back on the men to watch the children go into the house. She'd made her voice carry well-enough.

"That's a nice watch-tower on the barn. Liked to scare us to death when your man sounded the bell."

"Just so you know, he's not the only one on watch. We're the Troughtons of the 74th."

"So, Mrs. Troughton, you are a soldier?"

"I am, as are the rest of my people."

"We only need about three of your men. If we leave soon, we might be able to catch the boars still sleeping, as cold as it is."

Glynn walked up next to her and stared at the three men. "We're busy today, but thank you."

"Well, if you're busy, you're busy. So I tell you what, once we get the boars, maybe you'd like to trade us for some of the pork. A jar of lard for – say – a bottle of wine?"

"We don't have any wine," Chris lied.

The two brothers exchanged looks.

"What would you take for the horse?"

"The horse is not for sale," Glynn stated with finality.

Beau spread his hands out, "I'm just trying to be neighborly. We've got some canned tuna you might like in exchange for eggs.

Children need eggs, you know."

Chris softened at the mention of children. "I can spare a dozen eggs this morning, and throw in a can of black olives."

"I'll take the eggs, but I can't abide black olives."

His words froze in the air between them.

She drew a breath and grabbed her battle braid. "Now, what bizarre sins have black olives ever committed that you shun them so?"

Beau licked his lips, suddenly nervous. "Funny way of putting that."

"I'll keep your children safe. You go on and stick your pigs. But before you come calling next time, you need to shout out, so you don't get a pitchfork through you or something worse."

"A pitchfork?" Mason turned green.

Glynn repeated, "Or something worse."

"Have a nice boar hunt," Chris smiled.

They watched until the men slid back inside the wheat field.

Chris whistled twice. Jailbird held up three fingers and kept them raised until they were out of sight.

"Hunter, join Jailbird. Locked and loaded, gentlemen. Looks like Christmas might never come." Glynn ordered. He and Chris walked backwards to the porch, keeping their eyes on the fields.

Inside, Smartboard had the children snuggled under quilts and sipping hot honey-sweetened coffee. The girl was sucking on a wheat cake. The boy was staring, morose and shamed-faced, down at the table.

Chris looked at Glynn. He nodded and smiled at Smartboard.

"What grade are you in?" she asked innocently.

"I was in the third grade when the monsters came."

"How about you, Cody Patterson?"

The boy jerked. "Seventh."

"You said your last name was Patterson, but Beau's last name is Pellegrino."

"Tain't really. He got it off a water bottle."

Smartboard handed him another cake. "Is he really your father?"

The boy shrugged, "He takes care of us."

"He beats you. Pizzaboy saw it." Smartboard said this gently. "What kind of father beats his son?"

"A bad one," Sis exclaimed.

"You walked a long way this morning, before dark."

"Just over the hill. We were camping."

"Shut up, Lil Sis."

"We already figured it, son."

"Don't call me son. I ain't your son." He glared at Glynn.

"Neither is that man who murdered the people that used to live here," Chris clenched it.

The girl looked confused; the boy ashamed.

Smartboard placed her hands on the girl's shoulders. "How would you like a nice scrubby bubble bath and then sleep in a real bed?"

The girl nodded and followed her out of the room, a wheat cake still in her mouth.

Glynn held out the chair for Chris. She shook her head, "I'll see to my men, you see to him."

"My oldest son hated seventh grade." Glynn turned the chair and straddled it. "He was small, and the other boys and girls didn't take him seriously. Now he's a man – if he's still alive. Do you think your parents are still alive?"

The boy shrugged, and then shook his head. "Beau wears my momma's necklace around his neck. The only person she ever let wear it was me."

"Is Beau planning to kill us?"

He nodded.

"Divide and conquer?"

He nodded again. "They were going to kill the three men that went with them, and then come back for the rest of you. They wanted the women."

"They killed Yves and the other man. Did you know that?"
The boy didn't respond.

"Did you have a hand in that? Did you help kill Yves?"

"No!" he jumped up; the chair crashed behind him. Preacher glanced at them from his stance by the back door.

"You know why he wants the women?"

Cody took a deep breath and picked up the chair. He nodded as he sat back down. "I heard them talking. They've taken women before."

"He'll do the same to Lil Sis when she's old enough, if he hasn't already." Glynn kept his voice soft.

"He hasn't. I won't let him."

Glynn let the silence work on Cody's honesty.

"The other man, he was one of Beau's men. James – he got killed by Grandpa Yves, and the other men just went crazy."

"Did you see it happen?"

"Not all of it. We led Grandpa Yves into the barn where the men were waiting, then I took Lil Sis home. But I came back, when they sent me out gathering wood." The boys' shoulders hunched and his head fell to his chest. "They were dead." A tear plunked onto his shirt.

Preacher walked over and gave the boy a consoling pat on the shoulder, then returned to his place by the door.

"What was your job today?"

"Keep you in the house until noon, and then lead the men into the barn. Course, when Beau realized you had a guard on the roof, he changed plans and told me to lead ya'll out back, behind the oven."

"How were you to know when?"

"Just timing. He'd be lying in wait. Once they killed the men, he planned on keeping the women here and visiting. He liked the house." The boy had relaxed once he realized these sins were being lifted. "And he really wanted the horse."

"He's not taking my horse," Chris growled as she joined them.

"Go sit with your sister in the second bedroom to the right on the third floor. We'll come get you when we need you."

It took Chris and Glynn fifteen minutes to strategize. She ordered the Preacher to spread the word and then called for Cody to join them.

"We need you to do something. It's dangerous and if you aren't believable, you'll most likely be killed,"

Chris interrupted the colonel, "You betray us, and I know you'll be killed because I'll be the one killing you."

The boy's eyes widened. Glynn pursed his lips but didn't counter her threat.

"Go tell Beau that you found the door to the secret room and it's full of wine and food. Take him around the house, just outside that back door. You'll see the double doors in the ground. Will you do that?"

"Yes ma'am."

"Understand me, the United States is under Martial Law. Kidnapping, murder and looting are all punishable by death. If you lead those men back here, you need to understand – I mean to hang them."

"Don't hang Lil Sis. She didn't have anything to do with this." He squared his shoulders.

"We don't hang children," Glynn growled. "Once this business is finished, you and your sister are free to go."

"Or you could stay here, in the bunk house," Chris suggested.

"Lil Sis and I -- We'll stay with you."

"Preacher, tell Smartboard to take the girl down into the cellar; she'll be safe there. And bring up a bottle of wine. Cody can give it to Beau as proof." Chris continued, "Belly, take a pot of coffee to the watchmen and stay there. Hooting orders only."

"Hooting orders?" the boy asked.

"Never you mind, Cody." Chris didn't trust him. "But tell Beau we've all gone back to bed."

Preacher handed Cody a bottle. "Lead the men to the cellar

door, and then back out of the way. Go back to the barn – stay inside one of the stalls. If they ask, tell them you hid Lil Sis there and you'll take her home."

"You're afraid he'll use me as a shield again. I know."

Glynn paused, "He won't ever do it again. I promise."

Chris nodded and gave him a little smile.

23
MECHMON JUSTICE

Hunter whispered to Pizzaboy as they lay on the widow's walk of the barn.

Pizzaboy nodded. "Beau has a Wilson Combat autoloader rifle slung over his shoulder. Caliber: 5.56. Barrel: 18 inches. Weight: 8 pounds. Collapsible stock, no sights. Semi-auto, armor-tuff finish, 30-shot mag. It's listed for around $2450. The gun in his right hand is a piece of crap and just looks hot. It won't shoot straight and will most likely knock his wrist out of alignment. Now, the other rifle is impressive as hell. UA Arms Blackwidow autoloader rifle. Caliber: 5.56 Barrel: 16 inches. Weight: 7.2 pounds. Magpul CTR stock with adjustable sights. It's got a Piston system, 30-shot mag. And it sells for about $3200.

"Mason is carrying a Wilson Combat Speedfeed Pump Action twelve gauge. Barrel: 18.4 inches and it weighs 8.9 pounds. It boasts a collapsible synthetic stock. I think that's the border model with the multipurpose tactical sling, buttstock swivel and rigid mag tube sling mount, extra power heavy-duty stainless mag spring, high visibility follower, sidesaddle shell carrier, Armor-Tuff finish in green. It's only got six shots and sells between 665 to 1250 dollars. The other one Mason is carrying is a cheaper weapon –

about 880 dollars, but it looks wicked. It's a Kel-Tec KSG - Pump Action twelve gauge shotgun with 2 ¾ inch chamber and an 18.5 inch barrel. It weighs 6.9 pounds. Optics read, Picatinny rail, parkerized/anodized finish, 14-shot mag."

"What about the other guy?"

"Xander's got a Larue Tactical Costa Edition autoloader rifle Caliber: 5.56mm. Barrel 14.5 inches with apinned and wielded muzzle device. Weight 7.9 pounds and Magpul MOE stock. As I recall, it's a semi-auto, direct impingement with LaRue PST port selector system, Geissele SSA trigger, flat dark earth finish, 30-shot mag. $2895 or there abouts. The other rifle is 5.56 mm caliber Black Rain PG9 autoloader with a sixteen-inch barrel weighing in at about 6.7 pounds. It's semi-auto, low-profile bas block, skull finish, 30-shot mag."

Hunter whistled softly. "How much?"

"Two thousand thirty, give or take."

"So, bows and arrows against the riflemen of the apocalypse."

"Yeppers. Pretty much sums it up."

Stub followed behind them, carrying a hank of rope. They each carried sacks of ammunition and bandoleers of automatic bullets. They clanked and clinked like metallic mariachis as they made their way behind the house.

"Now keep real quiet, because they said they were going back to sleep. I hid Lil Sis in the barn, but I knew you'd want to see this." Cody's voice carried to Hunter, Belly and Jailbird on the widow's walk and to the people on the second and third floors.

"You better not be lying to me, Cody, or I'll take the strap to you."

"I'm not lying. You're about to get the biggest surprise of your life. One you really deserve." The marauders stopped. "There, those double doors lead down into an underground bunker that is huge and filled with treasure."

Beau glared at the boy and then the doors. "Xander, open them."

He stood back while the large ex-deacon tried to haul open one of the doors. It was locked but the smell of ripe apples and sour wine made the men smile.

"All right, boy. Go get your sister and head on home."

Cody nodded and turned away. He was smiling. When he passed the kiln, he began to run.

The boy heading into the barn was the signal for the Troughtons to act. As President of Troughtonia, Chris called out, "Beau Pellegrino, you and your men are under arrest for the murders of Yves de la Bois, Cody Patterson's mother, and six members of the Delaney Republic. You are also charged with looting and pillaging during time of war. These charges are all punishable by death. How do you plead?"

The bad men clutched their weapons and looked around, trying to find the source of the voice for a target. Xander sprayed up at the house with gun fire and the other two dashed to the kiln for cover. Mason cried out; the fletched part of an arrow stuck out of his thigh.

The ground began to tremble, but they were all so caught up in the battle, only Hunter noticed. He looked back over his shoulder to the west and grabbed Pizzaboy's arm. "Mechmons."

Three of them, side by side, traveling north to south across the wheat fields, were ignorant of the battle raging not far away to the east.

"Oh!" Pizzaboy stood up. A bullet pinged off the ship's bell; he crouched down again. "You're gonna love this!"

"Put down your weapons and surrender," Glynn shouted.

He was answered by a spray of bullets.

The Harley Breakout burst from the barn and headed west across the fields. The ship's bell began to clang. Three meant an all-call, five meant immediate return to home. Seven meant proximity alert. The bell kept ringing. The Troughtons in the house looked at each other in confusion. The earth trembled as if in syncopation to the bell.

"Sweet Jesus!" Preacher screeched from his post at the front of the house, overlooking the wheat. "Get out of the house! Jessica darling! Run!"

"What?" Glynn and Chris reached him at the same time. Preacher pointed west.

Hunter was riding the bike in zigzags at break neck speed, first veering north, then crossing his path to veer south, but heading toward the farmhouse. Behind him, lured by the metallic body of the bike, chomped three mechmons side by side.

"Oh my God!" Chris gasped. She ran to the side window overlooking the kiln where Beau and his men still crouched. "Beau, get out of here! Run! Mechmons! You're covered in guns."

He looked up at the sound of her voice which was drowned out by the bells. He aimed his piece-of-crap pistol. Glynn grabbed her and they both fell sideways to safety as Beau fired.

The bike jumped the road and raced straight at the kiln. Hunter skidded through the yard between the house and the barn and circled the house. The mechmons, following in hot pursuit, gobbled up the guns – and as it so happened - the bad guys attached to the guns. With the bike directly behind them, bouncing across the swatch made by the aliens and on the other side of the road, the mechmons continued their journey, now heading directly east.

The Troughtons all ran out to the fields to celebrate with Hunter.

The children came, too and found themselves in Preacher's and Smartboard's arms. The old friends looked at each other, and then embraced and kissed and whispered undying endearments. Hunter was hugged and thumped and kissed. The revelry finally subsided and they turned to head back to the house. The sun was setting behind them, casting it brilliance at the house.

Chris saw it first. She reached over and silently took Hunter's arm. He looked down at her and then heard gasps behind him. He glanced at Pizzaboy, who sank with Peggy to the crushed wheat.

Then Hunter turned and looked at the house. The tin roof caught and reflected the blazing light shining off the tin roof.

He smiled through tear-brimmed eyes at his family, "Troughton Company is home."

EPILOGUE

Hunter and Glynn rode the bike back to the Troughtons and got them moving toward the farmhouse, now named Jerry's Montana. Then Glynn took the bike four hundred miles further and tendered his resignation from the 74th Cavalry. He spent one night in the Delaney Republic and discovered a dozen Troughtons had decided to make the empty suburb their home. He enjoyed the barbeque the doctor's people threw for him, but stayed away from the tea. Dr. Arnold was packed and ready the next morning. His wife had passed away and he was ready to start over again.

"I heard I might have some patients up your way."

Glynn nodded and helped him climb on the back of the bike.

As they headed up to the farmhouse, they heard the ship's bell.

Chris stepped out onto the porch and flung her arms around his neck.

She turned him to the barn and pointed. In bright white letters, Hunter had painted:

TROUGHTON COMPANY IS HERE.

MECHMONS BEST BE A'FEARED.

In February, Mickey's wife Sally gave birth to a little girl. Lovenia and Stuart had twins the last week of February, early, but well-tended. March came in like a lion as Angel bore Jailbird a son. Peter and Chris Glynn had a boy the third week of June. Daisy-Mae and Belly had another girl, and on their second Christmas Eve in Jerry's Montana, Smartboard bore Preacher a little boy.

January, when all of the women seemed to be pregnant again, the skies filled with alien ships and humanity feared for their existence. It was with disbelief – joyous disbelief – when the Troughtons watched the aliens hover over the hibernating city-eaters, roadsters and mechmons. The metal beasties levitated and were swallowed up by the mother ships. Pizzaboy figured it was some type of electromagnet. Hunter figured it was just harvest time, like lobster fishermen bringing up their baskets. Or so he told his children.

Horses galloped unfettered and free across Troughtonia, and the penalty for harming one was severe.

The Troughtons planted crops and set snares and went sasquatch-hunting an awful lot. They would laugh when a child pointed out that they never seemed to bring back any sasquatches.

They were happy. Troughton Company was home.

ABOUT THE AUTHOR

Evelyn Rainey has published science fiction, fantasy, historical fiction, children's, and Christian books. She has been published in *Zero Signal, Lakeland Ledger, Polk County Democrat, World Treasury of Golden Poems, Youth Alive, Wesleyan Magazine* and the *Polk County Poetry Anthology.* She enjoys corresponding with people who have read her books and/or who want to discuss the Art and Business of writing.

With degrees and certificates in Early Childhood, Elementary, Middle School Integrated Curriculum, Gifted, ESOL, and Journalism, she retired after 38 years as a teacher. Currently, she is pursuing a Master's degree in Biblical Studies.

More information, including her blog and videos, can be found on http://ShelteringTree.Earth.

DISCUSSION GUIDE FOR BOOK CLUBS, SCIENCE FICTION CONVENTION PANELS, AND JOURNALS

1. Compare/contrast the Mechmons with other literary alien invasions. What's unique about them? What's believable and what's unbelievable about them?

2. Of the original Troughton Company, which character are you most like? Most different from?

3. Discuss Jerry Troughton and how he defused tension among his people and others, how he dealt with new people and obstacles, and how everyone felt about him. How do you feel about him?

4. Pizzaboy Joe Lloyd is both genius and moron. Why was he called Pizzaboy? What was his most endearing quality? What was his most amazing talent?

5. Hours and hours (and hours) of watching History Channel, Discovery Channel, and Unsolved Mysteries were part of gathering the background for this novel. Do you watch any of these and if so, what type is your favorite and why?

6. Most post-apocalypse novels and movies dwell on the characters and immediate emergences of the situation. Troughton Company goes beyond that and offers many different lessons on how to actually survive in the wild without electricity or metals. Reread one of these and discuss if you could follow the directions (brilliantly woven in as literary flow).

7. One of the themes of this novel is how humans deal with the loss of their way of life. If you were faced with the same apocalypse, how would your life change? How would you deal with it?

8. One of the themes of this novel is the need to belong. How does Jerry deal with this? How does Glynn deal with this? How does Beau Pellegrino deal with this? How do you deal with this?

9. If you were a member of one of the Legions, what would your laws be regarding marriage and age of majority? What would the name of your Legion be? Where would your Legion choose to settle?

10. Chris Troughton changes through the course of the story. What changes were the most significant? What caused them? Compare/contrast Chrissy Troughton (at the beginning of the story) to Chris Glynn (at the end of the story).

11. Of all the couples in the story, which ones were your favorite and least favorite? Explain why.

12. If you were a Troughton, would you stay with the Bachelor/Bachelorettes, the Women's Tent, or in a Family Tent? Explain.

13. Thinking about the Republic of Delaney, how would you prepare your neighborhood to defend against marauders?

14. Beau Pellegrino and his marauders needed to face justice. The Troughtons were divided on how to serve this justice. Which side would you be on and why? How satisfied were you by the demise of the marauders?

15. What is your opinion of the plight of women in a post-apocalyptic world?

16. If you were a Troughton, what would your nickname be and why?

17. Choose one of the characters and design a cosplay costume for him/her/it. Be specific in details, materials, and accoutrements.

We are a very exclusive publishing house. Our readers, once they finish one of our books, will be able to get up and face the world wiser, stronger, centered, and with the assurance that we are not alone: we are all a part of the Sheltering Tree on Earth. If you as a writer feel that same calling, please refer to

ShelteringTree.Earth/writer-guidelines

www.ingramcontent.com/pod-product-compliance
Lightning Source LLC
Chambersburg PA
CBHW060627260626
47161CB00008B/2819